Mariel wanted this as she had never wanted anything in her life.

He tasted of mint toothpaste and he smelled of soap, and when he touched the sides of her face as he kissed her she quivered, remembering that yes, this was exactly how it was, kissing Noah. This was how he had always begun when he kissed her—by touching her face, cupping her cheeks in his hands as he slowly moved his lips over hers.

It was good, so incredibly good, to be kissed by him again. When he opened his mouth she did as well, welcoming his warm, gently probing tongue. And when he leaned into her, she sank back on the bed, her hands on his shoulders, pulling him down on top of her. Her stomach was fluttering like mad and her mind was racing and she couldn't think clearly; all she could do was feel. And need.

She needed him desperately—had needed him for years—and now he was here. They were back in this inn in this town—

Then she remembered why.

BOOK YOUR PLACE ON OUR WEBSITE AND MAKE THE READING CONNECTION!

We've created a customized website just for our very special readers, where you can get the inside scoop on everything that's going on with Zebra, Pinnacle and Kensington books.

When you come online, you'll have the exciting opportunity to:

- View covers of upcoming books

- Read sample chapters

- Learn about our future publishing schedule (listed by publication month *and author*)

- Find out when your favorite authors will be visiting a city near you

- Search for and order backlist books from our online catalog

- Check out author bios and background information

- Send e-mail to your favorite authors

- Meet the Kensington staff online

- Join us in weekly chats with authors, readers and other guests

- Get writing guidelines

- AND MUCH MORE!

**Visit our website at
http://www.zebrabooks.com**

CAN'T STOP LOVING YOU

Janelle Taylor

ZEBRA BOOKS
KENSINGTON PUBLISHING CORP.
http://www.zebrabooks.com

To Joan and Fareed Betros, a truly romantic
couple and good friends, and to
McKay Daines who makes dreams come true.

ZEBRA BOOKS are published by
Kensington Publishing Corp.
850 Third Avenue
New York, NY 10022

All Kensington titles, imprints and distributed lines are available at special quantity discounts for bulk purchases for sales
promotion, premiums, fund-raising, educational or institutional
use.

Special book excerpts or customized printings can also be created to fit specific needs. For details, write or phone the office of
the Kensington Special Sales Manager: Kensington Publishing
Corp., 850 Third Avenue, New York, NY 10022. Attn. Special
Sales Department. Phone: 1-800-221-2647.

First Printing: May, 2001
10 9 8 7 6 5 4 3 2 1

Printed in the United States of America

Prologue

November, 1986
Strasburg, New York

"Two more minutes."

"Not even." Mariel Rowan looked up from the second hand on her watch to see Noah Lyons staring at his own. "So that's good. In one minute and fifty-six seconds we'll know."

"Not even," he echoed, and flashed a grim smile at her before looking down at his wrist again.

Seated beside him on the rumpled dorm bed, she inhaled deeply, then exhaled heavily through puffed cheeks. The waiting was torture, and there was absolutely no way to ease the tension. Nothing to do but sit here watching each second tick by so that they wouldn't have to look at each other—or at the opened pregnancy kit on the desk, plopped next to a stack of textbooks, an open and untouched can of diet soda, and a framed photograph of Mariel's smiling family, whom she hadn't seen in the three months since she had gone away to school.

If her parents ever knew . . .

Well, they wouldn't know. They were back home in Missouri, over a thousand miles away from here. Either way—no matter how this turned out—Mariel would never tell them. There was no reason to.

"What are you thinking?"

Noah's voice startled her. She turned to see him looking at her, an intent expression on his handsome face. She fought the urge to reach out and brush an errant lock of wavy dark hair out of his brown eyes, afraid that if she touched him, she would crumble. Right now, she had to be strong. There would be time for crumbling later. . . .

Later? In exactly thirty-one seconds, she realized, looking down at her watch again.

"Mariel?"

She shrugged. "What am I thinking? I'm thinking either my whole world is about to turn upside down . . . or . . ."

"Or everything will be okay," he finished for her. "We can go back to the way it was."

She nodded, but she didn't agree. Nothing would ever be the way it was. This had rocked her to the very core, had cast doubt on dreams she had—until now—been certain would come true.

Dreams were all she had had, growing up in sleepy Rockton, Missouri.

Maybe not *all.* She had had her parents, Andrew and Sarah, and her kid sister, Leslie. And she had had friends, too. Plenty of friends. But she had known from a young age that it was all temporary, that the day would come when she would flee Rockton and never look back.

Finally, late this past August, when the blazing summer sun had fried the heartland to an ugly brown and it seemed there would never be another season, it had happened. She had left home.

First stop: this small private college in upstate New York, where a hint of autumn had already been in the air a week before Labor Day.

Mariel had never even heard of Strasburg College until the summer before her senior year in high school, when she had made her first trip to the East Coast to sing with her girls' choir at Chautauqua Institution, a cultural arts community in western New York. The group performance in a packed amphitheater had concluded with her heartfelt solo from a Broadway musical. When it was over, she had received thunderous applause—and an invitation from an impressed drama professor who happened to be there. He had asked her to audition for one of a handful of theater arts scholarships at Strasburg—and miraculously, she had won one.

Her parents hadn't been thrilled. In fact, they had been pretty much devastated.

Their plan for Mariel was for her to go to a state university—preferably one that would allow her to live at home, dating only local boys—and become a teacher. That was what her mother had done decades ago, before she married Andrew. And it was what most of Mariel's friends were planning to do. As her best friend Katie Beth Miller always said, teaching was a family-friendly profession. If you couldn't afford—or, God forbid, didn't want—to give up your job after you were married and had children, you would at least have summers and school holidays off, and you would be home early every afternoon.

Working mothers weren't the norm in Rockton.

Working, unmarried women without children were almost unheard-of.

But that was what Mariel intended to be.

Not in Rockton, of course. She planned to go from Strasburg to New York City, where she would become a Broadway sensation. Of course, that might take a few years. And before it happened, she might spend some time in Europe after college—to study voice, or maybe just to travel.

That was the plan.

The dream.

The dream didn't include teaching, or Rockton, or a husband and children.

All Mariel had ever wanted was to be an actress. A footloose actress.

Well, that was *almost* all she wanted.

For the last three months, ever since she had arrived in Strasburg, she had also wanted Noah Lyons.

She had even started to fantasize that she might be able to have her dream *and* Noah.

But that was absolutely *it*.

There wasn't room in there for motherhood.

"Mariel?"

She blinked. "Yeah?"

"It's time. It's *been* time. I was waiting for you to notice, but you're a million miles away. What are you thinking?"

That this can't happen.

Not to me.

"I just—never mind. Let's just find out," she said, standing abruptly and walking toward the white plastic stick sitting on the desk. It was flat on one end and had a little window. She had read the pamphlet that came with it. If there was a dark circle in the window, it would mean she was pregnant.

Her hand was shaking as she reached for the stick.

Then Noah was behind her, one hand closing over her fingers as she picked it up, his other hand on her shoulder to steady her.

"Are you okay?" he asked, his voice low in her ear.

She didn't answer.

Her eyes were closed.

She couldn't look.

"Mariel, you have to move your thumb. It's blocking the window."

"Okay." Her voice came out small and frightened. She hated the sound. She hated being this person— this cliché. The preacher's daughter, away from the Midwest only three months and already missing a period.

But not pregnant. She *couldn't* be pregnant. It had to be the stress.

The stress of leaving home for the first time, starting college, falling in love. . . .

"Mariel?"

She took a deep breath. Moved her thumb. Opened her eyes. Looked at the stick.

There was a circle in the window.

"What does that mean?" Noah asked. "Does it mean you're not pregnant?"

She could barely hear his voice over the roar in her own head. She was screaming inside, shrieking in agony.

Somehow, aloud she only said, "No. It means that I am."

"You *are?*"

She nodded, head bent, still clutching the white stick helplessly. They hadn't moved. He was still holding her, but his hand suddenly felt heavy on her shoulder. She couldn't look up at him; couldn't bear to know what he was thinking. She was too consumed by her own whirl of thoughts, for the moment, to care.

"It'll be okay," Noah whispered in her ear.

Anger flared. Irrational maybe, but anger just the same. Of course it would be okay for him. He wasn't pregnant. This was happening to her.

She whirled around to look him in the eye. "No, it won't be okay," she snapped, wishing she could find something other than compassion on his face. His gentle expression only compounded her inner turmoil, adding guilt to the fury.

"Look, Mariel, I know you're upset, but we'll work this out." He reached out to touch her again.

She took a step backward and crashed into her roommate's dresser. "How can we work this out? I'm eighteen and pregnant, Noah. I've barely started college and it's all over. Everything."

"Of course it isn't over. There are ways—"

She gasped. "If you think I'm going to terminate the pregnancy, then you're—"

"Of course I don't think that!"

She swallowed hard. "Because that's just not an option. Not for me."

"I know, Mariel. I know your father—"

"This has nothing to do with my father being a minister," she interrupted, trying to quell her anger. Someplace deep inside she knew he was trying to say—and do—the right thing. Just as she was. But right now, he didn't count. "This has nothing to do with anyone else. This has to do with me. What's right for me. And I'm going to have this baby, Noah."

He nodded, staring down at her so tenderly that she had to turn away, because it made her torn between wanting to lash out at him—and wanting the impossible.

Her gaze fell on her own reflection in the mirror above her roommate's bureau. She was shocked to see that she looked pretty much the same as always. Her long, light brown wavy hair was slightly tousled. She must have raked her fingers through it at some point; she did that when she was nervous. And there were deep shadows under her wide-set green eyes, which wasn't surprising considering she hadn't slept in the two nights since she had concluded that her period wasn't going to put in a late appearance after all.

But other than those telltale signs of what she had been through, she was her usual self on the outside— just a pretty college girl in an oversized, navy hooded Strasburg sweatshirt.

And standing over her shoulder was a tall, lean, all-American-looking college guy wearing a green and black plaid flannel shirt, jeans—and a similar set of under-eye circles.

Things like this didn't happen to people like them.

But even as the thought crossed her mind, she forced it out, knowing it was ridiculous. Things like this happened *only* to people like them. People who were too caught up in each other to pay attention to details.

Like using birth control every time.

He put his hands on her shoulders and tilted his face next to hers. "Mariel—don't shut me out. Please. We're in this together."

She had to fight back a lump in her throat. "I wish I could feel like we were, Noah. But we're not. It's just me. My God, I've never felt so alone in my life."

"You're not alone," he said fiercely. "You'll never be alone. I'm going to be with you through everything, Mariel. I won't leave your side."

She shook her head, touched by his loyalty even as she was irritated by his lack of logic. "Noah, you don't have to make a choice. I'm going to have to leave school. The baby is due at the end of June or beginning of July, and—"

"It is? How do you know?" he broke in, his breathless tone suddenly taking on a hint of . . . was it wonder?

"Because when I went to the library yesterday I looked up gestation cycles, and they had this chart. I know when my last period was. I know when the baby is due."

He nodded. "The *baby*. When you say it like that it's so . . ."

She knew what he meant. There *was* a sense of wonder, no matter what else she was feeling. There was a human life growing inside of her. A life she had created with Noah, whom she . . .

No. She didn't *love* him. She couldn't love someone she had known for only three months . . . could she?

Maybe, if they had been given a chance to see where this relationship led, they would have fallen in love someday.

But they would never know now.

"You said you'll have to leave school, Mariel."

She nodded, steeped in misery again.

Noah cleared his throat. "Do you mean you're going to go back home? Because your parents—"

"My parents would probably throw me out if I came home pregnant, Noah."

He didn't look surprised.

And she realized what he must think of her parents. Had she made them out to be ogres when she talked about them to him? Probably. She did a lot of grumbling about what it was like to grow up with a minister father and a full-time mom who baked cookies and ran the PTO. About how they didn't understand her.

Both her parents were in their late fifties, far older than her friends' parents. They had married young and tried for years to have children. Long after they had given up hope, Mariel had come along unexpectedly, followed, even more incredibly, by Leslie five years later. As a result, Andrew and Sarah told anyone who would listen that their daughters were miracles from God.

And now here was Mariel, feeling the opposite. Feeling cursed because she was pregnant.

More guilt. Everywhere she turned, guilt.

"Maybe my parents wouldn't throw me out, Noah," she told him, needing him to know she had distorted the truth. "They're not horrible people. Just ultraconservative. And ultrareligious. And Rockton's a tiny town. They would die of shame if I turned up unmarried and pregnant."

"You don't have to be," Noah said quickly, a strange expression on his face.

She bristled. "I told you, I'm having this baby, Noah. I can't possibly choose to—"

"No, I didn't mean the pregnant part."

She stared at his reflection beside hers in the mirror, not understanding.

Or maybe not willing to understand.

But when he pulled on her shoulders, spinning her around to face him, she couldn't avoid it. He dropped down in front of her on one knee before she could say something to stop him.

Still, she tried. "Noah, please don't—"

He grabbed her hand, clasping it as he looked up at her. His voice was ragged when he spoke, his face raw with emotion.

But it wasn't the right emotion. It wasn't the one she would hope—expect—to see there on the verge of the announcement he was so obviously about to make.

"Mariel, you don't have to be alone. Ever," he said fervently. "I'm going to take care of you and our baby. I swear. If you marry me, I'll never let you down."

"Marry you?" It came out so high-pitched that she winced. She didn't mean to react this way, but she couldn't help herself. It was just too much. All of this, in the space of a few minutes. First the positive pregnancy test, and now a marriage proposal.

What he was doing was so noble. So sweet.

So *wrong*.

"Noah, we can't," she said, regaining control over her vocal cords if not her emotions. She felt as though she was on the verge of hysteria. Laughter? Tears? Maybe both.

"Yes, we can," he said, getting up off the floor, holding both her hands in his and bringing them up against his chest. She could feel his heart racing beneath her wrists, and she realized that somewhere inside of her their baby's heart was beating as well. For a split second, she was caught up in that—and in him. In the picture he had painted with his heartfelt, foolish words.

Then reality returned, and she forced herself to face the truth—and to convince him to do the same.

"Noah, listen to yourself. This is insane. You're talking about marriage."

"Exactly."

"We're in college. We have our whole lives ahead. Not just school, but travel, and careers, and—Noah, we can't get married. We're *eighteen.*"

"So? We're pregnant," he shot back, his eyes flashing at her. Finally, he was showing a trace of anger, and for that she felt oddly grateful. She didn't want—or need—him to be her selfless hero.

"I'm pregnant, Noah. Not *us.* Me. I'm the one who's having the baby."

"And I'm the one who was raised by a single mother," he retorted. "I'm the one who knows what that's like. I'm the one who's spent every day of my life thinking how differently things would have turned out if I'd had a father. A child—our child—needs two parents—"

"You're right," she said softly.

"—and there's no way I'm going to—what?" he asked suddenly, as if he had just heard what she had said. "Did you say I'm right?"

She nodded.

His face lit up.

He opened his mouth to speak, but she put her fingers against his lips before he could make a sound. "Our child does need two parents, Noah. But those parents aren't going to be you and me."

CHAPTER ONE

May, 2001
Rockton, Missouri

"Mariel? Where are you?"

Mariel paused with her hand on the study door, hearing her sister's voice in the foyer below. "I'm up here, Leslie," she called wearily. "What's wrong?"

"Can you come back down for a second? You won't believe this."

With a sigh, Mariel turned away from the study and headed back down the flight of steps to the first floor. She hadn't walked up them more than fifteen seconds earlier, confident her sister was headed out to have a manicure at last.

As sisters went, Leslie was usually pretty laid back and self-sufficient. But with her wedding countdown dwindling from months to weeks, she was becoming increasingly high maintenance. Luckily, the bridal shower would be over with by this time tomorrow, leaving only the wedding for Mariel to guide her sister through.

Only the wedding?

She was dreading that ordeal already. Not that she wasn't anxious to see her sister happily married to Jed Peterson, her high school sweetheart, who also happened to live right next door.

But Leslie was already fretting about the tiniest details—whether the type on the printed matchbooks would be the exact shade of dark pink as the frosting roses on the cake, and whether the faint scar on Jed's knuckle would show if the photographer decided to snap a close-up shot of their hands in their new wedding rings.

Mariel had no idea how she was going to make it through another seven weeks of listening to her sister's irrational worries without completely losing her sanity.

"What's wrong, Leslie?" she asked, finding her sister in the living room. She was sitting on the old-fashioned, uncomfortable couch—which their mother had always called the "davenport"—and there was a large, open gift box filled with what appeared to be layers of tissue in front of her.

"You have to look at this, Mariel," Leslie said in a choked voice. "The UPS guy delivered it just as I was walking out the door."

"What is it? A shower gift?" Mariel reached across the glass coffee table for the box, careful not to knock over the cluster of china religious figurines that had been there as long as she could remember.

"It's from Jed's two cousins," Leslie said.

"The twins from Texas?"

"Lord, no." Leslie looked horrified. "Mary Ellen and Pamela Joan aren't invited to the shower, remember? We knew they'd fly up for it, and it's already going to be hard enough on Jed's mom to have the two of them staying under their roof the weekend of the wedding. They never stop talking."

"Then, which cousins?"

"Millie and Helen."

"They sound like little old ladies," Mariel said.

"They are little old ladies. Spinsters. They're Jed's second cousins, or maybe third. They can't come to the shower because they play bingo at their retirement home every Sunday afternoon. Go ahead, Mar. Look what they sent."

Mariel parted the layers of tissue and pulled out something white and satiny. *Long* and white and satiny. And *lacy.* And *sequiny.* She looked up at Leslie, her arms clutching what seemed like yards and yards of the billowing garment. Something tickled her nose, and she sneezed. "Was that a feather? What *is* this, Leslie?"

"It's a peignoir set," her sister said in a strangled voice.

"Are you laughing or crying?"

"I'm not sure." Leslie sank back on the couch and threw her head back.

Mariel shifted the fabric, and something fluttered to the floor. She bent to pick it up and saw that it was a note written on old-fashioned floral stationery. The spidery handwriting read, *For your wedding night, dear Leslie.*

"For your wedding night?" Mariel looked at her sister. "But this is . . ."

"Hideous. I know."

"Les, this thing is covered in . . . stuff. Feathers, sequins . . . you name it."

"I know!" Her sister buried her face in her hands. "I can't wear it. Ever! Let alone on my wedding night."

"Just send them a nice thank-you and give it to charity."

"Mariel, you don't understand. They're going to ask me if I liked it. They're going to want me to model it for them. They're going to ask Jed—"

"Calm down, Leslie! You're getting carried away."

Her sister, the Drama Queen, groaned. "I can't take this. The stress is killing me. Why didn't we just elope?"

"You wanted a big wedding, remember?" Mariel attempted to stuff the peignoir back into the box and jammed the cover on. A feather wafted in the air. "I'm the one who said maybe we should keep it more . . . manageable."

"I know. But I kept picturing the kind of wedding Mom would have wanted for me. She always talked about our wedding days—mine and yours. I guess maybe I'm doing it for her, in a way."

Tears sprang to Mariel's eyes. Her mother had been gone almost two years, and she still became emotional at the mere mention of her. They all did. Especially Dad.

Luckily, he was out visiting Reverend Henry, the minister who had taken over the church when Dad retired last year and moved to Florida.

"Go have your nails done, Leslie. And forget all about this crazy getup. Nobody will know what you wear on your wedding night except you and Jed."

"You're right." Her sister smiled and picked up the

gift box, walking toward the door. "I wonder if he's back from St. Louis yet. He'll get a kick out of seeing this."

With the latest prenuptial crisis safely averted and her sister on her way through the lilac bushes to the Petersons', Mariel climbed the steps once again.

In her mother's former sewing room—which she had recently transformed into a study—she sat down at her desk and turned on the computer. As she waited for it to boot up, she looked around the room, admiring the navy-and-green striped wallpaper, the freshly painted white woodwork, and the braided rug on the hardwood floor. Her own bedroom across the hall seemed strangely empty now that she had moved her desk, chair, and bookshelf in here, but she was thinking of buying new furniture after Leslie moved out in July. Either that, or moving into the master bedroom suite.

But, much as it made sense, she wasn't entirely comfortable with that idea. She might have the small, white colonial-style house all to herself, but she wasn't certain it would ever feel as though it truly belonged to her, no matter where she slept or put her computer.

You can always buy a place of your own, she reminded herself.

But she pushed that thought out of her head. That would be almost like . . .

Like what?

Giving up?

Admitting to herself—and the world—that she was probably never going to get married?

Well, wasn't that what she had always wanted? To be single, and free?

Yes. But not like this, a small voice reminded her. Things were supposed to be different. She was supposed to be in New York, or London, or even Hollywood. Not in Rockton, Missouri, living in the town—and the very house—she had spent most of her youth trying to escape.

The computer clicked and hummed and the start-up screen appeared at last. She quickly logged on to the Internet. Her heart leaped when she saw the mailbox icon with the flag up and heard the disembodied voice that announced, "You've got mail."

E-mail.

Her one link to the world she had once thought she might actually experience. Now she did so vicariously through her on-line friendships.

She wondered who had written since she had last checked the mail early this morning, before Leslie woke up and went on a roll, deciding they should bake five dozen wedding-cake-shaped cutout cookies for the shower guests. Cookies that were even now spread all over the kitchen on sheets of waxed paper, awaiting icing and decoration, which Leslie had decided to leave up to Mariel. "You're much more creative than I am, Mar," she had said. "Maybe you can pipe my and Jed's names on each one in pink frosting with little rosebuds."

Maybe. But that could wait.

Mariel leaned forward in her chair, dragging the mouse to click on the mailbox. There were quite a few messages. She scanned the list, recognizing the user names.

One from her chat room pal Jackie, who was an actress up for a lead in the touring company of *Fiddler on the Roof.*

One from Anthony, another chat room acquaintance

who didn't seem to think she meant it when she said she wasn't interested in a long-distance web relationship.

One from an on-line bookstore, probably notifying her that her order had been shipped.

And one from someone she didn't recognize.

She stared at the unfamiliar screen name.

Who was *Indegrl?*

She had no idea. She clicked on it, and after a brief electronic whirring, a short document appeared.

> *Dear Mariel Rowan,*
>
> *I was born in St. Thomas's Hospital outside Syracuse, New York, on July 4, 1987. My parents adopted me. I'm searching for my birth mother. I think you might be her. If you think so, too, please write back. I'm sending a photo attachment in case you want to see if we look alike.*
> *Sincerely,*
Amber Steadman

Mariel couldn't breathe.

She couldn't move.

She couldn't think.

Someplace deep down inside, she had always known this day was coming.

Now that it was here, she suddenly couldn't recall whether she had anticipated it with dread . . . or with longing.

This girl—this Amber Steadman—this disembodied person . . .

This might be the daughter she hadn't seen since that dazzlingly sunny Independence Day almost fifteen years ago.

Independence Day.

At the time, she had told herself that it was fitting that she had given birth on that day, of all days. She had done her duty. Had her baby. All she had to do was place her in the loving arms of the childless, upper-middle-class married couple she had selected, and she would be free.

But it hadn't worked that way.

Even now, she rarely allowed herself to think of the awful day when she had said good-bye forever to the two people who mattered most in her world.

Independence.

Indegrl.

It has to be her, Mariel told herself, clicking on the download icon, suddenly desperate to see the picture.

Of course, it didn't really *have* to be. There must have been lots of babies born in St. Thomas's Hospital that day.

But how many were given up for adoption?

The picture was starting to appear in strips of color that filled in from the top of her screen downward.

She could see dark hair, parted in the middle.

Mariel's hair was lighter than that.

A high forehead, no bangs.

Mariel had always worn bangs.

So? Hairstyles aren't hereditary, she reminded herself, watching in fascination as a pair of straight, dark eyebrows appeared, and then green eyes fringed by thick lashes. The lashes were the same shade as the too-dark hair and brows, but the eyes . . .

They were Mariel's eyes.

Mariel's fifteen-year-old eyes, looking back at her from a stranger's face.

She bit her lip, clutched the arms of her chair, and

stared at the computer in trepidation, not sure what she was expecting. The eyes were proof enough. It didn't matter if the rest of her face didn't look the least bit like Mariel's—

And it didn't, she realized.

The nose was too long, the mouth too full.

Noah's nose. Noah's mouth. Noah's hair and Noah's brows.

Mariel's eyes.

She let out a shuddering sigh as the truth slammed into her full force at last, far too potent to deny or even second-guess.

This was positively, absolutely, the child she and Noah had handed over to strangers moments before they had walked away from each other forever.

"Hi, Mom."

"Where's Kelly?"

Noah kissed his mother on the cheek, suppressing a sigh. "You know she works Saturdays," he told her, noticing that she had colored her hair. Again. "I like the new tint," he said, patting her head before heading from the tiny entry hall into the galley kitchen.

His mother closed the door behind him, locked the two bolts, and followed him. "You don't think it's too blond?" she asked.

He did, but he wasn't about to tell her that. When he was a kid he had tried for years to get her to go back to her natural color, which was probably even darker than his hair. She had always told him that blondes had more fun.

Which had always struck him as odd, because his

mother rarely seemed to have any fun. She was always too busy working two jobs, struggling every month to make the rent on this run-down fifth-floor walk-up on Fortieth Street just south of Queens Boulevard.

"I brought you soup," he said, setting down the grocery bag he had lugged two blocks from the subway.

"I have soup. You didn't have to do that."

He opened the cupboard and saw only one red-and-white labeled can left from the half dozen he had brought her last Saturday. "So, you'll have more soup," he told her, taking out the cans one by one and stacking them in the cupboard. "Chicken and Stars, Chicken Noodle, Chicken Gumbo . . . geez, Mom, did I get you anything but chicken? Oh, here we go, here's some vegetable beef."

"I like that. I like chicken soup, too. You don't have to do this, Noah. What's that?"

"Black olives. You like black olives."

"Don't buy me olives, Noah. Don't buy me soup. You don't—"

"They were on sale," he lied, and handed her a box of Ring Dings. "For dessert."

"Are you staying for dessert?"

"Definitely." He pulled out a chair and sat at the table. It wobbled when he rested his elbows on it, and he bent to look at the legs. "Mom, what happened to that piece of wood I brought you to put under the short leg?"

"Isn't it there?" She folded the brown paper grocery bag neatly and put it into the cabinet beneath the sink. "You want some tea, Noah?"

"Sure." He should have brought tea bags, he realized, watching her take out a glass jar with only a few left, all herbal. He made a mental note to bring tea bags and another small piece of wood for the table leg.

"What time is Kelly coming home?" his mother asked, setting the kettle on the gas flame.

Never, Mom. She's never coming home.

But he couldn't bring himself to tell her that. It had been three weeks since Kelly had moved out, and months since they had come to the mutual decision that their marriage was over. He had even placed an ad for a roommate in the *Village Voice* classifieds, unable to afford the rent without Kelly's substantial salary, and unwilling to leave the apartment—and the eclectic East Village neighborhood—behind.

"Noah?"

He looked up to see his mother watching him, her hands on her hips. She looked old, he noticed. Old and shabby, in her faded jeans and a T-shirt emblazoned with a television network logo. He had given it to her, along with countless others—one of the perks of working in the creative department of a Madison Avenue ad agency. Free T-shirts, caps, nylon bags, plastic cups, key chains—all of them stamped with the names of various cable networks and publications.

Another perk was all the deodorant, laxatives, and condoms he could use, courtesy of the agency's biggest client. Now that Kelly was out of the picture, he supposed the condoms might come in handy . . . if he ever met a woman appealing enough to date, let alone sleep with.

He and Kelly hadn't needed condoms. She had an IUD—something most OB-GYNs didn't recommend for a woman who hadn't yet had children and intended to start a family. But Noah hadn't found out about that part until recently. He had always assumed that when they were ready for children, Kelly would have the IUD removed and get pregnant.

Theoretically, it could have worked that way, despite the doctor's recommendation. But Kelly hadn't wanted the IUD to be removed. She hadn't wanted to get pregnant, and she hadn't wanted children.

If only she had told him that before he married her. Before he fell in love with her.

She claimed she hadn't realized back then how she felt about motherhood. That she had assumed she would grow into the kind of maternal longing that seemed to seize all of their married friends. As it turned out, Kelly's biological clock was apparently defective, and she wasn't the least bit fazed.

Noah sometimes wondered if their marriage would have continued if she had been willing to have children.

Possibly.

Kelly had been easy to fall in love with back when they were both twenty-four and she was a gorgeous, witty, brilliant law student who was crazy about him. And she had been easy to fall out of love with now that they were both thirty-three and she was a gorgeous, witty, brilliant lawyer who was convinced that Noah wasn't living up to his potential.

Sooner or later, he would have to tell his mother that he and Kelly were getting divorced.

But not today.

He knew how badly his mother wanted him to have a normal life—the kind of life she never had, and could never give him. She wanted him to have a wife, and children, and a nice place to live, and a corporate job.

The corporate job, he had—although it was Kelly's idea, not his.

The nice place to live, he also had—and he would be able to keep it provided somebody promptly answered his ROOMMATE WANTED ad.

The rest—the wife and children—he would never have.

But even now, he couldn't help thinking about what might have been. Not with Kelly—with Mariel. After all these years, he still wondered about her, about whether they would have stayed together if she hadn't gotten pregnant.

Just as he wondered if he and Kelly would have stayed together if she had.

"Noah, is everything all right?" his mother asked, her probing dark eyes fastened on his face.

"Everything is fine, Mom," he lied, blotting Mariel's face out of his mind.

"Well? What do you think?" Mariel anxiously asked Katie Beth Mulligan, her closest friend for thirty years, since they were both in preschool and her name had been Katie Beth Miller. Now she was married to Patrick Mulligan, who had always sat behind her in classroom alphabetical order and had gone from pulling her red braids in elementary school to asking her out in high school.

Mariel had been maid of honor at their wedding the summer after Katie Beth graduated from the nearby state university with a teaching degree. By then Mariel was following in her footsteps. By the time she had earned her own master's in elementary education, Katie

Beth, the first grade teacher at Rockton Elementary, was going on maternity leave to have her first baby. She recommended to the school board that Mariel temporarily fill her position—and that she take it permanently when Katie Beth became pregnant again three months after giving birth and decided to become a full-time mom.

Now Katie Beth had four children, and Mariel had been the first grade teacher at Rockton Elementary long enough to have taught Katie Beth's oldest daughter, Olivia.

"I think she looks like you around the eyes," Katie Beth told her, glancing from the image on the computer screen to Mariel's face. "But I don't know about the rest."

"That's because you've never seen Noah," Mariel said. "She looks like a combination of me and him. Just seeing this picture is—"

She broke off, hearing a door slam downstairs.

"Mariel? I'm back," Leslie shouted.

"I'm up here with Katie Beth," Mariel called, quickly clicking on the *X* in the upper right hand corner of the screen that bore the downloaded photo of Amber Steadman. The computer complied, and the photo disappeared instantly.

To Katie Beth, she whispered, "What am I going to do about this? I'm sure it's her."

"Then, tell her."

"I can't tell her something like that with an e-mail," Mariel protested. "It's too impersonal."

Katie Beth nodded, her freckled face uncharacteristically serious. "Maybe you should call her," she suggested, her voice also low, lest Leslie overhear.

"Don't you think a phone call is almost as impersonal as an e-mail?"

"I guess you're right."

They looked at each other somberly.

Katie Beth was the sole person in whom Mariel had confided about her teenaged pregnancy and the child she had given up. Mariel hadn't even told her what had happened until she had been back in Rockton for a few years. By then, the pain of the experience had subsided to a dull ache, and Mariel had planned to keep it to herself forever. But when she visited Katie Beth in the hospital the day after her friend bore her first child, she was caught off guard by a flood of emotion the moment Katie Beth laid the newborn Olivia in Mariel's arms. She broke down sobbing and was forced to tell a bewildered Katie Beth what had happened.

They had rarely talked about it in the years since, but Mariel was glad to have unburdened herself—and glad to have Katie Beth to turn to now, when her lost daughter had suddenly materialized in her life.

"What are you going to do, Mariel?" Katie Beth asked.

"What *can* I do?" She leaned past her friend, who was seated in the desk chair, and grabbed the mouse, maneuvering it to shut down the computer. "It's the end of the school year, and on top of conferences, report cards, and science fair projects, I'm directing two dozen seven-year-olds in a musical version of *Snow White*. Plus I've got Leslie on my hands, and tomorrow I'm giving a bridal shower for sixty people—"

"Oh, before I forget, Pat is dropping off the punch bowl and extra chairs tomorrow morning because I'll be late for the shower—Ryan has a birthday party to go to, and Pat can't bring him because the other three aren't invited and he has to stay home with them."

Mariel smiled despite her dilemma. Katie Beth's home life was a constant flurry of pediatrician appointments, play dates, and lessons. Now that Pat was working full time down at the Ford dealership in addition to his part-time house-painting business, she really had her hands full.

"How do you feel about this, Mar?" Katie Beth asked, touching her sleeve as the computer whirred to a halt and the room went silent. "Do you want her in your life?"

"I live in Missouri, Katie Beth, and she lives in New York. I can't be in her life, even if she wants me to be there."

"But do you want her in yours?"

Mariel swallowed hard over a lump in her throat. The answer, of course, was yes. Yes, she desperately wanted her child in her life.

But this was far more complicated than what she wanted. Amber was no longer hers. Mariel had given her up so that she would have a mother and a father and a home and a future. Presumably, she had those things.

So why is she looking for me?

And then there was Noah. She hadn't seen him in fifteen years, and she had tried her hardest to put him out of her mind. The unexpected contact with Amber Steadman was a reminder that she wasn't the only parent involved here. Noah was the girl's father.

What if she's found him, too? Mariel wondered. What if somehow, by contacting Amber, she opened the door to a confrontation with Noah after all these years?

"Maybe she'll be better off if I don't tell her she found me," Mariel told Katie Beth, cringing at the thought of facing Noah again. "Maybe I should just write back and say sorry, wrong person."

"Maybe you should." Katie Beth's green eyes were troubled. "Or maybe you should tell her the truth. That you're her mother . . ."

"And I gave her away." Mariel felt hot tears stinging her eyes. "And then she can hate me, just like Noah did."

"From what you said, Noah didn't hate you," Katie Beth said gently. "He stood by you the whole time you were pregnant. He visited you in that home for unwed mothers, and he was there when you were in labor—"

"And afterward, to sign the papers he never wanted to sign." Mariel shook her head. "That was when it was over between us, Katie Beth. Whatever feelings he might have had left for me throughout the pregnancy were only because his child was inside me. Once she was out, and he realized I was going to go through with giving her up—I'll never forget the look on his face when he finished signing the adoption papers. It was just so . . ."

"Angry?"

"No. Just . . . dead. I can't think of any other way to describe it. He just wasn't there anymore, not the way he had been there for me. I guess he always had hope I would change my mind."

"And you never considered it?"

"How could I, Katie Beth? I couldn't marry him and raise a child. I was eighteen. And I couldn't come home with a baby after never telling my parents I was even pregnant."

"I can't believe none of us ever suspected when you

came home that Christmas," Katie Beth said. "I just figured you had gained the usual freshman ten pounds. We all had. Only mine never came off, and I added five more with each baby," she said ruefully, patting her ample hip.

"I couldn't believe nobody figured it out, either," Mariel said. "I spent half of that vacation throwing up and the rest of it sleeping. My parents figured I had the flu. And when I flew back east, they thought I was headed back to college. They never realized I was moving into St. Agatha's."

She closed her eyes, remembering what that had been like. She had taken a cab from the airport to the home for unwed mothers, conscious of the taxi driver's curious glances in the rearview mirror as he steered over the snowy highways. When she got out to walk up the icy steps of the big renovated Victorian home, he had hurried around to help her and insisted on carrying her bag for her. He had told her he had a one-year-old at home and that his wife was pregnant with their next child, as though they had something in common.

Even now, Mariel remembered the feeling of shame and utter loneliness that had seeped into her that day.

"You went through hell, Mariel," Katie Beth said, clasping her hand. "Maybe you should just leave it alone. Don't answer the e-mail at all. Let it go."

She nodded slowly. But she wasn't sure she could just let it go.

Amber Steadman had reached out to her. This was her one chance to connect with her lost child. And she knew in her heart that if she didn't take it, she would never get it back.

CHAPTER TWO

The sun was shining for a change in Syracuse, New York, but the June weather was far cooler than in Missouri, where the usual summer heatwave had kicked in earlier than usual this year.

As Mariel, lugging a large suitcase, walked through the airport parking lot toward her midsized rental car, she shivered despite the sunlight on her shoulders. She was wearing a sleeveless white cotton blouse, khaki shorts, and sandals. She would have been better off in jeans, a sweatshirt, and sneakers. She should have known better.

She couldn't help remembering the first time she had left the Midwestern heat to come east. It had been surprisingly cool here that day, too. But back then it had been summer's end, rather than its beginning. And back then, she had come here to embrace her future, rather than her past.

Almost three weeks had passed since she had received the e-mail from Amber Steadman. She had spent the time finishing out the school year and helping Leslie put away her shower gifts and decorate the small ranch house she and Jed were fixing up a few blocks away.

Every minute of every day, her daughter had been on her mind.

She knew what she had to do long before she went down to see Tammy Harper at All Aboard Travel to make reservations for a flight back to New York.

"Goin' on vacation, Mariel?" Tammy had asked. They had gone to high school together, and Tammy was the nosy, gossipy type.

Naturally, Mariel had responded with a simple yes.

"Syracuse, New York," Tammy mused. "That anywhere near New York City?"

"About four hours away," Mariel had told her, thinking that as a travel agent, Tammy could stand to brush up on her geography skills.

"So you're not goin' to New York City?"

"No."

"Why are you goin' to Syracuse on vacation? What's out there?"

"I went to college nearby," Mariel had said, gritting her teeth. "I'm going to visit an old friend."

That was what she had told Leslie and her father, too—that she had decided to attend a Strasburg reunion.

"But I'm getting married in less than a month, and you were only there for two semesters," Leslie had protested.

One semester, really, Mariel thought now as she opened

her suitcase and grabbed her jean jacket to wear. She got behind the wheel and started the engine.

Actually, maybe the fact that Leslie was getting married in a month was part of the reason Mariel suddenly felt as though she had to get away from Rockton. It wasn't just her sister's self-centered dependence on her to handle all the wedding details. She could do without Leslie's daily dramas, yes. But she could also do without the constant reminder that her sister was about to get married and leave home.

And leave Mariel.

Everyone had left. Her mother, her father, and now Leslie.

Ironic, because Mariel had been the one who had tried to leave them.

She wondered what people were saying in town about her now. Had they written her off as a spinster schoolteacher yet? Probably.

And she didn't care.

Rather, she shouldn't care.

But it hurt, being left alone in a house—and a town— she had never wanted to call her home.

At least when Mom and Dad and Leslie lived with her, she had a family. Now she had no one.

Except a daughter who lived half a continent away and who still had no idea that she had found her mother.

Mariel had decided against e-mailing Amber Steadman in reply, or even calling her. She had decided that an encounter like this should take place in person—it seemed the least potentially traumatic alternative.

So here she was, back in Syracuse, heading south on the winding, hilly highway that led out of the city toward the foothills of the Catskill Mountains. Strasburg was almost an hour's drive away, with Valley Falls another twenty-five miles beyond that.

Tammy had made her a reservation at the Super 8 just off the highway exit for Strasburg. Mariel had told her that was fine.

But when she pulled into the parking lot and eyed the functional, cement two-story building, she realized that this wasn't where she wanted to be.

Impulsively, she turned the car around and headed back out to the main road, making a right in the direction of a green STRASBURG 2 MILES sign with an arrow.

As she drove along the tree-lined highway, with the window down and a crisp breeze billowing through the car, she noticed town house complexes and businesses that weren't there fifteen years ago. Back then, everything had seemed shabby. Now quite a few of the rambling nineteenth century homes along the familiar route seemed to have had face lifts, with fresh paint, wicker porch furniture, and blooming window boxes. Some were fronted by BED AND BREAKFAST signposts. As she drew closer to town she saw that the old mediocre A&P had been replaced by a twenty-four-hour superstore with a bakery, pharmacy and florist. Nearby, a crumbling barn had been turned into an upscale antiques center.

As she turned along Main Street, she saw a row of quaint, tidy storefronts. The used bookstore was now a New Age boutique, and several bars had been transformed into cafes with sidewalk tables. Pots spilling over with bright pink and purple impatiens and petunias hung from every lamppost. In the small town green, surrounded by benches, the crumbling fountain she remembered had been restored with a statue at its center and streams of sparkling water spilling from tier to tier.

She had almost reached the end of Main Street. There, adjacent to the entrance to the campus, a three-story Victorian loomed.

So it was still here.

Mariel pulled into a diagonal parking space on the street in front of the building and sat for a moment, staring up at the familiar structure through the windshield.

It used to be a muddy yellow color, with black trim.

Now it was painted in a period palate—shades of rose and mauve and eggshell adorning the ornately scrolling gingerbread trim, the wooden shutters, and the rows of fish-scale shingles way up under the gables. The big wraparound porch was still intact, but the white rocking chairs she remembered had been repainted a dark maroon to match the color scheme. The place looked, all in all, like a rose-colored valentine.

Over the years, she had often thought about the Sweet Briar Inn.

It was here that Noah had brought her on the September night when they had been alone together for the first time. It was probably here, in the pretty white iron bed she remembered so clearly, that their child had been conceived.

She opened the car door and got out, walking briskly toward the front steps before she had a chance to change her mind, to question the wisdom of staying in a place that would only bring back memories of her first love.

Hell, her only love.

There had never been another man in her life.

She had dated, back in college. She had tried to make herself fall in love with one after another of the nice local boys who were interested in her. But every time she went out with one, she felt as though she could see what her life would be like if she married him. With every boy, the vision was the same.

It was the life her mother had, and Katie Beth had, and Leslie was about to have.

It was the ordinary life she never wanted.

Or maybe, she thought as she mounted the wooden steps, she just didn't want it with the wrong person.

There had been a time when she had glimpsed a future like that with Noah—marriage, and a home, and a family—and it hadn't made her want to cringe or run away.

But she had lost Noah, and she had kept the local college boys at arm's length, and when she graduated and started teaching, she had found herself the lone unmarried, twentysomething woman in Rockton, aside from Pat Carver, the middle school gym teacher, who lived with another woman and whom nobody liked to talk about.

There simply wasn't anybody for Mariel to date as long as she stayed in Rockton. And at this point, she was past considering leaving. It was too late to recapture her dream of becoming an actress, even if she were motivated. The truth was, she had long since lost the burning desire to be onstage. She no longer needed the adoration of thousands—though the adoration of one might be nice. One special person who loved her more than anything else . . .

But that wasn't meant to be.

Her plans to see the world had evaporated, too. This

trip east was the first solo vacation she had taken. Until now, her travels had been limited to yearly trips to Florida with her family, and then alone with Leslie for Thanksgiving and Easter after Dad had moved there. Now that Leslie was getting married, their visits to Dad on holidays wouldn't even be the same because Jed would be along and Mariel would always feel like a third wheel.

Having reached the porch, Mariel hesitated only a moment in front of the antique double doors with their oval beveled windows. Then she opened the door on the right and stepped into the hushed, carpeted foyer.

Classical music was playing in the background. Pachelbel's Canon in D, she noted. It was one of her favorite pieces, and the familiar strains eased the tension in her shoulders a bit.

Inhaling the cinnamon-apple scent of potpourri, she looked around. Slowly, her eyes adjusted to the dim interior. As she gazed at the floral-print wallpaper, the french doors opening onto the large restaurant dining room, the built-in curio cabinets, and the vast stairway leading to the second and third floors, she realized that she didn't recall what any of it had looked like back then. And no wonder. She had known why Noah had brought her here, and all she could think about was that she was about to make love for the first time. She didn't remember being nervous or afraid—only that she had wanted to be here with him; that she had been crazy about him and knew that what they were doing wasn't wrong. That it couldn't be wrong.

Lord, had she really believed that? Had she really been that naive, that innocent?

"I'm afraid we don't start serving dinner until five-thirty," a voice said. "And we stopped serving lunch at three."

Startled, Mariel realized that there was an elderly lady standing behind a tall counter in the far corner of the room. She had a cloud of snow-white hair, wire-rimmed glasses, and wore several long strands of pearls over her sand-colored summer sweater.

"Oh, I'm not here to eat," Mariel told her. "I was wondering if you had a room vacancy."

There. She had said it. It was too late now to go back to the sterile Super 8 on the highway.

"Yes, we do. But the ones on the second floor with private baths are all occupied. We do have rooms on the third floor with shared bathrooms—right down the hall. Will that be all right? You'd be the only guest up there."

"That would be fine, thank you."

The woman reached for a clipboard, introducing herself. "I'm Susan Tominski—my son owns the inn, and I work the desk most days. For how many nights did you need a room?"

Mariel fumbled for an answer and settled on "Two." Then she cleared her throat and amended, "Maybe longer, though. Or . . . maybe just one."

Yes, just one if she changed her mind about finding Amber Steadman and decided to board the first plane back home in the morning instead of waiting until Tuesday, when she had scheduled her return flight.

The old lady looked confused.

"I'm sorry," Mariel said. "I'll definitely take it for two."

If she had to leave tomorrow, she would just pay for two nights.

"Are you vacationing here?" Susan Tominski asked—pleasantly, not nosily as Tammy had. Still, Mariel's guard went up.

"No, not really," Mariel said, and changed the subject. "It sure is chilly today, isn't it?"

"Oh, the heatwave is on its way," the woman said with a smile. "They're saying on the Weather Channel that it's going to be in the high nineties by this time tomorrow. Hard to believe, isn't it?"

"It sure is."

"You know, you look familiar," Susan said, looking more closely at her, and Mariel's stomach turned over.

Could she possibly recognize her from that night she and Noah had been here all those years ago? Could she possibly know that Mariel had gotten pregnant and dropped out of school and—

"You're Sam Crowe's niece Linda, aren't you?" she asked, pointing a finger as though she had suddenly placed Mariel.

"No . . . no, I'm not." Relief coursed through Mariel. Of course the old lady didn't remember her. Chances were that nobody in Strasburg remembered her. And nobody in town other than Noah had ever known what had happened to her.

After she found out she was pregnant, she had distanced herself from her roommates and the handful of other friends she had made in her first few months at college. Before she went home for Christmas, while everyone was distracted by finals, she started telling people she had decided to transfer to a college back in Missouri because she was homesick. They actually seemed to buy it.

"Oh, you look just like that Linda," Susan chattered.

"But then, I haven't seen her in twenty years since she moved to Buffalo, and I guess she wouldn't look like that anymore, would she? She'd be middle-aged by now." Chuckling to herself, she turned to look at an old-fashioned grid of key cubbyholes.

And then it struck Mariel belatedly that this old woman might not be the only local who thought she looked familiar. It was entirely possible that if she ran into anyone who knew Amber Steadman, the resemblance might be noticed. She should probably prepare herself for that. . . .

Or you can just leave now. Just go home and forget she ever found you.

Her hand clenching the rental car key at her side, she realized that it was what she wanted to do. Why confront the past and dig up all of those unresolved emotions? Why put herself through the turmoil of meeting the daughter she had given up? For all she knew, the girl was filled with resentment for a mother who had placed her into a stranger's arms, then turned her back forever . . . or for what she had thought—hoped— would be forever.

She didn't want to face Amber, and she didn't want to face the aftermath of what she had done. She wanted to go home to Rockton and try to forget, just as she had been doing for the past fifteen years. She wanted to assume she had done what was best—even if Noah had felt differently at the time. If it had been up to him, they would be married and raising a teenaged daughter right now.

She swallowed hard, wanting that scenario to seem as horrible as it had a decade and a half ago.

But strangely, it didn't.

Who are you kidding, Mariel? You wouldn't still be married to him. Shotgun teenaged marriages never last. You would probably be long divorced by now, a single mother trying to make it without a college degree.

So she had done the right thing, hadn't she? Shoving aside her doubts, she opened her mouth to announce that she had changed her mind about the room. If she hurried back to the airport, she might be able to catch a flight back home this evening—

"Here we are, room eight," Susan said, turning back to face Mariel, key in hand. "Just go right up both flights of stairs to the third floor. It'll be the last room on your right."

Mariel closed her mouth.

Opening it again, "Thank you," was all she said as she dropped the car key into the pocket of her shorts and reached out to take the one for room 8.

Noah flipped through the stack of mail he had just removed from the mailbox in the entryway as he walked up the fourth and last flight of steps. Nothing but bills— Con Ed, cable, his *Writer's Digest* subscription, and his Banana Republic charge account.

He didn't want to see that one. He had bought himself several new shirts and a few pairs of khakis and jeans last month, right after he had found a new roommate. His thinking had been that he could afford to splurge a little now that he didn't have to worry about paying the entire rent single-handedly this month.

But somehow, he was still broke. His twice-monthly paycheck from the ad agency never seemed to stretch far enough, thanks to the ridiculous cost of living in

Manhattan. Maybe he should chuck it all, move away, and start over someplace where he could get more than eight hundred square feet for two thousand dollars a month.

But where would he go? And what would he do? There wasn't a tremendous demand for advertising creatives outside of New York City. He had fallen into this career more out of necessity than ambition, but the ad industry was where his experience lay, and it was based in New York.

He made his way along the hallway—which smelled of frying onions and Pine Sol—toward his apartment, making a face as he heard the music spilling out into the hallway from beyond his closed door.

Maybe he should just give up this place and move out into one of the boroughs or into Jersey, where rents were cheaper and he could get more for his money.

After all, this roommate thing wasn't really working out so far.

It wasn't that he didn't like Alan Henning, because he did. Well, he supposed he would, as he got to know him better. Right now they were little more than strangers. Alan was quiet, and pleasant enough, and he cleaned up after himself. The trouble was, it seemed as though the guy was always there, underfoot.

Noah had chosen him from more than a dozen applicants in part because he said he worked odd hours, rather than nine-to-five. Since Noah worked regular business hours at the agency—aside from frequent killer overtime—he had figured that would mean he and Alan wouldn't be in each other's way.

As it turned out, Alan, who was a bartender and musician, never seemed to leave the apartment until very late in the evening, right around the time Noah went to bed. And he invariably came home at about the same hour Noah's alarm went off. He used to enjoy watching the *Today Show* as he got ready for work and made coffee, but Alan was usually sprawled on the couch watching music videos by the time he got out of the shower. It was disconcerting to feel as though his apartment was no longer his own.

Of course, it never had been his own, really. He had shared the place with Kelly ever since they moved in almost seven years ago, right before they got married. But living with a wife wasn't like living with a roommate—not until the end, when he and Kelly had realized their marriage wasn't going to last. That was when they had entered that stage of awkward politeness, same as Noah had with Alan now.

All he really wanted, he thought as he inserted his key into the deadbolt, was to feel like he was home. He hadn't felt like that here in months. Years, really, because even when he and Kelly were companionably married, he had always thought that it would take children to transform their lives into that comfortable domestic mode he craved.

He felt a pang for the life he would never have—the life he had always assumed lay right around the corner.

Stepping over the threshold into the small entry hall, he fought the urge to cover his ears. The rock music was blasting from the stereo speakers in the living room. Still clutching his keys, with his black canvas briefcase-style bag slung over his shoulder, he poked his head into the room and saw Alan on the couch. He wore only a pair of gray sweatpants and lay on his back, eyes closed, elbows bent, hands tucked under his neck.

Noah went over to turn the volume down.

Alan immediately opened his eyes and sat up. "Oh," he said, "you scared me."

"Sorry. I just thought it was a little loud. The neighbors might complain."

"They haven't said anything."

"But they might tell the super, and that's the last thing we need. Trust me, you don't want to make an enemy out of Nelson Santiago. He can be a real SOB."

"So you've said." Alan yawned lazily and rubbed the scruffy half beard on his chin. With his shoulder-length dark hair and slacker wardrobe, he wasn't the kind of roommate Noah had pictured finding when he placed the ad. But the others who had shown up had either seemed vaguely shady or were right out of college or new in New York and eager to make friends. At this stage in his life, Noah had enough male pals, and he certainly wasn't in the mood to play tour guide.

Alan, who was about Noah's age and had lived here all his life, had seemed relatively low maintenance, and thus the safest prospect.

Noah supposed he would get used to him always being around, and he seemed to mind his own business for the most part. Then again, there had been a few occasions when Noah had been certain that somebody had gone through his drawers. He suspected that Alan might have been looking for clothing to borrow, since his own wardrobe seemed to be fairly limited. At least, that was what he wanted to believe. He doubted the guy was a kleptomaniac, and besides, nothing had ever been missing. Just rumpled or moved around a bit, as though somebody had snooped.

Even that made Noah uneasy, but he had to give his

roommate the benefit of the doubt until he actually caught him in the act. Besides, maybe it was his imagination. He had been pretty distracted lately.

In an effort to be friendly, he asked Alan, "How was your day?"

"It was cool. How was work?"

"The usual," Noah said. "Crazy pace. Crazy clients. I'm lucky I got out by eight tonight." If he hadn't ducked out the door when he did, he would have been there until midnight. That would have made three nights in a row.

There would probably be hell to pay Monday morning, but right now, that seemed a long way off. The weekend had finally arrived—not that he had big plans. Or any plans.

With a sigh, Noah tossed his bag over the back of an imitation Stickley chair. Kelly had taken the real thing when she moved out. This was one they had picked up a few years ago at a tag sale while they were visiting friends up in Westchester.

The apartment had once been furnished mainly in tag sale and secondhand store finds, but as Kelly's salary climbed, she had purchased increasingly stylish furniture. Some of it looked just like the junk, but was what she called "shabby chic," and cost far more. She had taken all of it with her to her new two-bedroom floor-through in a brownstone on the Upper West Side.

Noah looked around the living room, thinking that it basically resembled one of the houses in Whoville after the Grinch got through pillaging it in the old Dr. Seuss cartoon. There were bare hooks on the walls where pictures had once hung, and a worn spot on the carpet that had once been hidden by a potted plant. He really had to buy some curtains for the windows, which were now covered only in the ugly aluminum blinds that had come with the place. And he should go shopping for a real bookcase instead of leaving those stacks of paperbacks in a couple of plastic crates he had picked up at a bargain store on Canal Street.

There was a lot he would do, if he ever had time.

No, he had time.

If he ever was inspired—that was more like it. Because it wasn't easy to invest time, money, and energy in fixing up an apartment that was little more than a roof over his head.

When Alan had moved in, Noah had told him to feel free to contribute to the decor if he felt like it. Apparently, he didn't, because he had brought little more with him besides his clothes, his guitar, his CDs, and the box spring and mattress that served as his bed.

"Did anyone call?" Noah asked, glancing at the answering machine.

"Nope."

Noah fought the urge to ask if he was sure. Just last week, his friend Craig had said he left a message for Noah on the machine, but Noah had never got it. He figured Alan must have accidentally erased it.

That could happen to anyone, but Noah couldn't help feeling increasingly irritated with his omnipresent roommate. If he could just have some privacy, maybe he would be able to relax. Sit on the couch with a beer, catch a Yankees game . . .

But the couch was full of Alan, as usual, and he wouldn't be able to hear the announcers above the blasting stereo.

Too bad Kelly had taken the big-screen television she

had bought him for his thirtieth birthday a few years back. She had left him their bedroom TV, which he had moved to the living room. Now he wondered if that had been a mistake. At least with a television in his bedroom, there would be something to do other than lie on his bed and brood.

His computer, too, was in the living room. There wasn't adequate outlet space for it in the bedroom. At least Kelly hadn't taken that, leaving the bulky desktop here in favor of the state-of-the-art laptop she had brought with her.

Piled on the floor beside the computer were stacks of manilla folders, each containing portions of various screenplays Noah had been writing for years. He always told himself that some day he would finish one and send it off to Hollywood, and that would be the end of his nine-to-five misery. But that day wouldn't come if he didn't work on his writing, and he hadn't worked on his writing in ages.

He could blame it on Alan always being in the living room, but the truth was, he had gradually lost his motivation to write as his marriage to Kelly became less and less fulfilling. He couldn't remember the last time he had worked on his latest project, an international intrigue thriller that he was convinced would be perfect for Harrison Ford or Bruce Willis . . . if Noah ever got past writing the opening scene, finished the damned thing, and sold it.

He sighed and sat at the desk in the corner beneath one of the two tall living room windows that faced Broadway. The blinds were open, and he gazed out as he waited for the computer to boot up. There wasn't much of a view since he was on a low floor—just the ever present traffic dotted with yellow taxicabs and buses, and the tall, white stone-faced building across the wide avenue, with rows of apartment windows on the upper levels and several shops with brightly lit display windows on the first floor.

Noah turned his attention back to his computer. He clicked on the Internet access icon, then, when his screen came up, clicked on the Sign On icon. His name and password were automatically entered in the system, so the dial-up was immediate.

He remembered how, toward the end of their marriage, Kelly had changed her own Internet access screen so that her password had to be entered each time she signed on. He didn't know the new code, and he didn't ask her why she had changed the system so that a password was necessary. It was obvious. She didn't want him to have access to her e-mail.

He had wondered—often, at first—if that meant she was involved with somebody else. But by the time their divorce was inevitable, he had stopped caring. Now he doubted that she was romantically involved with anyone, or had been during their marriage. Kelly was wed to her work and her lifestyle, a lifestyle that included shopping and the spa and the gym and her uptown friends. That was fine with him. He only wished it hadn't taken them so many years to discover that they were moving in opposite directions.

As the Internet came up on his screen, Noah was disappointed to find that there was no little flag popping up from the mailbox icon, and the voice was silent after a computerized "Welcome."

No mail.

Not even junk mail.

Disheartened, he considered surfing the net for a while. Then, with a glance at Alan lounging on the couch two feet away and showing no hint of any other plan, Noah signed off abruptly and stood up. He might as well go to his room, where he could unwind in peace and relative quiet, now that the stereo volume was lower. Maybe later he would scrounge up something from the kitchen to eat or have a pizza delivered. It was almost nine, and he was too exhausted to go out, even just to pick up takeout.

"No e-mail?" Alan asked casually, opening his eyes again as Noah crossed the room and opened the door that led to his ten-by-twelve private space.

"Not tonight," Noah replied. "I'm going to lie down in my room for a while."

"Okay. I'll see you later."

I'm sure you will, Noah thought grimly as he closed the door behind him, unable to believe that his life had come to this.

As dusk settled over the quaint buildings nestled on Strasburg's Main Street, Mariel emerged from the Sweet Briar Inn wearing the jeans, sweatshirt, and sneakers she had wished she had on earlier. She had spent the past few hours curled up on the bed, asleep. She had been so nervous about the trip that she had tossed and turned restlessly the past few nights back home, and exhaustion had finally caught up with her. Now, feeling slightly refreshed if no less apprehensive, she intended to find someplace to eat where she wouldn't feel conspicuous dining alone.

Back home, nobody ever ate out alone, aside from

the retirees who filled the stools at the local coffee shop, where the waitresses knew everyone and spent as much time chatting with the regulars at the counter as they did serving and clearing tables.

As she strolled away from the inn toward the row of shops and cafes, Mariel decided to buy a newspaper so that she would have something to look at while she ate. It should be such a simple thing for a grown woman to do: to eat solo in a restaurant.

But she couldn't help feeling jittery about the prospect. Maybe it was because she was here, in Strasburg, after so many years of revisiting the place in her mind.

The town was more quaint than she remembered, she thought, as she walked beneath the leafy canopy of towering, centuries-old maples and oaks. Crickets were buzzing, and the air seemed more still, less chilly, than it had this afternoon. Maybe Susan had been right about the weather, although Mariel couldn't imagine this part of New York State being in the grip of a heatwave. What she mainly remembered of the ten months she had spent here, aside from the glorious autumn when she had fallen in love with Noah, was snow, snow, and more snow. Snow that started the first week of November and lasted into April.

By the time the weather warmed, she had been hugely pregnant and spent most of her time indoors, staring at the wall, contemplating the decision she had made about the baby—the decision she intended to stick to, no matter what.

And she had.

She realized that she was in front of a small stationery and tobacco store that sold magazines and newspapers. It was right next door to a small cafe with tables out on the sidewalk. A few of them were occupied, but it appeared to be the kind of quiet, casual place she was looking for. She decided to buy something to read and head over.

Two minutes later, she was seated at a small, round table located right next to the sidewalk, her back to the other patrons. The hostess hadn't seemed fazed that Mariel had asked for a table for one, but she couldn't help feeling self-conscious dining solo.

A good-looking college student–type appeared beside her table. "Hi, my name is Kevin and I'll be your waiter tonight. Are you waiting for somebody to join you, or . . . ?"

"No, I'm here alone," Mariel said uncomfortably, glancing over her shoulder toward the couples at the other tables. She realized that most of them were young— undoubtedly students spending the summer semester at college.

She pushed aside the wistfulness that crept in and turned her attention to the waiter, who was telling her about the specials. She ordered a pasta dish and a glass of white wine, then unfolded the local newspaper and scanned the front page.

Not much national or international news here, she noticed—how like the *Rockton Gazette* back home. Apparently, small towns everywhere were more caught up in local issues than global ones. Mariel skimmed an article about an upcoming controversial zoning board hearing and one about scholarship winners who had just graduated from Strasburg Central High School. She flipped to the second page and read through incidents listed in the police blotter section—a runaway dog, a

shoplifting incident at the 7–Eleven, and a couple of
fender benders.

Her wine arrived as she was reading the letters to the
editor on page four. She took a sip of the cool, tangy
sweetness, thinking she should have bought additional
reading material. At this rate, she would be finished
with the entire newspaper before her salad arrived.

As she turned her attention to the next page, a name
jumped out at her, and her breath caught in her throat.

Amber Steadman.

She had glimpsed it almost subconsciously and assured herself that she had to be mistaken as she scrutinized the print, searching for it again.

But she hadn't been wrong.

There it was.

Amber Steadman.

In the lead paragraph beneath a headline that read

VALLEY FALLS GIRL REMAINS MISSING.

The next few hours were a blur for Mariel.

She had made some excuse to the waiter and left the
cafe after paying for her meal, turning down his offer
to wrap the salad and pasta for her to take with her.
She had absolutely no appetite left.

She returned to the newsstand and bought a copy of
every other local newspaper she could find, including
the bigger ones from Syracuse, Binghamton and Utica.

Back in her room, she combed through them page
by page, line by line, searching for more information on
the missing Valley Falls teenager. But there was nothing
else, aside from an article in the *Valley Falls Ledger* that
basically recapped what she had read back at the cafe.

Amber Steadman had disappeared more than a week ago without a trace. She had been last seen leaving for school. There was no evidence of foul play, but the police were working with her frantic parents to track down any possible leads. A hotline number had been set up, and the parents were offering a reward for information leading to her safe return.

Now, seated at a microfiche machine in the nearly empty Strasburg college library, Mariel had spent the past hour scanning previous issues of the local newspapers for stories about the disappearance. It had made the front page headlines in all of the papers, accompanied by photos of Amber, and one, in the *Valley Falls Ledger,* of her parents. Carl and Joanne Steadman were a moderately attractive middle-aged couple—Carl balding with glasses, Joanne petite with short blond hair. The strain of their ordeal was evident in the photo, which had apparently been snapped outside police headquarters. They looked like distraught, worried parents.

Ever since she had found out about Amber's disappearance, a growing sense of panic had taken hold inside of her. What if Amber had been abducted by one of those twisted serial killers she occasionally heard about—the kind that preyed upon teenaged girls? What if she had been raped, tortured, killed?

Mariel felt sick as one horrific scenario after another played through her mind, and she realized that for Carl and Joanne Steadman, the nightmare was hundreds, thousands of times worse. Mariel might be Amber's birth mother, but Carl and Joanne were the ones who had raised her, nurtured her, protected her, loved her.

Or had they?

In several accounts covering the story, there was mention of the fact that the police suspected that Amber might not have been abducted. Some of her possessions were missing, and more than one of her schoolmates had told a detective that Amber had been talking about running away.

Mariel sat staring into space, her arms wrapped around her churning middle as she contemplated that. Why would Amber have run away?

Could it possibly have anything to do with the fact that she had e-mailed Mariel and gotten no response?

Logically, Mariel didn't see how that could possibly be the case. Amber didn't know that she was her birth mother—only that it was possible. Surely if Amber was that upset about not hearing back from her, she would have contacted her again.

But even if that hadn't been the reason Amber had run away—*if* she had even run away—could it have contributed somehow to the situation? What was Amber running from? What had led her to contact Mariel in the first place? And would she still have run away if Mariel had written back to her, or called her, instead of waiting until now?

Her mind whirling, Mariel turned off the microfiche machine and pushed back her chair. She had to do something. She couldn't just sit here reading about her daughter's disappearance. She had to see if she could help.

But how?

Should she call the police? If she did, she realized, they might suspect that she had something to do with Amber's disappearance. Of course they would. They would find it coincidental that she turned up in town now, after years of silence . . . wouldn't they?

But it wasn't coincidental. Amber had contacted her out of the blue, possibly because Amber was troubled. That made sense. If something had been bothering her—especially something involving her home life—she might fantasize about her birth mother coming to the rescue.

Well, Mariel had failed miserably there.

But she wasn't the only birth parent Amber might have tried to find.

Noah's name had been on the adoption papers. Whatever source had led Amber to Mariel could also have led her to Noah. Had she tried to contact him, too?

Had she found him, too?

Mariel walked slowly through the maze of study carrels, finding her way back to the reference desk, where a lone librarian was on duty. The place was nearly deserted at this hour on a Friday evening in June.

"Excuse me," she said to the woman behind the desk, who had earlier shown her how to use the microfiche machine. "I was wondering if you would mind helping me again?"

"I don't mind," the woman said, "but I do have to remind you that the library is closing in ten minutes."

"Oh, no."

"I'm sorry." She offered a sympathetic smile. "We have abbreviated hours at this time of year. But you can always come back in the morning. We open at—"

"No, actually, this shouldn't take long, if you can point me in the right direction. I need help locating somebody. He went to Strasburg, actually, so maybe

there's some kind of alumni data base that would list
current addresses and phone numbers?''

"There is, but he would most likely be listed there
only if he graduated. Did he?''

"I don't know,'' Mariel admitted. She had no idea
what had ever become of Noah after he walked out of
that hospital room on the Fourth of July fifteen years
ago. Now she was struck by the realization that with any
luck, she was about to find out.

"Well, we can start there,'' the woman said, rising
and walking toward a bank of computer terminals.

Minutes later, Mariel was staring at a listing on the
screen. According to this, Noah Lyons lived on Broadway in New York City. There was no phone number,
but an e-mail address was provided. That was it. No
marital status or family or employment information.

Well.

He was still in New York.

"Do you think this is the person you were looking
for?'' the librarian asked.

Startled, having forgotten she wasn't alone, she nodded. "I'm sure it is.''

"If you want to take a moment to copy down the
information . . .'' The woman looked pointedly at her
watch.

"I'll do it quickly,'' Mariel promised, and the woman
smiled briefly before walking away.

Mariel fumbled in her bag for a pen and something
to write on.

Are you married, Noah?

Do you have children?

*What kind of job do you have? Are you happy? Do you ever
think about me?*

Tears blurred her eyes as she scribbled the information onto the back of a cash machine withdrawal receipt. She wasn't prepared for this flood of emotion, nor was she prepared to contemplate speaking to Noah again.

So, instead of contemplating it, she acted—before she could have time to change her mind.

The computer had Internet access. She hurriedly got on-line and typed Noah's e-mail address into a blank letter, then sat there, fingers poised over the keyboard, wondering what to write.

"Ma'am? We're closing now," the librarian called politely from her desk.

"All right, I'll be finished in a second," Mariel murmured, beginning to type. Her fingers flew over the keys as sections of overhead lights began to click off around her. She didn't bother to reread the message, just hit Send and pushed back her chair.

"Did you find what you needed?" the librarian asked as Mariel scurried toward the door, where a second librarian stood waiting, jangling a key ring impatiently.

She could only nod, her throat too choked with emotion to respond.

CHAPTER THREE

"Another Saturday night, and I ain't got nobody . . ."
Noah stopped singing the old Cat Stevens tune as he
opened the fridge and took out a beer. He twisted off
the cap, admiring the mist that swirled from the neck
of the green bottle. Then, wiping a trickle of sweat from
his right temple, he carried the beer into the living
room and sat on the sill in front of the open window,
hoping for a breeze.

No such luck.

It was hotter than hell in this apartment, and thanks
to Kelly, he no longer had the window air conditioner
units that had cooled down the entire place in summers
past. The heat and humidity had moved in from the
west, striking the city just as the sun came up this morning. After meeting his friend Danny for a racquetball
game, Noah had spent the afternoon at his mother's
apartment, tinkering with an old floor fan that she

couldn't get to work. Nothing he did could salvage it, and he wound up going with her to Duane Reade so that she could get a new one.

He would go buy a fan for himself, too—tomorrow. He was too hot and exhausted to go in search of one now and then lug it home through the streets.

He sat with his back leaning against the window frame, one knee bent and his foot on the sill. He took a big gulp of the cold beer and looked out over Broadway below, listening to the traffic and watching people walking along the sidewalk that teemed with people at every hour of the day.

He wondered, as he had been prone to wondering lately, what it would be like to live someplace else. Someplace where peace and quiet didn't cost more than he could afford on a nearly six-figure salary. Where he wouldn't be in a constant state of exhaustion, and could actually get some writing done.

But tonight, if it weren't for the heat, he would have almost been content for a change. Alan was out, so he finally had the apartment to himself. He liked to stay in on Saturday nights, relishing the lazy hours at home, knowing he didn't have to rise early with an alarm the next morning.

When he was married, Kelly had planned almost every minute of every weekend. There were parties and art gallery openings and dinners out with friends—nearly always her friends and their boring spouses, at pretentious restaurants where minuscule entrees were presented on enormous white plates with adroitly placed green sprigs or scrolls of artfully dribbled sauce.

When he was in the mood to go out, Noah liked pizza and spaghetti and Mexican food, and he liked noisy, crowded places where he could wear jeans and drink beer from a bottle or sip a strong frozen drink.

Tonight, he had been invited to join Austin, one of the copywriters at work, and his wife, who were going to a nearby cabaret with some friends. Considering the way Austin had asked several times yesterday if Noah was absolutely sure he wasn't interested, Noah had assumed that the friends included unattached females.

Austin wasn't the only one who seemed inclined to believe that Noah was sitting around moping and lonely now that Kelly had left him. Several of his friends had extended invitations for blind double dates lately, and Danny, still happily single at thirty-five, had tried to talk him into taking a half share in a house in the Hamptons for the summer. He had heard about Danny's summer escapades for a few years now and wasn't the least bit tempted by the promise of wild nights in clubs with beautiful, promiscuous women.

He was too damned tired for that.

Not necessarily physically—because the truth was, he ached to hold a woman, to make love again after months of celibacy.

But emotionally, he just couldn't handle the party scene—the fleeting, meaningless flings that had never even appealed to him in his college days. That wasn't where he had expected—or wanted—to be at this stage of his life.

He sighed, drained the beer, and went to the fridge for another. As he pushed aside the cartons of take-out Chinese left over from dinner a few nights ago, he realized that there was only one beer left from the six-pack he had bought recently on the way home after a particularly trying day at the office. There should have been three.

Obviously, Alan had helped himself.

Terrific.

Noah would have to have a talk with him about sharing the grocery expenses. That, too, was something he hadn't expected to be doing at this stage of his life. Dealing with roommates was something a student did while away at school, or a young adult just starting out in the city. He was a grown man with a corporate job—he shouldn't be living like this.

Christ, he thought grimly, opening the last beer, how many times was he going to be astonished all over again that this was how his life had turned out? The reality of his world seemed to catch him off guard several times a day. One would think, sooner or later, that he would be used to it. But he wasn't.

He returned to the living room and glanced at the pile of half-written screenplays on the floor by the computer. He could work on one. . . .

No, he couldn't.

He was too drained to create.

Noah restlessly turned on the television. He flipped channels on the remote, marveling that the renowned Manhattan cable television system, with more than a hundred stations, was showing nothing that captured his interest.

What would capture his interest?

"A new life," he said aloud, clicking off the television and tossing the remote onto the couch. That would do it. If he could move someplace, start over, find something he loved—somebody he loved—he would be at peace.

Okay, great. Now he had a plan. All he had to do was implement it.

Yeah, right. He must have drunk that first beer down too fast. In this frame of mind, anything seemed possible.

So maybe it was, he told himself as he put on an old Steely Dan CD. Maybe all he had to do was find out what was out there, and then go after it.

He sat down at the computer desk and turned on the monitor, figuring that the Internet was a good place to start. Not that he knew how to go about finding whatever it was he was looking for. He could hardly type "new life" into the search engine Find prompt.

Or could he?

Holding the bottle in his left hand, he sipped more beer as he maneuvered the mouse with his right, using the swift one-click sign-on to the Internet.

"Welcome. You've got mail," the automated voice announced.

"I do?" he said aloud. He raised an eyebrow and clicked on the mailbox icon.

He didn't recognize the sender's user name.

When he opened the e-mail, he automatically glanced first at the bottom for a signature.

When he read the name that was typed there, he gasped.

Instantly trembling from head to toe, he set the beer bottle on the floor beside his chair and leaned forward, forcing himself to read the message through from the beginning.

Dear Noah,

I know that this e-mail from me, out of the blue, will catch you off guard, and I'm sorry. I'll get right to the point. The child we gave up for adoption is in trouble, and I thought you deserved to know. I'm in Strasburg, staying at the Sweet Briar Inn, in Room 8. You can reach me there. I would have called you, but there was no phone number listed in the alumni database.

Sincerely,
Mariel Rowan

A flurry of thoughts crossed his mind as he finished reading—disparate thoughts, as he struggled to get hold of himself in response to the shocking, sudden connection to a woman he had never thought he would speak to—or see—again.

I never should have listened to Kelly. . . . She had told him never to give out their phone number for anything, ever. They were unlisted, and she didn't want to end up getting telemarketing calls. Nor did he, but that was beside the point. If he had listed their phone number on the form the alumni council had sent him years ago, Mariel could have called him directly instead of resorting to electronic communication.

Our child is in trouble.

What kind of trouble? His heart lurched at the thought of the daughter he had never forgotten, not for one day of his life in all the years since he had silently told her good-bye and wished her a good life.

She signed it Mariel Rowan—that means she's still single.

Or did it? Mariel wasn't the kind of woman he could imagine taking her husband's name. He wasn't even sure he could imagine her married. Or maybe that was just because he was reluctant to think of her with another man, even now.

Over the years, he had occasionally wondered what had become of her.

Occasionally?

Hell, often, before and after the few good years he had spent at the beginning of his relationship with Kelly.

Now he could pick up the phone and call Mariel Rowan at the Sweet Briar Inn in Strasburg. She was there, only a few hours' drive away from here.

Because their child was in trouble.

Why the hell did she know about this? Why was she telling him? Had she been in contact with their daughter over the years?

A wave of jealousy swept through him, trailed by a flicker of long-dormant anger as all the old feelings came rushing back. He had wanted so desperately to keep their baby. Even after he had realized that she really wasn't going to give in and marry him—even after he had realized that it was probably for the best—he had struggled to figure out a way that he could raise their daughter on his own.

But in the end, he had realized that Mariel was right. There was nothing to do but give her up to parents who couldn't possibly love her any more than Noah did, but who would give her everything he couldn't.

Yet they hadn't kept his baby safe from harm. Dammit, she was in trouble.

What kind of trouble? Frantic, he rose from his chair and stalked over to the telephone, picking it up.

There was no dial tone.

Cursing, he jabbed the Talk button a few times.

Still no dial tone.

What the . . . ?

Oh.

The line was tied up by the computer. He strode back over to the screen and quickly signed off, then pressed the Talk button again.

This time there was a dial tone.

He dialed information, his heart racing.

Susan Tominski was behind the desk in the lobby when Mariel returned at dusk from an evening walk around campus. After a day spent mostly brooding in her room and scanning today's editions of all the local papers, she had decided that it would be a good idea to get out for some air. So, despite the heat and humidity that had set in today just as Susan had forecast, she had wandered along the paths, staring at the familiar ivy-covered brick buildings with their freshly painted trim and white six-over-six windowpanes.

A lifetime had passed since she had been here, and she felt the years. She barely remembered what it had been like to live in Canterbury Hall, the freshman girls' dorm, and she didn't recall what kinds of meals had been served in the dining hall, or whether she had ever gone to a soccer game out on the athletic field.

For all her vivid memories of what had come after—those horrid, lonely months in the Syracuse home for unwed mothers—her days here at Strasburg seemed to have faded into a series of hazy images. Except for the memories involving Noah.

Those were still vivid.

But those, she pushed away—even as she wondered if he had gotten her e-mail yet. What if he was away? Or what if he was one of those people who never checked it? Or what if he had changed his e-mail address and had never received it in the first place?

Her fears were instantly forgotten when she stepped into the lobby and Susan stopped her and handed her a folded sheet of paper. "Somebody called for you while you were out, Ms. Rowan," she said. "I rang him through to your room, but I'm afraid we don't have one of those voice mail systems like newer hotels. He called me back at the desk when he didn't reach you, and he left his number."

He.

So it had been Noah.

But of course it had been.

Who else knew she was here? Leslie and her father had only the number for the Super 8 where she had initially made her reservation, and she couldn't bring herself to call them today and tell them she had changed her plans. She was afraid they would hear in her voice that she was troubled, and she couldn't begin to explain what was wrong.

With trembling fingers, she unfolded the paper and saw Noah's name, alongside a telephone number with a 212 area code.

"Thank you," she said to Susan, turning toward the stairway.

Safely in her room, with its cheery navy-on-white

floral-print wallpaper, she sat on the edge of the bed and dialed Noah's number.

She took a deep breath as it rang, her mind racing as she tried to brace herself to hear his voice again after all these years.

When it happened—when she heard his voice at last—it was an answering machine's recorded outgoing message. Even then, it had an impact on her.

"We can't come to the phone right now. Please leave a message at the beep and we'll get back to you."

We.

So he didn't live alone.

Well, what did she expect? He was probably married with several children by now.

She hung up at the beep, unable to find her voice, too shaken by the haunting sound of his.

She could try him back later.

But when she did—a half hour later, and every fifteen minutes after that—she got only the machine. Each time, she hung up. If she left a message, the ball would be in his court again. If he didn't call back, she would be helpless, left to wait until she heard from him. She was much better off trying until she got a human voice—preferably Noah's—on the line.

She shuddered at the likelihood that the phone might be answered instead by his wife or one of his children. What would she say if she found herself speaking to the woman he had married? How would she introduce herself? As an old friend?

But maybe she wouldn't have to. Maybe Noah had already told his wife about the e-mail. Maybe he had long ago told her about his old girlfriend Mariel. Or maybe Mariel hadn't been a significant enough part of his life to warrant mention. Maybe he had never thought about her at all.

No. She couldn't believe that. However Noah had felt about her in the end, he couldn't have forgotten her. What they had been through together was too heart-wrenching to simply get past and move on. Surely he had thought about their child over the years. Surely he had thought about her.

But surely not as often—or as wistfully—as she had thought about him.

Finally, well after midnight, she gave up trying to call him. It was too late now. Maybe he and his wife were out on the town, or had gone away for the weekend. Maybe he had checked his e-mail from another location. Maybe he was a traveling businessman with a laptop and a summer house in the Hamptons.

It seemed strange, now, that she had no idea what his life was like or who he had become.

Mariel paced restlessly across the light blue carpet and looked out the window at the silent, empty stretch of Main Street below. The window was open, but there was no breeze to stir the starched white priscilla curtains. The sound of crickets drifted up to her ears, and, from one of the college hangouts up the block, she could hear the faint music of a live band.

Stretching and rubbing her aching neck muscles, she decided she might as well go to bed. She was physically exhausted, though she doubted she would get much sleep this evening now that Noah had called.

She hadn't slept last night, either, when she had finally crawled beneath the crisp white coverlet—her thoughts had whirled with concerns about Amber, wherever she was. Every frightening movie she had ever seen had come back to haunt her, particularly movies of the week about kidnaped teenagers, and slasher movies about psychos and serial killers. She envisioned hundreds of different scenarios, all of them terrifying, all of them making her physically ache with worry.

Now she wearily changed into the sleeveless babydoll-style summer nightgown she had brought. Last night she had worn the flannel pajamas she had thrown into her suitcase as an afterthought, and it had been a good thing she had brought them. But the weather tonight was drastically different. Even this almost-sheer pale yellow cotton felt like too much fabric on a hot, sticky night like this.

Should she put on a robe before she walked down the hall to brush her teeth and wash up?

No. It was simply too hot, and even though it was a shared bath, she had it all to herself, as there were no other guests staying on the third floor. In fact, maybe she would take a shower to cool off before bed, she decided. It might help her to relax so that she could fall asleep.

Mariel picked up the small quilted floral bag containing her toiletries and headed down the hall. The inn was quiet, although she could hear faint strains of the classical music that was always playing in the lobby.

Her footsteps scarcely made a sound on the dark green carpeting as she moved along the corridor, which was dimly lit by candle-style electric sconces. The doors to the other three third-floor guest rooms were ajar, and she gave in to her curiosity and peeked into each one as she passed.

Like her room and the hallway, they were all papered in floral Waverly print—one in shades of lavender, another in yellows, and the third in reds. All the furniture was of polished cherry wood in classic Queen Anne style. Rooms 5 and 7 each had two double beds, and room 6 had a single queen-sized bed, just as Mariel's room did.

It was in one of these four rooms that she had spent that fateful night with Noah. She was certain that they had been on the third floor, because she knew they hadn't had a private bathroom. But which room was it? She couldn't remember, and snooping beyond the open doors didn't trigger anything in her mind.

At the end of the hall, she went into the bathroom and locked the door behind her. Then she took a long shower. Her mother always used to say that if you took a shower to cool off in the summer heat, you should use the hottest water you could stand. That way, you would feel cooler when you stepped out.

Her mother was right, she thought, five minutes later. She was far more comfortable as she wrapped a towel around herself after drying off. She knotted it just above her breasts and used another towel to wipe the condensation from the mirror, thinking about Sarah Rowan— about how often the wise words she had shared came to Mariel's mind, and how unfair it was that she hadn't had more time to do what a mother did naturally and best: guide her children.

She had died two years ago this August, and it had been almost ten years since she had been diagnosed with Alzheimer's.

Mariel hadn't wanted to believe the dire prognosis at first, despite the unmistakable signs that something was seriously wrong. Her usually organized mother had become increasingly forgetful, but Mariel had figured it was simply old age. After all, her parents were in their sixties by then. It was obvious that they weren't going to be around forever, and Mariel should have been prepared. Her mother, often mistaken by strangers as her grandmother, had gone gray back when Mariel was still in high school, before Katie Beth's mother had even celebrated her fortieth birthday.

But when Alzheimer's struck, she refused to face it at first. Unlike Leslie and her father, who were openly devastated by the news, Mariel remained cheerful and optimistic. That was probably why it had hit her so hard later, as her mother's condition spiraled downward. She had been vehemently opposed to institutionalizing her toward the end, until the day Sarah wandered out of the house and was nearly killed trying to cross the busy interstate that ran through Rockton.

Mariel had finally tearfully agreed with her father and Leslie that it was time their mother left the house where the four of them had lived for so many years. Sarah had lived another eighteen months in the nursing home, and Mariel had visited her there faithfully long after her mother stopped recognizing her.

That was the hardest part—seeing the blank look in those familiar green eyes as they gazed at her.

Now, Mariel gazed into the mirror and noticed how much she resembled Sarah. She had the same wide-set moss-colored eyes and the same high cheekbones, even the same freckles across her nose like a dusting of cinnamon. Her mother's hair had been much straighter and a darker brown than Mariel's own light brown waves, and Sarah had always worn it pulled back in a bun while Mariel usually wore hers hanging loose. But right now, it was wet from the shower and combed straight back from her forehead, and . . .

I look like her, Mariel realized. *I look like she looked in the pictures of her when I was born.*

Sarah had been several years older then than Mariel was now, at thirty-three, but the resemblance was close. Closer than Mariel had ever noticed.

A wave of homesickness washed over her. Not for the place, for Rockton—but for a time that had long-since passed and for a woman who was dead.

I want my mommy, she thought desolately, gazing at herself in the mirror, the reflection blurred by tears. *I need my mommy.*

But she couldn't let herself cry, because if she did— if she let go—she might never stop. She wanted to cry not just for her own lost mother, but for the daughter she had given up, the daughter who might be in danger now. And for the love she had been denied when Noah turned his back on her.

No.

No.

She couldn't allow herself to think of it that way, because it simply wasn't true. He hadn't turned his back on her. He had been there, as much as he could be, throughout that endless winter when she lived in the home for unwed mothers. He had visited her regularly, and brought her little gifts even though he was always broke. He had gone to her prenatal checkups and held her hand through labor, and he had signed the adoption papers only for her sake—and perhaps, for their child's.

She wanted to think that—that she hadn't forced him into doing anything that really felt wrong for him.

He must have realized, in the years that had passed, that it had been the right decision for both of them. He must have.

Hot tears flooded her eyes and spilled over, running down her cheeks. She took off the towel and wiped them away, then put on her nightgown. Already, the bathroom felt uncomfortably warm again, and she splashed cold water on her face and neck.

As she was turning off the faucet there was a knock on the door.

Startled, she called, "I'll be right out."

Who could it be? Maybe it was Susan. Maybe she had been in here too long or used up too much hot water, she thought—perhaps irrationally, she realized. After all, there were no other guests on the floor; the rooms had all been empty on her way to the bathroom, and there was little chance that somebody would be checking in at this hour.

Mariel quickly gathered her things and opened the bathroom door. The first thing she noticed was the welcome blast of relatively cooler, drier air as she stepped from the steamy bathroom into the hall.

The next thing she noticed was that the door to the room directly opposite the bathroom—Room 6, the one with the yellow wallpaper and the queen-sized bed—was now closed.

So somebody had checked in while she was taking a shower.

What kind of person would show up at a hotel at this time of night? Then it dawned on her that it was probably a couple looking for a place to spend the night together, just as she and Noah had done so many years ago.

The thought of sharing the third floor with passionate young lovers made her dread even more the prospect of another restless night in the big bed, alone. But she couldn't dwell on that. It shouldn't be any different now, here, than it ever was. She was, after all, used to sleeping alone. There had been no lover for her after Noah. Even if she had met somebody she wanted to make love to, she would never have taken another chance of winding up single and pregnant. The only birth control that was fool proof was abstinence.

She knocked lightly on the door of room 6 as she passed and called softly, "The bathroom's all yours."

Then, without waiting for a reply, she continued on down the hall, went into her room, and closed and locked the door behind her.

Noah froze at the sound of her voice.

It was Mariel. He would recognize her anywhere.

He had suspected as much, when she had called to him from behind the bathroom door moments earlier.

Actually, he had suspected Mariel was in there when he first climbed the stairs to the third floor, found the bathroom door closed and heard the sound of a shower running. Not that he was certain that it was her, but something had told him it was likely that she inhabited the other third-floor room.

When he had checked in a few minutes ago, he had been told that the rooms on the second floor were larger—suites, with private baths—and that they were all occupied. The old woman had mentioned that there was only one other guest on the third floor, and had added—almost slyly—that the guest was a female.

That meant that Mariel was here alone.

Did it also mean she was still single?

Not necessarily, he realized, as he heard her footsteps retreat down the hall moments before a door closed firmly behind her.

And, he reminded himself, he had no business wondering about her love life, or lack of one. He was here for one reason alone: his daughter was in trouble.

When he couldn't reach Mariel at the inn, he hadn't thought twice about driving up here. It had been an automatic response; he couldn't wait any longer to know what was wrong.

Strasburg was a tiny town, and he knew where Mariel was staying.

At the same inn where he had brought her the night they first made love. A yearning, boyish part of him wanted to think that she had chosen to stay there for sentimental reasons that had something to do with him. But the realistic, jaded man he had become knew better. He remembered Strasburg well enough to know that if one wanted to spend the night there, the choices were fairly limited to the Super 8 and Best Western hotels out on the highway, or the Sweet Briar Inn in the heart of town. There wasn't much choice involved. The Sweet Briar was quaint and charming, as opposed to the modern concrete lodgings located on the fast-food strip off the Strasburg exit.

After failing to reach Mariel at the inn, he had tossed some clothes into a duffel bag and borrowed his friend Danny's car, explaining that it was a family emergency. He didn't go into detail, and Danny didn't push him— nor was he reluctant to lend Noah the seven-year-old Toyota. Danny was always complaining about having a car in the city—about the hours he wasted each week driving around in search of one of the elusive legal parking spots on the Manhattan streets. Letting Noah have the Toyota for at least the next twenty-four hours meant Danny didn't have to worry about parking it for a change.

Noah had made the drive up to Strasburg in record time. He knew the roads fairly well, having made the trip countless times back in his college days, and a few times since for alumni weekends and reunions. He had always wanted to bring Kelly with him, but she had begged off every time. She had attended Radcliffe and wasn't the least bit interested in, as she put it, "sitting around twiddling my thumbs while you're busy reminiscing with a bunch of washed-up frat boys."

Maybe Noah's old buddies were washed-up frat boys. Maybe he was, too. So what? He sometimes thought that he was lucky he had any fond memories of college after the way his freshman year had turned out. He had realized, over that long, desolate summer back in Queens after they had given away their baby and Mariel had gone back home, that he could either let the loss ruin his life, or he could return to Strasburg in the fall and try to make a fresh start. He had opted for the latter and joined a fraternity as a way to meet more people and find a social life. It had been the right thing to do, looking back. Life in the Phi Sig house had been rowdy and frequently hilarious, and it definitely had taken his mind off his troubles.

Now, those troubles had stormed back to haunt him in a way he had never anticipated.

And here he was, knowing that Mariel Rowan was a few yards down the hall, close enough to talk to, if he

chose—or to touch. Not that he intended to touch her.
Look where that had landed him last time. He didn't
dare allow himself to become captivated by her again,
no matter what she was like as a grown woman.

He had no doubt that she was as seductive as ever.
How well he remembered what it had been like to entan-
gle his fingers in her long, silky hair, and how right her
taut, slender body had felt when he held her in his
arms. He could still hear her throaty laugh low in his
ear, still feel the weight of her head on his chest when
he held her after making love to her.

Forcing the memory out, he grabbed his contact lens
kit and headed out the door, shutting it behind him.
He hesitated in the hushed hallway a moment, staring
at the closed door at the other end of the hall. All was
silent behind it. He couldn't knock. Not now.

He would wait until morning to speak to her. It would
be much easier after a good night's sleep. The drive
might have been familiar, but it had still been nearly
four hours long and was exhausting. He wasn't ready
to face Mariel again until he had time to grasp the fact
that he was really here, about to confront the past he
had avoided for so long—and news about his child that
would no doubt be unsettling, whatever it was.

He turned and crossed the hall to the bathroom. It
was still warm and damp from her shower. He steadied
himself against the door frame as he stepped over the
threshold, caught off guard by a whiff of the steamy air.
If he hadn't heard her voice calling to him from the
hallway minutes ago, this scent, so uniquely hers, would
have confirmed that she was here. It was a fresh, herbal
fragrance—lotion, or shampoo, or some kind of co-

logne. He had never known what it was, and he hadn't smelled it since they had parted; but now here it was.

He stood there for a moment, breathing deeply, lost in the heady scent that carried him back, not to the hard times, but to the sweetest, most intimate times they had shared.

Then, as reality nudged its way back in, he stripped off his sweat-soggy shirt and splashed cold water on his face.

She had forgotten her hairbrush in the bathroom.

Mariel sighed, setting down the toiletries bag she had just searched in vain. She would have to go back down the hall and get it. If she slept on her naturally wavy hair without spraying on conditioner and brushing it out, it would be a mess of snarls by morning.

So much for having the third floor to myself, she thought as she padded barefoot down the hall and found that the bathroom door was closed. She considered knocking, then decided that wouldn't be polite. She might as well sit on the upholstered hall bench beneath the window at the head of the stairs and wait, hoping that whoever it was wouldn't be long. The shower had relaxed her, and the strain of the last two days had caught up with her. She was anxious to crawl into bed.

She had barely settled on the bench when she heard the bathroom door start to open. She rose just as the occupant emerged into the hallway a few feet away . . .

And found herself face-to-face with a shirtless Noah Lyons.

CHAPTER FOUR

"Mariel."

He heard her name escape his lips as her scent enveloped him, and his eyes took in the incredible sight of her standing before him. She was all bare skin and damp hair and enormous green eyes, and it was all he could do not to sag against the door frame beside him. She was framed by the window behind her, and the moonlight that spilled in left little to his imagination, rendering her short summer nightgown all but sheer.

She was still slender, still beautiful, yet the angular girlish figure had been replaced by a grown woman's soft curves: rounded hips and full breasts and the slightest swell of belly where she had carried his child.

With that thought it all came rushing back to him: the shock of her pregnancy, her refusal to marry him and her decision to give up their child, followed by the numbing months waiting for the birth and the inevitable devastation of the aftermath.

Plunked firmly back on earth, Noah found his voice again and said, "I tried to call you back. When I didn't reach you, I drove up here."

She nodded. She hadn't yet spoken, nor had her gaze budged from his face. He reminded himself that she was stunned to see him here, now—even more stunned than he had been to walk out of the bathroom and find her there, scantily clad. He, at least, had known she was under this roof. She had been given no advance warning, no time to prepare.

Or was he assuming too much? Was he wrong to believe that his presence had as soul-searing an effect on her as hers did on him?

Judging by the silence, he was not. He had once known her well enough to have grown accustomed to the look that melded with the shock in her eyes. She was attracted to him. Still. After all these years, after all that had happened, she had feelings for him.

Hope took flight in the vicinity of his heart, only to crash land when a veil dropped over the raw emotion he had glimpsed in her face and she spoke at last. "You didn't have to come, Noah. I only wanted to talk to you about what had happened, to see if—"

"I didn't have to come?" he cut in angrily. "Am I any less her parent than you are? For Christ's sake, Mariel, I'm the one who wanted to keep her."

Her jaw dropped, and fire flashed in her eyes. "You wanted to keep her at her own expense. You weren't thinking about what was right for her. You were being selfish."

"No, Mariel, *you* were being selfish," he shot back before he could stop himself.

He hated that he had said it—hated that he still felt that way, after a decade and a half of trying to convince himself that she—that *they*—had done the right thing. Intellectually, he knew that they couldn't have kept her, stayed together, raised her. Yet emotionally, he had never given up the sense that he—that they—had abandoned their child. That they hadn't lived up to their responsibility.

Hell, she hadn't even considered giving it a shot. She hadn't been willing to risk what his mother had, alone and pregnant at roughly the same age. His mother, unlike Mariel, hadn't even had the option of marrying his father; she had valiantly struggled to raise him alone, and she had triumphed.

"So you still hate me after all this time," Mariel said flatly. "I'm not surprised."

Well, Noah was. He was shocked at the intensity of the anger that had bubbled so readily to the surface. What was done was done. He had accepted it, put it behind him. Hadn't he?

Couldn't he?

He wanted to explain himself, defend himself. But he couldn't begin to find the right words. All he could say, in as level a tone as hers, was, "What happened to her?"

"She's disappeared," Mariel said simply.

"Disappeared?" Countless questions whirled through his mind. He faltered, then uttered the most obvious. "How did you find out?"

She took a deep breath. "It's a long story. It can wait until morning—"

"No."

"Noah, it's late." She brushed past him without touching him and stepped into the bathroom, retrieving a hairbrush from the sink. He had noticed it when he was there, but hadn't considered that it might be hers. If he had . . .

No.

He wasn't a lovesick schoolboy who would swipe one of her belongings to keep, to treasure. He was a grown man who felt nothing for this woman but deep-seated resentment, and he would do well to remember that.

"We should both get some sleep because this is complicated and I have no idea what we're getting into," she continued, pushing past him again, clutching the brush. This time, her hip grazed his thigh, and he was infuriated when he felt his jeans tighten around his arousal at the passing contact.

"Mariel, I didn't drive four hours in the middle of the night to get some sleep. You were the one who called me. Now tell me what you know."

She sighed, looking around the hallway and, as if in afterthought, down at her skimpy nightgown. He saw her try to hide behind her arms as she folded them across her breasts, and he felt another stir of desire for her despite his irritation.

"Can we at least go someplace private to talk?" she asked, apparently resigned to the fact that she wasn't going to be rid of him, not even temporarily.

He nodded. "Come into my room."

"Come into mine."

Touche, he thought. She was already striding down the hall, and he hurried after her, still carrying his bathroom kit.

She opened the door to her room, and he followed her in, glancing disinterestedly at the blue and white wallpaper, antique furnishings, and open suitcase on the luggage rack. She hadn't unpacked her clothes, he realized. Either she had only arrived today, or she didn't intend to stay long.

"Tell me," he said sternly, closing the door after them.

She was reaching for a terry cloth robe draped over one knob at the foot of the four-poster bed. She pulled it on and swiftly belted it at the waist before turning to face him. "You can sit," she said, gesturing at the wing chair across from the bed.

"I'll stand."

She shrugged, and sat on the edge of the bed, positioning herself so that her back was three-quarters turned to him. He couldn't see her face as she said, "I got an e-mail a few weeks ago from her."

"From who?" he asked, even as he realized what she meant. From their daughter. Their daughter had been in touch with Mariel. Jealousy sparked through him, and he fought to hold it back.

"Her name is Amber Steadman now," Mariel said, brushing her hair as she spoke.

Amber Steadman, he thought. The name was foreign. A stranger's name. He couldn't seem to link it to the squirming, dark-haired newborn he had held so briefly that long-ago July day.

"She wrote to me, Noah, asking me if I'm her mother."

"So this was the first time you'd heard from her?" He walked around the foot of the bed and stood in front of her, needing to look at her. She had stopped brushing, and her head was bent, her hand rubbing her forehead as though she was having a difficult time with this.

"Yes," she said, nodding. "I hadn't seen or heard anything since that first day—that *last* day—in the hospital. When they took her away."

He realized that her voice was choked, and he quelled the urge to say something comforting. It had been her decision to give away their baby. She had to live with the consequences. If it had been up to him—

But it hadn't been. And he had been through this far too often already in the last few minutes, to say nothing of the last fifteen years.

"So she contacted you by e-mail to see if you were her mother," he recapped. "And you wrote back to her?"

"No. I couldn't. Not then. I wanted to wait to see her in person. That's why I flew here. . . ."

"From where?" he asked, realizing he knew nothing about her life or what had become of her. He couldn't even begin to guess.

"From Missouri," she said—one more surprise in a night of surprises.

"You're living back in Missouri?"

Her laugh was bitter. "Right back in Rockton, where I started."

"Since when?"

"Since I left here," she said shortly. "Anyway, I flew here yesterday, and I was planning to go to see her . . . or maybe call her first. I don't know what I was planning. I only knew that I couldn't do this long-distance. And when I got here, I found out by accident—through a newspaper article—that she's been missing for over a week."

Dread seeped in. "She was kidnaped?"

She shrugged, looking up at him for the first time. He was caught off guard by the desolate expression on her face. "The police think she might have run away. Her parents are beside themselves with worry, according to the press."

Her parents. Yes.

The strangers who had raised her were her parents. He and Mariel were not.

But it was their long-ago bond that had given her life; their blood ran through her veins. He knew nothing about what had happened to the missing girl after the first precious hours of her life; yet her well-being was suddenly intrinsic to his own, and he knew he wouldn't rest until he knew she was alive, and safe.

"If she ran away," he said slowly, pondering what Mariel had told him, "then something was wrong. Maybe something at home."

Mariel nodded. "I keep wondering if there was abuse, or . . ."

Noah swallowed hard. The guilt in Mariel's troubled expression was palpable, and suddenly, he didn't want to add to it. He wanted to ease her hurt—which was insane, because she was the one who had caused this, and she was the one who had hurt him.

"Who have you spoken to about this?" he asked her, trying to focus on one thing at a time, the important things first. How he felt about Mariel was unimportant now—or so he told himself as he fought the urge to move closer to her. He stood his ground a few feet from the bed, facing her, watching her.

"I haven't spoken to anyone but you," Mariel said, running the brush through her damp hair, the bristles getting caught in the tangle of wavy strands. "I didn't know what else to do. I was afraid that if I went to her parents, or to the police, they would somehow think I had something to do with this."

He wanted to point out that she was doing it again—putting herself first. But he bit back the words.

She went on speaking, asking him if he had heard from Amber.

"Don't you think I would have told you already if I had?" he asked sharply. "Do you think I'd be sitting here, keeping it to myself?"

"Stop it, Noah!" she said in disgust.

"Stop what?"

"Stop talking to me that way. If you're so angry that you can't be reasonable, then you should just go."

"I'm not going anywhere, Mariel. I have as much a right to be here as you do. She's my daughter, too."

She's my daughter.

He had never spoken the words out loud. Hearing them made it all so surreal. Here they were, parents arguing over their child, as countless sets of parents had done since the beginning of time. If he tried hard enough, for a moment he could forget that they had given up the baby and gone their separate ways.

But they weren't a family, he and Mariel and Amber Steadman. They were three isolated human beings who had lived separate lives except for the briefest interlude, and this didn't change anything.

"Noah," Mariel said, and he realized that uncomfortable silence had hung between them as his thoughts careened on another tangent. "I called you because I needed to know if she had tried to reach you. I thought maybe she had. Your name is on the papers.''

"Well, she didn't try to reach me," he said, filled with disappointment and regret and, yes, envy. He envied Mariel, who had been given a chance that hadn't been given to him. If his daughter had contacted him, he would have jumped at the chance to know her. To help her. And maybe to fill the gaping hole in his life.

He drew a deep breath and told Mariel, "I'm going to call the police and find out what they know, because if those people who raised her have hurt her in any way—"

"Noah, you can't just call the police," she cut in. "They'll think you're involved."

"Well, they'll figure out soon enough that I'm not. I'm just an outsider."

"Exactly."

Her voice was suddenly soft. He was startled by the shift in her tone and saw that she was looking directly at him for a change.

"You and I are both outsiders, Noah. We're strangers to her," she said. "You're the only other person in the world who knows how I feel. How it's possible to care so much about someone whose life only slightly touched yours."

"Slightly? Her life turned ours upside down," Noah said with a shudder of emotion. "If none of this had happened . . . well, who knows."

He couldn't tear himself from her somber green gaze. His own gaze locked on her face, he took a step closer, speaking without allowing himself to think, to censor. "I swear, I have wondered every day for fifteen years what happened to you, and to her," he told Mariel, his voice ragged.

"I've done the same thing," she said, barely above a whisper. "I wanted her to be alive, and okay. And I wanted you . . . I wanted you to be—"

"What?" he asked, when she didn't finish.

She said nothing.

He swallowed over the lump that had risen in his throat. This was Mariel. He had known her so intimately, yet so fleetingly, so long ago, and now she was here in front of him and it was as though time had stood still. He still wanted her, Lord help him, and he could swear she felt the same about him.

"Where have you been, Noah?" she asked finally, still staring at him. "Are you married? Do you have children?"

"No children," he returned. "Just her. If you count her."

"I do," she said softly. "What about a wife?"

"No wife." His hands clenched into fists at his sides. "There was a wife, but not anymore."

Her expression was impossible to read as she asked, "What happened?"

She chose herself over having a family with me. Just like you did, Mariel.

"Irreconcilable differences," he said aloud. "We wanted different things."

"How long were you married?"

"Seven years. The divorce will be final this month. What about you?"

"Me? I'm not divorced."

His heart plummeted. "Oh," he said, his tone carefully neutral.

"I've never been married."

His heart soared. "Oh." His tone was still neutral. He didn't want her to know what an impact those words had on him. Hell, he didn't want them to *have* an impact. Her marital status was none of his business. He couldn't care less if she had a husband and five kids back home in Rockville or wherever the hell she was from.

Yeah, right.

"What do you do?" she asked, and it took him a moment to comprehend the question.

"I work in the creative department of an advertising agency."

"Really?" She looked impressed. Well, she always did want to be an actress, he thought wryly. There was nothing impressive about his job.

"Do you enjoy it?" she asked.

"Not at all," he said truthfully. "It's not what I ever envisioned myself doing."

"Then, why are you doing it?"

Because my wife made me.

"Because I needed to earn a living in New York, and screenwriters who don't sell anything can't afford astronomical rent."

"You're a screenwriter?"

"In my dreams," he said on a bitter laugh. "I've got a dozen half-written screenplays, and I keep telling myself that someday I'm going to sit down and finish one and sell it."

"Why haven't you?"

"Burn out, I guess," he told her, unsettled by his own candor, yet unable to do anything about it. "My job is a rat race. I spend my days catering to demanding clients and reworking lines of copy hundreds of times. It's hard to feel inspired after that. But I don't know, maybe now that . . ."

"Now that what?" she asked when he trailed off.

He had been about to say now that Kelly was gone, but he didn't want to go there. Not now. Not with her. Instead, he said honestly, "Now that I'm getting older, maybe I'll give it another go. Maybe I'll leave the rat race and go someplace where life isn't so hectic and the cost of living isn't so expensive, and I'll just . . . write."

She nodded, a faraway expression in her eyes.

"What are you thinking?" he asked.

"That you're describing Rockton. Life isn't hectic there, and it's definitely affordable. But the rat race sounds a lot more appealing to me," she said. "I mean, New York is where I always pictured myself living. I was going to be a big star. And now look at me."

He was looking at her. He couldn't take his eyes off of her. "What do you do in Rockton, Mariel?"

"I teach first grade. Careful, don't fall over," she said, catching sight of his astonishment. "I know. It's not what I ever imagined myself doing, either."

"Do you like it?"

"I love it," she said with a smile. "The children are so sweet, and I like to think that I make a huge difference in their lives. That's amazing to me, that I have such an opportunity to help guide all these little people at the beginning of an important path. I never knew I had it in me to do something so . . ."

"Noble," he supplied when she seemed to be searching for a word.

"Noble? I never thought of it that way." She leveled

a gaze at him. "And I never thought I'd hear you call me that, Noah. Not when five minutes ago you were telling me how much you hate me."

"I never said I hated you," he told her, his mind whirling with thoughts he was powerless to stop or even pin down and consider.

"You didn't have to say it. It was obvious."

"It's obvious that I hate you?" he echoed, his heart pounding. "Right now? You feel as though I hate you?"

She looked up at him, studying his face.

And then, seized by an impulse he couldn't control, he bent his head and kissed her.

As Noah's lips came down over hers, Mariel met him hungrily, too far gone to think clearly. She wanted this as she had never wanted anything in her life.

He tasted of mint toothpaste and he smelled of soap, and when he touched the sides of her face as he kissed her, she quivered, remembering that yes, this was exactly how it was, kissing Noah. This was how he had always begun when he kissed her—by touching her face, cupping her cheeks in his hands as he slowly moved his lips over hers.

It was good, so incredibly good, to be kissed by him again. When he opened his mouth she did as well, welcoming his warm, gently probing tongue. And when he leaned into her, she sank back on the bed, her hands on his shoulders, pulling him down on top of her. Her stomach was fluttering like mad and her mind was racing and she couldn't think clearly; all she could do was feel. And need.

She needed him desperately—had needed him for years—and now he was here. They were back in this inn in this town—

Then she remembered why.

She froze, then turned her head, breaking off the kiss.

"What is it?" he whispered, but when she opened her eyes she saw that he, too, had just remembered what was going on.

They sat up, and for a moment the only sound in the room was their breathing. She waited for her pulse to slow, for the aching need to subside, but it didn't happen. Every ounce of her energy was focused on the overwhelming desire to throw herself into his arms again, to beg him to finish what he had started and damn the consequences.

"What the hell are we doing?" he asked, standing.

She gazed up at him, standing there without a shirt, taking in his strong biceps and upper arms and his broad, hairless chest and the taut muscles of his torso. He wore a pair of faded blue jeans that hugged his hips and couldn't hide the blatant fact that he was as passionately drawn to her as she was to him.

She dragged her attention to his face—that darkly handsome face that had haunted her dreams all these years. It was the same in so many ways—the same thick, dark lashes fringing his dark eyes, the same strong jaw and full lips and cleft in his chin. Yet there was no sign of the sweet, earnest boy she had once known, only a rugged man who was determined to be nobody's fool.

"We can't do this," she said, but she was trying to convince herself more than him, and he wasn't arguing.

He shook his head, disgust blatant on his face. When he spoke, she realized that he was disgusted with himself as much as he was with her—or maybe, instead of her. The hatred and resentment and anger she had glimpsed

earlier were no longer evident as he _____
Mariel. I don't know what I was thinking. ___ sorry,
ing—that was the problem. But it won't hap_ think-

"No," she said, wondering if he could hear again."
of disappointment in her voice. "It definitely warble
pen again."   ap-

"What are we going to do?" he asked, pacing ___
to the window, his hands shoved in the pockets of h__
jeans. She wondered if it was to relieve the pressure or
to hide his arousal from her, and she felt a pang of
regret. She hated this. Yet she had done it to herself.
She had summoned him to Strasburg, and now she had
to deal with the consequences.

"We're going to keep our hands off of each other,"
she said firmly. "That's what we're going to do."

He turned, amusement flashing in his dark eyes. "I
didn't mean that. That's a given."

"Oh." She felt a hot flush on her cheeks.

"I meant, what are we going to do about Amber
Steadman? Now that we're both here ... what's our
next step?"

She hadn't thought beyond finding out whether
Amber had e-mailed him. She certainly hadn't thought
about the two of them in Strasburg, dealing with this
together.

There was such comfort in the realization that she
was no longer alone that she shoved aside the turmoil
and embarrassment over what had just happened
between them, focusing at last on the more pressing
issue at hand.

"We have to find out what happened to her, Noah."

"I agree. But if the police are working on it, we
should—"

Janelle Taylor

"...an't go to the police," she cut in firmly.

"...you're wrong. I think we have to go to the ...e need to tell them that she contacted you. ...reaching out to find her birth mother, and now ...disappeared. That can't be a coincidence."

"...hat's exactly what I thought," Mariel told him. "...instead of going to the police, maybe we should start with the parents."

"I think that's just asking for trouble. They'll be suspicious. Besides, if they're guilty of treating her badly or doing anything that would lead her to run away—"

"Then we'll probably sense it, Noah. We'll probably be able to tell if there was something going on there."

"Not necessarily. We're not detectives, Mariel. We're just—"

"Strangers. I know. Strangers who—" Her voice broke, and she felt tears building in her eyes.

"Strangers who care," he said gently, walking back over to stand above her.

He seemed to hesitate before laying a hand on her shoulder and patting her. "Look, I feel the same way you do, Mariel. We're in the same boat. So let's help each other with this, okay?"

She nodded, wanting to lean into him for support, but knowing that the slightest physical contact between them was dangerous.

"We'll go see her parents in the morning," Noah conceded. "You look as exhausted as I feel. For now, let's get some sleep."

"Okay."

But sleep was the last thing on her mind when he left her alone in her room and she climbed into bed at last.

For countless recent nights, her daughter had occupied her thoughts.

Now, as she tossed and turned in the hot, humid third-floor room, all she could think about was Noah.

Seeing him again—kissing him again—had reawakened feelings she had tried so hard, for so long, to escape.

Now he was here, and there was no possible escape.

She couldn't leave Strasburg until she found out what had happened to Amber.

She would just have to be strong enough to resist her attraction to Noah, and hope that he would do the same.

CHAPTER FIVE

Mariel met Noah in the dining room at nine o'clock Sunday morning, just as they had arranged.

She had planned to be there first, so that she could be settled in and compose herself to see him again. But the alarm she had set on the bedside table didn't go off, and she found herself scrambling to get ready on time. It was ten past nine when she finally showed up in the big, elegant dining room and found him seated in the far corner at a round table for two.

The place was crowded with other guests and what appeared to be local families coming from early mass. As Mariel made her way through the dining room she felt self-consciously casual in her khaki shorts, sandals, and pale green, sleeveless T-shirt, her hair pulled into a high ponytail to keep it off her neck in the heat.

She had taken a few moments to put on light makeup, though—mascara and a hint of brown shadow to make her eyes look bigger, and a pale pink gloss on her lips. She had told herself that it wasn't for Noah's benefit, but now, as she saw him sitting there and felt her body react in anticipation, she admitted to herself that of course it was. She wanted him to be attracted to her—she just didn't want him to do anything about it.

Yeah, Mar, that makes perfect sense, she thought wryly as she arrived at the table.

He was reading a newspaper, a steaming cup of coffee in front of him. She saw that he, too, was dressed casually. Like her, he had on khaki shorts, and he also wore a navy, short-sleeved polo shirt with a collar and two buttons, and a pair of Docksiders without socks. He was intent on his newspaper until she cleared her throat and spoke.

"Hi, Noah."

He started, then said hello and jumped up to pull out her chair.

She remembered how impressed she had always been by his manners. He was the first boy who had ever treated her like a lady, holding doors and chairs for her and helping her with her coat, even offering to carry her backpack for her. He had grown even more courteous when she was pregnant, but by then, she had found herself annoyed by his chivalry, rather than flattered.

Now, as she slid into the chair he held for her, she tried to be annoyed but couldn't be.

She smiled at him as he seated himself again, and she said, "Thanks. You always were a gentleman."

"My mother taught me well."

Her smile faded. The mention of his mother reminded her of his long-ago argument for getting married and keeping their baby—he had said he didn't want their child to grow up without a father, as he had.

"How'd you sleep?" he asked, busy refolding his newspaper. She saw that it was the local one and wondered if he was looking for articles about Amber.

"Not that great," she answered his question. Then, not wanting him to think she had lost any sleep over him, she said quickly, "It's just so damned hot." She thrust out her lower lip and blew her bangs off her forehead as if to punctuate the point.

"It is hot," he agreed. "I only spent one summer here—the one before senior year—and I don't remember the sun ever shining or the temperature getting above eighty. You know what they say. There are only two seasons in this part of New York State—winter and the Fourth of July."

She froze.

So did he, when he realized what he had said.

The Fourth of July.

Amber's birthday.

"Sorry," he mumbled, looking down at the newspaper in his hand.

"It's no big deal," she told him, but her hands were shaking as she spread her cloth napkin on her lap.

When she glanced up at him again, he was handing her one of the menus that had been propped against the vase of fresh cosmos in the middle of the white cloth tablecloth.

"The waitress was already by," he said. "She told me that the challah french toast is amazing."

"Did you order it?"

He shook his head. "I waited for you. I'm a gentleman, remember?"

That broke the ice again, and she smiled.

For a few minutes, until the waitress returned, they chatted about food. The small talk was a relief, and she found herself caught up in the details he shared about himself—that he had cut back on eating meat and cheese because his cholesterol was high, but that his favorite thing to eat for breakfast was a bagel piled with cream cheese and lox and onions.

They looked at the list of tantalizing specials printed on the menu. He said he wanted to try the raspberry pancakes, and she said she was thinking of having the spinach quiche. Then the waitress came, and they both ordered french toast. They laughed about it after she had walked away.

"I thought you were having quiche," Noah said.

"I thought you were having raspberry pancakes."

"I'll have them tomorrow. I'm in the mood for french toast."

"Tomorrow?" she echoed, poised with her hand on a packet of sugar for the coffee the waitress had just poured her. "Are you going to stay, then?"

"I'm not sure." His eyes stopped twinkling. "I'm supposed to be at work, but until I know what's going on up here . . . I just don't see how I can leave."

"What will you do? Call in sick?"

He shrugged. "I wouldn't mind quitting, but I guess I shouldn't do that, huh? What do you think? Should I just quit tomorrow?"

She couldn't tell if he was teasing. There was a bitterness in his tone that seemed out of character, but then, she reminded herself, what did she really know about his character? He wasn't the same person he had been.

She no longer knew him, despite the glimpses of familiarity.

"Are you serious?" she asked.

"I wish." He dumped another sugar packet into the coffee the waitress had just warmed up for him, then stirred it moodily.

"I take it you really don't enjoy your job."

"Not in the least bit."

"So how did you fall into it in the first place?"

He looked her in the eye. "It was my wife's idea."

The phrase *my wife* gave her a little twinge of pain. Yes, he was divorced—or almost divorced—but he had loved another woman.

Another woman had been his bride and shared his bed and his world while Mariel was off living her lonely life in Rockton.

"She wanted you to be in advertising?" she asked, hoping he didn't sense what she was thinking.

"She wanted me to fit into her world," Noah said, surprising her with his blunt, straightforward reply. Last night he had seemed cagey when he was talking about his marriage.

Now, he said, "Kelly's an attorney. She's from a privileged background, and she's used to a certain standard of living. A struggling writer wasn't her idea of husband material. I guess it wasn't mine, either. I was getting my master's in English from NYU when I met her, and she was impressed by that. But after I got it, she set up a bunch of interviews for me through connections she had. Most of them were for creative positions in ad agencies. She said PR and publishing didn't pay enough."

"You would rather have been in PR or publishing?"

"I would rather have been a bartender or a word processing temp while I worked on my screenplays," he said with a shrug, and sipped his coffee.

"So you went into advertising for your wife, and you were miserable." Mariel shook her head. "Now that she's out of your life, can't you do something else?"

"I was about to," he said, setting his cup carefully back on the saucer.

"When . . . what?"

"Hmm?" He looked up at her blankly.

"You were about to do something else, when what happened?"

"When you e-mailed me," he said with a shrug. "I was sitting there last night in my apartment—God, it seems like months ago—and I was about to get on-line and start looking for opportunities."

"What kind of opportunities?"

"I don't know. Cheap places to live, or interesting jobs . . . something different. Something that would take me out of my life. And then I got your e-mail, and I just blew out of town, and here I am."

"You're here because of Amber, though . . . right?" she asked, suddenly wondering how sincere his worry had been.

"Of course I'm here because of Amber." The urgent, troubled expression on his face instantly erased her doubts. "And as soon as we finish eating, we're going to head over to talk to the Steadmans."

She nodded. "I was wondering if you thought we should call first."

He shook his head and said darkly, "Why give them a chance to prepare? Let's see what they're really like."

"It's probably a long shot, Noah, that we're going to

find out anything from them that will be a clue to what happened to Amber. They're her parents. They're not going to want to talk to us when they find out who we are, and they're probably going crazy trying to find her. Chances are, they had nothing to do with what happened to her."

"You said yourself that the police think she ran away."

"But that doesn't mean—"

"Kids don't run away from happy homes, Mariel," he said.

She just shrugged, thinking of her own past. Of the parents who had doted on her, tried to give her everything, and of how she had spent every moment of her childhood waiting for the moment when she could flee.

But then, she hadn't really run away.

She had been eighteen, going off to college.

Amber had simply disappeared on her way to school one day.

The chilling implication settled over Mariel, and she met Noah's intent gaze across the table. "You're right," she said. "Something had to be wrong. Unless she didn't run away. What if she was abducted?"

His face was grim. "One thing at a time, Mariel, okay?"

She nodded, once again grateful for his presence. "Okay," she said, as the waitress arrived with maple syrup and butter.

The drive to Valley Falls took longer than Noah expected. He and his frat brothers had made road trips there a few times back in his college days, to go to the mall or to a club called the Black Door, where there were live bands and a two-drink minimum on weekends. Now there was a Cracker Barrel Restaurant where the club used to stand, and the two-lane highway was under construction in several spots, mostly to accommodate new shopping centers or town house developments.

"I don't remember any of this being here," he commented to Mariel as they passed a sprawling plaza with a big Home Depot and a bigger Wal-Mart. "This whole area is being built up."

"It's great," she said. "I wish there was a Wal-Mart in Rockton."

"It's great? How can you say that?" He slowed the car, spotting another orange-clad flag man ahead. "Places like this should stay rural. That's what makes them desirable."

"Spoken like a true city boy," she said with a laugh. "Or maybe not. Maybe that's a sign you need to get out of the city."

"When I come up here and see them tearing down trees and putting up those ugly concrete dime-a-dozen buildings, it makes me crazy."

"You wouldn't say that if you'd ever lived in a place like Rockton. Most of the time, I would kill for decent pizza or a place to buy a pair of jeans without driving for forty-five minutes."

"I guess I never thought of it that way," he admitted. He wanted to ask her why she was there, then, if she wasn't happy with small-town life. But she had turned her head away, toward the window, and he took that as a signal that she sensed what was on his mind and didn't want to talk about it.

They drove in silence for a few minutes. He thought about how one minute, it was strangely comfortable to

be with her again, and the next, it was awkward as hell.
He felt as though he had been on a roller coaster ever
since he had seen her in the hall last night. Kissing her
certainly hadn't helped matters any, considering that
he had spent most of the time since wondering when
and how and if he could do it again.

This, after he had sworn to himself, and to her, that
it wasn't going to happen again.

But now that he had reconnected with Mariel again,
he couldn't think straight. He never had been able to
when she was around; that was the problem. She had
a way of working her way in so that he couldn't focus
on what he should be doing. It had always been like
that with her, and he should have known it wouldn't
change.

If only she didn't look as appealing as ever—and so
drastically different from Kelly. His wife had been one
of those super-thin, high-strung city women—elegant
and sophisticated and well dressed. Kelly was beautiful
enough to turn heads on the street, with her perfect
features and her straight, pale blond hair and statuesque
figure. She had certainly turned his head, Noah reminded himself.

But he had definitely had his fill of her. And in the
end, she had turned out to be an ice princess.

Whereas in the end, Mariel had turned out to be . . .

Well, it wasn't the end with her yet, after all, and he
didn't know *what* she was.

Hard as he had tried to convince himself that she
was selfish and cold and undeserving of his forgiveness,
much less his love, he now realized that nothing was as
cut and dried as he had tried to make it. He wanted to
believe that she had given up their child—and him—

so that she could go off and become a globe-trotting actress.

But here she was, back in the hometown she had always said she hated, teaching first grade. She was living the life she had never wanted. He remembered conversations they had had early in their relationship, right after they had met—how passionately she had talked about what she was going to do with her life, and how she was going to make something of herself. She didn't want marriage or children—he clearly remembered that she had said that. It had struck a chord in him when she said it because even at eighteen, he knew that someday he wanted to be a husband and a father, and he thought that was what most people expected from their lives.

Not Mariel.

And here she was, still single. No children.

Why couldn't he just accept that she had known her limitations even back then?

"Noah! Turn here," she said abruptly, and he realized that he had been about to pass the intersection of Route 21, which led into Valley Falls.

He steered the car around the corner and headed down the wide road toward town. On both sides were large old-fashioned houses fronted by porches and green lawns and towering maples and oaks that cast dappled shade. Everywhere he looked there were American flags and flower boxes spilling over with blooms; swingsets and sandboxes and romping dogs and children on tricycles.

As they got closer to town there were a few more cars, a few more people. The road and parking lot in front of a picturesque white church were lined with cars, and the steeple bells were chiming. They passed a family walking hurriedly toward the church, obviously late for mass—the wife enormously pregnant and walking with the typical bow-legged backward tilt, the husband bending toward the toddler, whose arms were up stretched, and swinging the child up to be carried on his shoulders.

That's what I want, Noah thought. He wanted it so badly that he ached inside.

He wanted it all. The small-town life, the house with the yard, the wife, the child, the baby on the way. He wondered if the man he had passed knew how lucky he was—whether he was content and grateful every day for what he had.

Mariel's voice interrupted his thoughts.

"You should probably park so that we can ask someone where Berry Street is," she said, clutching a piece of paper on which she had scribbled the Steadmans' address back at the inn. They had found it by simply dialing information. "Unless you want to just drive around and see if we come across it. Valley Falls isn't that big."

"No, we'll stop and ask someone," he said quickly. He didn't want to drive around catching glimpses of other people's lives—lives he coveted and would never have. The sooner they found the Steadmans, the better.

Mariel stared up at the house on Berry Street.

It was a white colonial with black shutters, a tidy, sunny yard, and an attached two-car garage. Along the brick foundation on either side of the small concrete stoop, clumps of healthy peony shrubs bent under the weight of their colossal pink blooms, fronted by a border of white impatiens that looked as though it needed a good soaking and some shelter from the hot midafternoon sun.

Mariel found herself irritated by the fact that whoever had planted the impatiens didn't know that the annuals needed lots of water and shade. What kind of person would just plop the plants into an unsuitable environment?

The kind of person who would mistreat an adopted daughter.

She knew she was being ridiculous—rather, that she was possibly being ridiculous—but she couldn't help herself. She was looking at the Steadman residence with a critical eye, seeking evidence that the people who were raising her daughter were lousy human beings.

"What do you think?" Noah asked beside her, and she remembered that he was there.

She turned to look at him and saw that he, too, was giving the house an appraising, narrow-eyed stare.

"They don't take proper care of their garden," she said darkly.

He blinked, then motioned at the flowerbeds. "In all fairness, the garden looks pretty good to me."

"That's because you're from New York City. Anything remotely green looks good to you. The peonies are low-maintenance perennials, but trust me, they're abusing their impatiens."

He shrugged. "Whatever that means. Come on, let's go."

They got out of the car and headed up the short walk toward the house. Mariel glanced at the other houses on the residential block and concluded that this was an upper-middle-class neighborhood, probably with many of the houses occupied by young families judging by the number of lawns scattered with various plastic riding toys and wagons. A few of the neighbors were in sight—mothers watching over toddlers, and senior citizens watering or mowing lawns. But aside from a casual glance or two, nobody seemed to be paying any attention to Mariel and Noah as they walked toward the Steadmans' front door.

As Noah raised his hand to knock, Mariel saw a movement out of the corner of her eye. She looked sharply at the picture window to the right of the door just in time to see the curtain flutter back into place.

Somebody had been watching their arrival.

The door was answered immediately.

Mariel recognized Carl Steadman from the photo in the newspaper. He wasn't a handsome man, with aviator-style glasses and a fringe of dark hair around a broad patch of shiny scalp. He wasn't much taller than Mariel's five-six, and he wore a white polo shirt that was almost identical to Noah's, but he had matched his with navy shorts, navy socks, and sandals. Mariel couldn't help comparing the two men, and realized that she might feel sorry for Carl Steadman if she were convinced that he had done nothing to cause his daughter's disappearance. As it was, she regarded him warily, and noticed that the attitude was mutual.

"Yes? How can I help you?" the man asked as a woman appeared behind him.

Mariel saw that it was his wife, and knew instinctively that it was she who had been watching from the window. She hadn't known to expect company. Did she often sit in the window, looking out into the street? Was she distraught, restless, keeping an eye out for her lost daughter?

Realizing that it wasn't a far-fetched scenario, Mariel pushed away any empathetic feelings she might have for Joanne Steadman. As far as she was concerned, the woman was the enemy until proven otherwise.

It didn't help her case that she looked so distinctly . . . motherly. So different from Mariel herself. A pair of glasses was perched on her short blond hair, and the frames were connected to a chain she wore around her neck. Her eyes lacked make-up and were faintly lined with middle age, or worry. Possibly both. She wore pale blue slacks, flats, and a short-sleeved white blouse—a nondescript style typical of middle-aged midwestern PTO mothers, Mariel thought.

She was a matronly woman who probably never wore jeans and sneakers, and didn't get David Letterman's jokes, and had her car radio tuned to an easy listening station. Mariel couldn't help comparing herself to Joanne Steadman and wondering which of them Amber would choose for a mother, and hating herself for wondering that.

"Hello, Mr. and Mrs. Steadman," Noah was saying. "We're sorry to bother you . . ."

We're sorry to bother you. Mariel found herself noticing his casual use of the pronoun—noticing that it seemed to come naturally for him, as though they were still a couple.

She knew it meant nothing, yet she found a strange comfort in it. A strange sense of belonging that she hadn't felt since . . .

Well, since those early days in his arms, before the world had come crashing down around them.

"How can we help you?" Carl Steadman asked Noah, looking from him to Mariel.

"We're concerned about your daughter," Noah said after a moment's hesitation.

Again, his use of a pronoun jumped out at Mariel. This time it was *your*. *Your daughter.*

But Amber isn't their daughter—she's ours, she thought illogically, as the Steadmans' expressions tightened noticeably.

There was silence.

Feeling the edge of her own rising anxiety, Mariel jumped to fill it, blurting, "We were wondering if you've had any new information about where your daughter might be."

"Who are you?" Joanne Steadman asked finally, visibly upset.

And as her eyes met Amber's adoptive mother's eyes, Mariel realized that the question was inconsequential.

She knows, she thought.

Somehow, Joanne Steadman had guessed their identity. It was too late to play games.

"We're Amber's birth parents," Mariel managed to say. She felt Noah stiffen beside her. She couldn't look at him.

To their credit, the Steadmans managed to retain their composure, their expressions equally blank and inscrutable.

"Come in," Carl Steadman said at last.

Mariel noticed that he hadn't looked at his wife to gauge her reaction to their announcement, and he didn't now before extending the invitation. This was a stiff, formal couple, she thought distastefully, though she knew, somewhere inside, that the judgment might be unfair. They had been, in all likelihood, traumatized by their daughter's disappearance. What did she expect? To find them holding hands and smiling?

She found herself gazing around the house with blatant curiosity as she and Noah stepped over the threshold and followed the Steadmans to a living room adjacent to the entry hall. Her attention was drawn to the collection of framed photos on the wall alongside the staircase, and she realized that they were all of Amber.

Amber as a pudgy baby; Amber as an impish toddler; Amber as a gap-toothed elementary school student with pigtails.

The photos took Mariel's breath away, and it was all she could do not to stop in her tracks and gape at them.

She stole a glance at Noah as they were ushered into the living room and saw that he, too, was transfixed by the pictures of their daughter, turning his head to catch another glance over his shoulder, and then scanning the similar row of framed photos on the mantel above the white brick fireplace.

Mariel scrutinized the room as she accepted a seat on the couch at Carl Steadman's invitation, searching for, and finding, more evidence of the teenaged girl who had grown up in this house. There was sheet music open on the upright piano in one corner, and she pictured Amber sitting there, playing. The Harry Potter series and a row of young adult paperbacks mingled with the best-sellers and reference books lining the built-in bookshelves alongside the fireplace. And there were pictures everywhere—framed photographs on every surface. It was all Mariel could do not to rise and go to them, not to pick them up and examine them as thoroughly as she longed to do.

She sat as if frozen on the couch, poised for whatever was to come next, her mind whirling with foreign emotion. She didn't know how to react to this place, or these people. She hadn't allowed herself to envision this situation even when she had made the decision to come here. And even if she had tried to imagine what it would be like, she couldn't possibly have anticipated the intense mingling of pain and pleasure at this glimpse into the home her daughter had known.

This was an orderly room, yet comfortable—much in the way that Mariel's childhood home had been. Her mother had been an avid housekeeper and tended to their well-worn furniture as lovingly as she would tend to priceless antiques. As Mariel took in the outdated plaid fabric couch, the scarred coffee table, and the slightly faded wall-to-wall carpeting, she wanted to see it as alien and uninviting, but she couldn't. This was a small-town, middle-class home, just like small-town, middle-class homes everywhere. Just like the one in which she had been raised, and in which she still lived. She couldn't have done any better for Amber herself— not in providing material things.

But did the Steadmans love her? Had they treated her well?

"I don't know what to ask," Joanne Steadman said abruptly, now that the four of them were seated in the living room. She sat in a wing chair facing the couch, and her husband perched on the edge of a rocking chair.

Noah and Mariel sat side by side, not touching, though she was incredibly aware of his weight on the cushion beside her. She longed to lean on him, knowing that he was experiencing the same barrage of emotions that were sweeping over her—knowing that he alone understood what she felt. But she kept her distance. She had to. She couldn't give in to the illusion that they were anything more than strangers bound by a long-ago experience. Perhaps a long-ago mistake.

"My name is Noah Lyons," Noah said, and cleared his throat. "And this is Mariel Rowan."

"We know," Carl said awkwardly. "The names were on the adoption papers."

Silence. Again.

Mariel thought about the adoption. She hadn't met the Steadmans fifteen years ago—rather, had selected theirs from a sheaf of applications that had been handed to her by one of the nuns at the home as her pregnancy progressed and she insisted that her mind was made up. They had looked good on paper, Carl and Joanne Steadman.

He was an insurance salesman whose hobby was woodworking. She had imagined him building a dollhouse for the child she knew, without being told, was a daughter. She had shoved from her mind the unwelcome images of Noah filling that role—of Noah being father to the child she carried, of Noah making doll furniture or cradling a small pink bundle in his arms.

Just as she had forbidden herself to imagine someday being Mommy to her unborn baby. She had convinced herself that this stranger, Joanne Steadman, was far better suited for that. A former nurse, Joanne had been born and raised in Valley Falls, and her parents had still lived in town, along with both of her sisters. Mariel's child would have grandparents and aunts nearby, a family that would love her and care for her. Or so she had wanted desperately to believe.

"How did you hear about Amber?" Joanne's voice cut into Mariel's memories, and she didn't miss the chill in her words.

"I read about it in the local newspapers," Mariel said when Noah didn't answer right away.

"And you're here because you're—"

"Concerned," Noah interrupted the woman. "We're both very concerned about—your daughter."

Not *our* daughter. Not really. Not as far as these people were concerned.

"We thought we might be able to help," Mariel said, needing to ease the tension in the room.

"Help . . . in what way?" Carl asked. "You were asking us for information just a few minutes ago, not offering it."

"That's true," Noah told him. "As I said, we're concerned."

"Why?"

Mariel turned her own startled gaze on Joanne, whose one-word question had unexpectedly flared dangerous emotions in Mariel's gut. How dare this woman ask why she and Noah were concerned?

"You should know," Noah said with a dangerous gleam in his eye, "that Amber contacted Mariel recently, asking her if she was her birth mother."

For the first time, the Steadmans looked at each other.

Mariel saw that they were both startled and distressed, and she felt a twisted sense of satisfaction. Suddenly, she wanted to hurt these people who had ostensibly been hurt already by their daughter's disappearance. She wanted to rob them of their sense of parental rights—to let them know that Amber was aware that she had had, for however brief a time, another mother. And another father.

Mariel glanced at Noah.

He was watching the Steadmans, waiting for their response.

"When did Amber call you?" Carl Steadman asked Mariel.

"She didn't call me. She e-mailed."

Again, a look passed between the other couple, but this time, Mariel couldn't read it.

"What did she want?"

"To know if I was her mother," Mariel said simply, and saw Joanne flinch at the last word. She could have distinguished—could have said *birth mother*. But she had chosen not to.

"And how did you respond?" Joanne asked.

"I didn't respond," Mariel said. "I thought it would be better to deal with it in person. So I flew here to see her."

"You flew here? You no longer live in the area?" Relief was plain on Carl's face.

"I live in Missouri," Mariel told them.

"And you're married to each other now?" Joanne asked.

Though she had realized earlier that it might be their assumption, Mariel was caught off guard by her words. These people thought she and Noah were married. They were strangers who had no idea of the turmoil that had passed between them, or the wreckage of their relationship in the wake of the baby's birth and adoption.

These people thought that Mariel and Noah had simply picked themselves up and moved on . . . together.

"We're not married," Mariel said, and found herself voicing the words in unison with Noah, who had also quickly spoken up.

"I live in New York City now," he said. "When Mariel told me what had happened, I came right up here."

"And you found out accidentally, from the papers?" Carl asked, turning a probing gaze on Mariel.

She shifted uncomfortably, willing herself to act and sound casual as she said, "Yes."

And it was the truth, of course. She had no reason to squirm in her seat or avoid making eye contact with him. Yet she couldn't help it. She felt guilty.

Why?

It wasn't simply guilt over how she had responded to—or rather, failed to respond to—Amber's e-mail. It was deep-seated, age-old guilt stemming from a decision she had made fifteen years ago, and she still hadn't worked through it, no matter what she wanted Noah— and the Steadmans, for that matter—to believe.

Suddenly she felt entirely alone once again. Noah's presence was no longer a comfort, but an affliction. Having him here meant that she must defend herself and her actions not to two people, but to three.

"It seems coincidental that you showed up in town right on the heels of our daughter's disappearance," Joanne Steadman commented.

And in that instant, Mariel hated her. Not just for

what she said or the way she was looking at Mariel, but for the precious gift she had been given—and the precious gift that Mariel had willingly, perhaps foolishly, lost.

"If you're trying to tell me you're suspicious of me, you're wasting your time," Mariel said, her voice tight. "I had nothing to do with Amber's disappearance."

The woman just shrugged.

Noah stood. "I don't think this is as helpful or enlightening as Mariel and I had hoped it would be," he announced. "We'll be at the Sweet Briar Inn over in Strasburg if you want to contact us. We would appreciate it if you could fill us in if the police come up with any leads, or let us know when Amber comes home."

Yeah, right, Mariel thought, following his lead and getting to her feet. Her legs felt like liquid. There was no way these people were going to make them a part of the investigation or even tell Amber that they had been here.

The four of them stiffly made their way back to the entrance hall with its looming photo gallery of Amber. At the door, Mariel turned to the Steadmans, needing to ask one last question. "Do you believe what the police say—that Amber is a runaway?"

"Absolutely not," Carl replied instantly, and his wife nodded vehemently.

"Our daughter would never willingly leave home," she chimed in. "She loves us. She loves it here. She's well-adjusted and happy." Her voice became choked, yet she continued, "Somebody took Amber away from us. And Carl and I are determined to find out who. And why. And we're determined to find her alive."

Mariel swallowed hard over the lump that rose in her

throat at those chilling words. In that instant she truly believed that this was a mother who refused to prepare herself to confront her worst fears. Joanne Steadman clearly thought Amber was in danger.

And the reality was, she might very well be right.

CHAPTER SIX

"Now what?" Noah asked Mariel as they headed back along the highway toward Strasburg.

Neither of them had spoken for the first few minutes of the drive, and he assumed she had been as lost in her thoughts as he was in his own. He felt numb, having come face to face with the reality he had avoided all these years.

His daughter belonged to somebody else.

Amber's presence in that household was as palpable as if she had suddenly come bounding in the door. The Steadmans appeared for all the world to be doting parents. Noah hadn't missed the framed snapshots, the bronzed baby shoes on an end table, the glimpse of framed crayon artwork on the wall of the adjoining den.

He realized that he would rather believe that the Steadmans were inept parents and that they had done something to cause their daughter to run away than the alternative, which was that Amber had met with foul play.

It was far easier on his aching heart to imagine her homeless on the streets of Syracuse or Albany or even New York than to speculate about what might have happened to a pretty teenaged girl who had set out for school one sunny June morning and never been heard from again.

"I still think she's a runaway," Mariel said, her voice hollow.

Startled, he glanced at her. "You really believe that?"

"I don't know. Maybe I just want to believe it," she said bleakly, and he knew that her thoughts were following the same grim path his own had taken.

"Well, no matter what we think, we aren't just going to give up and go home now and leave this to the Steadmans and the police," Noah said, his stomach churning. "At least, I'm not."

"I'm not either."

His heart fluttered as he heard the conviction in her voice.

Well, what the hell had he been thinking? That she didn't care? Of course she cared. She had flown all the way here from Missouri, had summoned him here, and had already repeatedly voiced the worries that were now plainly written on her face. He knew that she cared about Amber Steadman.

He wanted to believe that she cared about him—that she was staying here, in part, because of him.

He knew that it wasn't true, yet he couldn't help yearning for the impossible.

"Don't worry," he said, casting a glance at her. Her

face was turned toward the car window. "We'll track her down, Mariel. We'll start looking on our own."

"Where do we even start?"

"We'll talk to her teachers, and her friends. We'll talk to anyone who might have some idea what could have happened to her."

"But the police are probably doing just that," she pointed out. "What are we going to learn that they won't?"

He bristled. "The police are treating this as a runaway case. They might not be following up on every possible scenario."

"So you don't think she ran away. You think somebody took her. Like one of those serial killers or pedophiles who prey on little girls . . . I feel sick, Noah," she said, and her voice had an edge of hysteria.

"I don't know what to think, Mariel, but I'm not ruling anything out. For all we know, Carl and Joanne Steadman are a couple of miserable people, and she couldn't stand living with them, so she took off. It isn't that hard to imagine, is it?"

She hesitated, then said, "I guess not."

He thought about the couple and the house they had just left. It was hard to judge the family dynamics under the circumstances. The Steadmans had been tense when they answered the door, and even more tense as the conversation wore on and they discovered their visitors' identity. By all appearances, they doted on their daughter. Yet appearances didn't count for much, he reminded himself, remembering that the Steadmans had assumed that he and Mariel were married.

"Are you hungry?" he asked Mariel, looking over at

her as they stopped at an intersection surrounded by fast-food and chain restaurants.

"No," she said, stifling a yawn. "But I could use some coffee. I didn't sleep well last night."

The telltale way in which she flinched as soon as the words left her mouth told him that he was the reason she hadn't slept last night, and again, he felt his heart jump-start.

She had no doubt lain awake thinking about that kiss, just as he had. Not that he believed that was all that was on her mind. Of course she was worried about Amber, and so was he. But even that—even their mutual worry—was a reminder of all they had once shared. And being back here, together, was bound to arouse feelings that had never been fully resolved when their relationship ended so abruptly.

Or had it?

Over the years, whenever he thought back on what had happened between them, Noah had mainly remembered the shattering day—July Fourth—when their daughter had been born, and the papers had been signed, and he had walked out of the hospital in a daze.

When he had returned the next morning, Mariel was gone.

He had known she would be.

Because their breakup hadn't been defined in that one last dramatic day; it had been a gradual process that began back in her dorm room the moment she turned down his proposal. The months that had followed had been one long, drawn-out good-bye, he had realized when they were over.

"So do you want to stop for coffee?" she was asking, dragging him back, once again, from the past.

"Coffee? Yes," he said, his mind scrambling to catch up. "Food, too."

"You're hungry?"

"Starved," he admitted.

"You were always so hungry," she recalled, almost fondly, as though she had momentarily forgotten who—and where—they were now. "All you ever wanted to do was eat. Before class, and after class, and . . ."

"Always," he said, watching her as he automatically pressed the accelerator when the light changed.

And he knew by the way she had trailed off, her hands clenching in her lap, that she was remembering what he was remembering. The first night they had made love, the night he had brought her to the Sweet Briar Inn and seduced her in a four-poster antique bed in one of the third-floor guest rooms.

When they lay naked and spent in each other's arms, drowsily stroking each other in the light of the flickering votive candles he had brought, he had asked if she was hungry. Then he had brought out the basket he had so carefully put together that afternoon—splurging all of his meal tickets for the day in the dining hall for the strawberries and grapes, the crackers and cheese and chocolate. She had teased him about his voracious appetite as they feasted on the makeshift picnic, and then he had indulged his appetite for her once again, making love to her until the gray morning light filtered through the shade and she drifted off to sleep in his arms.

A car horn honked, jarring him out of his reverie, and he swerved just in time to avoid an SUV making a left-hand turn in front of him.

"I guess I need coffee, too," he said, his nerves shot. Better to vocally blame his distraction on exhaustion, rather than on his haunting thoughts of her—of *them,* together. He spotted the Cracker Barrel restaurant up ahead and pointed. "Let's stop there."

"Cracker Barrel?" She shrugged. "Fine with me. They have great sundaes. Maybe I'll go for some sugar along with the caffeine."

"You've already been there?" he asked, surprised. She had said she only got into town yesterday.

"A zillion times, back home."

"Oh," he said, getting it as he pulled into the parking lot, past the misleadingly quaint building with its down-home, rocking-chair-lined porchlike entryway. "It's a chain."

She looked amused. "You've never heard of Cracker Barrel?"

"I live in Manhattan, remember? We've got delis, we've got five-star restaurants, we've got fast-food chains. We haven't got Cracker Barrel."

"You'll like it," she said. "They've got meatloaf."

Her comment caught him off guard.

She remembered.

He only dared to look at her when he had pulled the car into a parking spot, and he saw that she was busy checking her reflection in the pull-down rearview mirror.

"Meatloaf," he echoed.

She dragged her gaze up to his, then shrugged, but there was nothing nonchalant about her, hard as she tried. "I remembered that you like meatloaf. You do, right?"

It wasn't a real question. She knew the answer.

They had talked about it one day, as they were lying in each other's arms—about how he had always wanted the kind of family life where he came home and the house was clean and smelled delicious and his mother was waiting with a home-cooked meal, like meatloaf with gravy and mashed potatoes. His reality was that his mother always worked two jobs and was never there when he came home, and that most of his dinners, growing up, had come out of a can or box and been prepared by himself.

And Mariel had kissed his neck and his cheek and promised him that someday, she would make him meatloaf and gravy and mashed potatoes. He had teased her about it from that point on, pretending, whenever he popped into her dorm room, that he was expecting a meatloaf dinner—until, of course, she was pregnant and there was no more teasing, ever.

"I like meatloaf," he agreed slowly, his eyes searching her face for some sign of the girl he had once cared for so deeply. He knew that she was there somewhere, kept finding himself tantalized by glimpses of the Mariel she had once been. The Mariel he had asked—and wanted—to spend the rest of his life with.

Not the angry, bitter, frightened Mariel who had turned him down.

"So," he said, turning off the ignition. "Cracker Barrel."

"And then Robbie said, 'Miss Rowan, Melvin's fur looks kind of funny, and he's been taking a really long nap,' and I said, 'How long?' and he said, 'Since last Tuesday.' " Mariel laughed as she remembered the little boy who had been one of her favorite students this year.

Noah laughed, too. A true laugh. It was a sound she

had heard repeatedly in the last half hour or so, as they sat across from each other in the big family-style restaurant and she entertained him with anecdotes about her students.

"That'll teach Robbie's parents never to get him another pet," Noah said, sipping root beer from the glass mug in front of him.

"Oh, Melvin wasn't a pet," she said. "He was a caterpillar. Robbie has allergies, so that's about as close to being a pet owner as he's ever going to get. I helped him catch Melvin and put him into a jar, and Robbie fixed it up with leaves and twigs. He wanted to see Melvin turn into a beautiful butterfly. Instead, I helped him make a little coffin out of a matchbox, and we had a funeral."

"Poor Robbie," Noah said, shaking his head and toying with his straw. "He was lucky to have a teacher like you."

"I was lucky to have a student like him. They all have their charming qualities, but he was one of my favorites this year."

"You really enjoy teaching," he observed.

"I really do," she said, and she felt mildly surprised by her own admission. It wasn't exactly news to her, but she rarely thought about her career when she wasn't actually immersed in it—about how right it felt, despite the way she had fallen into it by default.

"I never would have seen it coming if anyone had asked me way back when," he said, resting his chin in his hand, watching her.

She pretended to be very interested in finishing the last crumbs of corn bread on her plate, though she was absolutely stuffed. Noah had talked her into ordering a meal, too, and she had found herself chowing down on chicken and dumplings and sides of southern greens and fried apples.

"I always assumed you would become an actress," Noah went on, obviously unwilling to let it go.

"Well, that was the plan."

"So what happened to change it?"

"Gee, I guess the problem was that it's really hard to get work as a stage star in Rockton," she said wryly.

"But you never wanted to live in Rockton. When you went back after . . . everything—I thought it was going to be temporary. For the summer. I thought you would resurface someplace else."

This was tricky, she thought, not wanting to look up from the last crumb of corn bread she was chasing around her plate with her fork. She had known that sooner or later they were going to get back onto the topic of the past—not even their past together, but the more recent past, apart. She wanted to know more about his life, and his marriage. . . .

Or did she?

She shouldn't feel threatened by the wife who was no longer his wife, she reminded herself.

And she should expect that he would be just as curious about what she had been doing in the years since they had last seen each other. Which was why she had been regaling him with tales from the first grade front. It had been fun, really, telling him about her students, seeing him react with genuine interest. He wasn't just being polite; he was really listening, really laughing, really caring.

And now he was waiting intently for a response to his

question about why she had settled in the hometown she had once hated.

The truth was, she had settled there because it was safe, and it was as far away from him and Strasburg as she could get. There was no way, even with him safely back at Strasburg for his sophomore year, that she was going to reclaim her dream of living in New York City— not when it was where he had grown up, and where his mother lived, and where she had assumed he would someday return after college.

And he had.

Good thing she had played it safe.

Then again, New York was a huge place. Big enough for both of them, if she had dared to take a chance. But the Mariel who had emerged from that traumatic freshman year hadn't been game for anything. She had wanted only to retreat, to hide, to heal.

And she *had* healed.

"I decided that being an actress in New York wasn't what I wanted after all," she said.

"But you wanted it so desperately when I knew you."

"You only knew me for a few months, Noah," she pointed out.

"And in those few months I didn't get the sense that you were given to flights of fancy. You were strong-willed, Mariel. You were driven, and ambitious. You knew exactly what you wanted, and you were going to go after it. You used to say you wouldn't go back to Rockton for anything ever again, unless it was Christmas, or you were on your way to be buried in the family plot."

"Wow, did I say that? I guess I always was a drama

queen," she said, trying to sound light. But the upbeat, casual mood of the conversation had been altered.

She thought about her life as it was now, and she realized that although she wasn't entirely content, her career and her location weren't the elements in her life that were lacking. When you came right down to it, she liked living in Rockton, and she liked teaching.

"Did you fall in love with somebody back home, Mariel? Is that why you stayed?" he asked, so unexpectedly that reaching for her coffee, she nearly knocked over her cup.

"No!" she said immediately—then instantly wished that she hadn't denied it.

Maybe she should have made up something—given herself an imaginary fiancé back home. Then Noah would be sure to keep his hands off. . . .

What was she thinking?

He had already promised to do just that, and so had she. There would be no more kissing or touching. They were here to find out what had happened to their daughter, period.

She opened her mouth to steer the conversation back to Amber's disappearance, but he was already talking.

"There was never anyone, then?" he was asking her. "After me? You never fell in love again?"

His words hung in the air between them, and she saw the look of dismay that crossed his face as soon as he realized what he had said.

Love.

They had never discussed love.

They had never acknowledged that they were in love even when it was happening . . . if that was, indeed, what had happened.

Had she been in love with him?

She didn't want to analyze that.

Nor did she want him to assume.

"I've never been in love, period," she said in another unsuccessful attempt at levity. "So don't flatter yourself, Lyons."

He recovered quickly; she had to give him that. He tilted his head to one side and looked at her, then grinned as he speared a green bean with his fork. "Oh, my wounded heart," he said flippantly, adding to an imaginary audience, "And so, ladies and gentlemen, that concludes the awkward portion of our conversation."

She smiled.

"You want one of those mug sundaes you were talking about?" he asked, picking up the dessert menu the waiter had left.

She groaned. "I can't fit in another morsel, Noah."

"Are you sure? Because I'm having one."

"You are incredible," she said, shaking her head.

She didn't mean it the way it came out. And she didn't like the way his eyes warmed at her words, twinkling at her before he said, "Right back at ya, Rowan."

"We're closing in five minutes," the librarian said, coming up behind Noah.

Startled by her voice, he looked up at her, and then at his watch.

He couldn't believe it. He had been sitting here at the microfiche machine in the Strasburg library for a full two hours. He glanced at Mariel, who was seated at a computer terminal a short distance away, copying notes off the screen.

"I'll wrap things up," Noah told the librarian, who smiled, nodded, and moved on to give Mariel the same warning.

Noah began to rewind the spool of microfiche in the machine, an expert at it now. Funny, but the librarian had had to teach him how to do it when he had first arrived tonight, even though he remembered using the library—and old newspapers on microfiche—to do research when he was a student here. It wasn't difficult to spool the film onto the roller, but one needed a certain level of expertise to operate the scanner in a manner that would move the film along at just the right rate to search for articles that contained relevant information.

In this case, he had searched back issues of every local and regional newspaper for articles about Amber Steadman.

He had read everything he could find on the subject of her disappearance. He had written every possibly important detail in the black-and-white marble notebook he had bought when he and Mariel stopped at the Staples Office Supply superstore after eating at Cracker Barrel. Mariel had a similar notebook, and now he saw her snap it closed and shut down the computer.

He replaced the microfilm into its canister, dropped it into the designated bin, and turned off the machine. He met Mariel by the exit doors just as the overhead lights were clicking off.

"This is the second night I've closed down the Strasburg library," Mariel said with a slight laugh as the librarian used her jangling key ring to let them out of the locked doors. A wall of muggy night air awaited them just beyond the air-conditioned library.

"Did you find information we can use to investigate Amber's disappearance?" Noah asked as they walked down the broad concrete steps of the modern building.

She nodded, gesturing at the notebook tucked under her arm. "I've got the names of teachers and administrators at her school, and an enhanced street map of Valley Falls showing the route she would probably have walked when she left home that morning."

"And I've got the names of all of her friends and neighbors who were interviewed by reporters, plus the names of local places she probably frequented, like stores at the malls and fast-food restaurants. We can interview employees about her."

"Where do we start?" Mariel asked, pushing a wisp of hair from her already damp forehead.

"I think her teachers would make the most sense. And her friends. We'll make a short list and cover them in the morning," Noah said as they walked across the broad, grassy quad. A chorus of cicadas created rhythmic background noise, and not a breath of breeze stirred the tree branches overhead.

"We're not going to start until morning?" she asked in dismay.

"I don't think we can show up on people's doorsteps at night," Noah pointed out.

"I guess you're right."

He wiped a trickle of sweat from his neck.

They walked in silence for a few moments.

"Too bad I decided not to stay at the Super 8 after all," Mariel said. "At least they had a pool. I'd love to go swimming right about now."

"I know. I'm used to oppressive heat in the city, but up here it seems even more stifling, somehow," Noah commented. "Although there was one spring, during finals—I think it was junior year—when we got a real heat wave. The frat house wasn't air-conditioned—"

"Frat house?" she echoed. "I didn't know you joined a frat, Noah. You don't seem like the type."

For a moment, he could focus only on the unaccustomed sound of his name on her lips. He used to love the way she said his name—the way her midwestern accent drew out the syllables, as opposed to hurried New Yorkers who rushed everything, including speech. Now he allowed himself a moment to savor it before responding to her comment.

"You mean you never suspected I was a frat boy at heart, Mariel?"

"I can't quite picture you living in one of those run-down, dirty places." She was referring to the row of ramshackle Victorians bedecked with Greek letters that lined Hudson Street not far from campus. The Phi Sig house had been the last one, perched on top of the hilly street, and it was known as the rowdiest of them all, with the best parties.

"It wasn't that dirty," he said with a chuckle. "Not after we'd made the new pledges scour the whole place on their hands and knees. And we had a regular exterminator to take care of the mice and bugs."

She shuddered.

He grinned. "I had a great time being a Phi Sig, Mariel. I'm still in touch with quite a few of my brothers. In fact, one of them, Danny, loaned me his car to drive up here." And though she had offered to drive her rental, he had insisted on driving to Valley Falls today, for some reason wanting to be the one at the wheel.

"I'm glad you have such good friends, Noah," she said sincerely.

"How about you? Do you have good friends back in Rockton?"

She nodded. "I've actually known one of them, Katie Beth, since our preschool days. And then there's my sister Leslie, and Jed."

"Jed?" A prickle of jealousy shot through him. She had said there was no one in her life, but . . . who was Jed? He pictured a rugged cowboy type and felt instantly inadequate in his polo shirt and shorts.

"Jed is my sister's fiancé. They're getting married in a few weeks, and she's probably panicking without me right about now. I'm sure my father has his hands full."

"What about your mother?"

He saw a shadow cross her face. "She died," she said simply.

"I'm so sorry, Mariel."

"So am I." She sighed. "It's been almost two years, and sometimes I wonder if I'll ever be over it."

They had reached the campus gates that led back to Main Street. The Sweet Briar Inn was directly across from them, with soft lamplight spilling from the windows and guests in rocking chairs creaking on the wraparound porch.

"You know, it's still early," Noah said suddenly, not wanting to call it a night just yet.

"You just said it was late." She sounded amused. He took that as an encouraging sign.

"Too late for interrogating strangers. Not too late for a cold drink." He gestured toward a small Mexican restaurant a few doors down from the inn. "What do you say?"

"I don't say no to a cold drink when it's over ninety degrees after sundown, that's for sure," she said.

They headed in that direction and a minute or two later were seated across from each other at a table for two. The place was small and not air-conditioned, with terra-cotta tile and shimmering candles, and fairly deserted. A ceiling fan whirred overhead, and another floor fan stirred the air nearby, but did little to cool things off. There was a sign on the wall above the bar advertising live mariachi musicians on Saturday nights.

A smiling Hispanic waiter appeared, set down a basket of chips and a crock of salsa, and asked if they wanted to see a menu.

Noah looked at Mariel, who shook her head. "I'm still stuffed from Cracker Barrel this afternoon."

"Me, too. We'll just have drinks," he told the waiter, who stood with his pen poised, waiting for Mariel's order.

"I'll have an iced tea," she said, then changed her mind. "Wait a minute, I'd better not have more caffeine at this hour. I need to get a good night's sleep for a change. Do you have anything decaf?"

The waiter grinned. "No caffeine in a Margarita."

"That's what I'm having," Noah decided. "Frozen. No salt."

Mariel hesitated, then threw up her hands. "Okay, count me in on that. But with salt."

"Coming right up."

The waiter disappeared into the kitchen.

They crunched their chips and talked about Mexican

food, then about television cooking shows, then about movies.

When their drinks arrived, Noah lifted his glass and said, for lack of anything profound, "Here's to a cold drink on a hot night."

She clinked her glass against his.

Noah swallowed some of the citrusy slush, savoring the chilling sensation on his tongue. He could taste the tequila, which meant he had better not toss this back as though it were ice water. But it was hard not to in this heat, especially after such a trying twenty-four hours.

He noticed that Mariel wasn't exactly sipping her drink, either.

"Goes down easy, doesn't it?" she asked, catching him watching her.

He offered her the basket of chips. "Never drink on an empty stomach."

"My stomach is definitely not empty after today," she said, but she helped herself to a couple of chips anyway.

Their conversation turned back to movies they had seen, and he got the impression that she, like he, caught most of them on cable or video. He wondered if that was because Rockton was too small a town for a movie theater, or because she didn't date and didn't want to go to the movies by herself.

He told himself that that was a broad assumption. After all, people went to movies all the time without being on a date. They went solo, or with friends, or family members. He should stop looking for clues into her personal life and simply come right out and ask if he wanted to know more.

But he couldn't bring himself to do that, because he wasn't supposed to be interested. So he changed the subject from movies to music to the weather. By that time, he was definitely feeling the effects of the tequila, and assumed she was, too. Her cheeks were still flushed, and she was smiling a lot, leaning forward in her chair, her elbows propped on the table. She seemed so relaxed, he thought, almost flirtatious, even though all they were talking about was the weather.

When she once again commented that she should have stayed at the Super 8 so she could go swimming and cool off, he took the bait.

Okay, maybe it wasn't bait. In fact, he knew her comment wasn't deliberate. When she had made it earlier, he had started to bring up the story of that May heat wave junior year in total innocence before she had unwittingly interrupted.

But this time, there was absolutely nothing innocent about his intentions.

"Like I started to tell you before, I was once here in Strasburg during a heat wave back in college," he said.

"Oh, right, when you were living in Delta house or whatever it was."

"The Delts were a sorority," he said, with mock offense. "I was a Phi Sig."

"Oops, sorry."

"*Anyway*"— he was determined not to get off track, here—"the brothers and I went swimming late one night, and it was great."

"What did you do? Go sneak into somebody's backyard pool?"

"Even better than that," he said. "There's a swimming hole in the woods not far from here. We all went over and jumped in. The water was cold and it felt incredible."

Her eyes sparkled at him, and she said, after taking another gulp of the almost-melted remains of her drink, "That sounds so good right about now, Noah."

"Which is why we should do it."

"Do what?"

"Go swimming," he said, and asked devilishly, "Why? What did *you* think I meant?"

It was a suggestive question, and he said it without thinking, buoyed by liquor-inspired giddiness. As soon as the words were out he expected her to scowl or shut down or stiffly suggest that they call it a night.

But she grinned back at him and said, "Never mind what I thought. Swimming sounds great."

"Are you serious?"

"I'd love to cool off before bed," she said with a shrug. "And it's been a while since I've dived into a swimming hole. We used to go to one in the woods when I was a kid. My mother worried constantly. And with good reason, I'm sure. One time my friend Katie Beth dove in and barely missed hitting a big rock."

"Well, okay then. No diving allowed." He could see she was hesitating.

"I wish I'd brought my bathing suit, or that there was someplace around here to buy one at this hour," she hedged.

"Swim in your clothes," he said with a shrug. "Come on, Mariel. I'm going with or without you. It's too damned hot. What do you say?"

"I say, let's go."

How on earth had Mariel gotten herself into this? Now, as she emerged with Noah from the wooded path into a small, tree-fringed clearing centered by a pool of moonlit water, swimming didn't seem like such a good idea.

In fact, it seemed like a really, really bad idea.

This place was completely isolated. After leaving the restaurant, they had strolled down to the end of a residential cul-de-sac a few blocks from the inn, then followed the short path through the trees. Here, away from the streetlights and the proximity of other people, she was acutely aware of being alone with Noah—of the steamy night air around them and the crickets chirping and an occasional thrashing in the underbrush as wildlife creatures scampered out of their way.

Mariel stopped at the edge of the clearing and looked at the water, conscious that Noah had gone still beside her.

"It's just like I remembered it," he said, his voice hushed.

"It's beautiful." She just stood looking at the pool of shimmering water that reflected the heat-hazy moon and stars above and cast their fluid light back into the trees.

Her body was damp with sweat, and she yearned to plunge into the refreshing depths.

But that would mean walking back to the hotel dripping wet, something that hadn't seemed like such a bad idea back at the restaurant, under the pleasant I-can-do-anything tequila glow. Why hadn't they at least stopped back at the inn for a couple of towels?

Noah still had both of their notebooks under his arm, for Pete's sake. This was insane.

"Last one in's a rotten egg," Noah said abruptly, and

carefully placed the notebooks on a flat rock at the edge of the water before pulling his shirt over his head.

"I've changed my mind," she said, and plopped down on a large moss-covered rock. "I'll just sit here and wait for you."

"Are you sure?"

She nodded.

He looked as if he wanted to say something more, but didn't.

Instead, he reached for the button on his shorts and unfastened it.

She realized, startled, he was going to take them off. Well, what did she expect? He was probably going to go in wearing his boxer shorts. Probably? Of course he was, because the alternative was . . .

She shoved the thought of Noah, naked, from her mind, remembering that he had worn boxers back in college. She wondered if he still did. It certainly looked as though she was about to find out.

It was all she could do not to stare as he stepped out of his shorts and placed them beside his shirt and the notebooks on the rock. She felt a dribble of sweat running down her neck and another starting at her hairline above her temple. She thrust out her lower lip and attempted to blow her damp bangs off her forehead, but they were plastered there with sweat. Lovely.

It was sweltering out here. She would kill for a dip in the pond.

"Sure you don't want to come in?" Noah asked, as though he had read her mind. He seemed to be almost taunting her.

"I'm positive." She fought the urge to lift the weight of her ponytail from her neck and wondered why she hadn't just pinned the whole mass of hair on top of her head this morning to keep cooler.

He shrugged and hooked his thumbs on the elastic waistband of his boxer shorts.

"What are you doing?" she blurted.

"Taking off my boxers," he said, all innocence.

But she saw the gleam in his eye.

"Don't you dare, Noah."

"Huh?" He paused, on the verge of pulling them down, looking at her as though he was shocked she would make such a command.

"I mean it. If you take off your boxers, I'm leaving."

"Why, Mariel?" He took a step closer to the rock where she was sitting, as though daring her to hold her ground. "You've seen me naked before."

There.

He had said it, and now she could no longer banish the image from her mind. She remembered what he looked like naked, and the lower region of her body clenched in response to the vivid thought. He had been the first, the only man she had ever seen without clothes, the only man whose naked flesh she had ever touched, and not just with her hands. He was the only man she had ever made love to, and it was impossible not to remember that now, as he stood before her, ready to bare himself once again.

It had started as a game moments ago. Now it was much more than that. He was directly acknowledging the intimacy they had shared, after both of them had alternately skirted around it or joked it off for the past twenty-four hours.

What should she do?

She couldn't think straight, couldn't think past her

body's betrayal and the explicit recollection that refused to leave her mind.

Noah looked at her, and she looked down, staring at her hands clenched on her lap.

"It shouldn't bother you, Mariel, because it's nothing new," he said, and his tone was light, if the meaning was anything but.

With that, he removed his boxer shorts, tossed them casually to the ground, and dove in.

Water droplets splashed her, and she looked up just in time to see him surface, sputtering. He lolled onto his back and swam a few lazy strokes out into the middle of the water, then paddled back toward her.

"You should come in, Mariel. It's incredible."

"I'm sure it is." If he only knew how she longed to shed her own clothes and join him . . . .

Or maybe he did know. Maybe that was why he was doing this.

But what would happen if she threw caution to the wind?

Nothing, she told herself. Nothing would happen because they had sworn it wouldn't.

"Come on," he coaxed. "You'll dry, you know."

"I know." Her voice sounded defensive even to her own ears.

"And you'll feel so much better. You'll *sleep* so much better."

No, she wouldn't. She wouldn't sleep easily until he was out of her life once again and her daughter was safe and she was back home in Rockton, where she belonged.

"Mariel," he said, flicking water at her.

She ducked. "Cut it out, Noah."

"What's the matter? Did you get splashed?"

He did it again.

She ducked again, but felt the cooling spray on her cheek. She giggled. "God, you're like a junior high school boy, Noah."

"In more ways than one," he said, catching her eye as he moved closer to her with languid strokes until his head was just beneath where she sat.

And she was locked on his gaze. She couldn't look away.

"What's that supposed to mean?" she asked, finding her voice.

He reached up and took her hands. The contact with his wet skin stole her breath, and she heard herself gasp.

"It means that junior high school boys usually have only one thing on their minds."

She couldn't reply to that. Her mind was swirling, her body aching with need sparked by the seductive expression in his eyes. He wanted her. She knew that without a doubt—knew that he was breaking their deal, and she was no longer safe.

And heaven help her, she didn't care.

She wanted what he wanted, and to hell with the consequences.

He tugged her hands, and his voice was softer when he said, "Come on in, Mariel. The water's beautiful."

She struggled to reclaim the argument that was lost in the maelstrom of wanton contemplation. "I told you . . . I don't want to get my clothes soaked," she said futilely.

"So don't wear any."

With that, he reached up and tugged the hem of her shorts.

"It's only me," he said in a low voice.

"That's the problem," she managed, her whole body trembling at his touch. She looked down and saw droplets of cool water glistening on her thigh just below the fabric of her shorts, and she shivered.

"Look, Mariel, I don't know what the hell I'm doing, and if you want me to stop it, I will," he said.

But she didn't want him to stop. She was engulfed by a craving so fierce that it left no room for rationale, or even further discussion. She uttered the only two words that came to mind, and they were enough for him.

"Don't stop."

She heard his breath catch in his throat.

"No, wait," she said, as the past crashed into her brain and she realized what they were about to risk. She was furious at herself for having forgotten for even an instant.

"What's wrong?" he asked in dismay.

"We can't, Noah. Not without protection. What the hell was I thinking?"

He laughed. "I have it," he said, reaching for his shorts, pulling a small silver packet out of the pocket.

She laughed, too, a giddy sound of relief. There was nothing else to hold her back now, no reason she should hesitate.

And then she was undressing herself, untucking the sleeveless T-shirt and pulling it over her head, unfastening the hook at the waistband of her shorts and pulling down the zipper, then lowering them over her hips. She was wearing a plain white lace bra and white lace-edged panties, garments she had never imagined he would see when she had unthinkingly pulled them on this morning.

Now, with the heat of his gaze on her body, she wished she was wearing something silky and seductive; but it didn't matter, because she was unfastening the bra and freeing the weight of her breasts, and she was shimmying out of her panties, and now she was naked, standing on the rock above him.

She heard the slow release of breath and wasn't sure if it had come from her own throat until she looked down and saw that it had come from his. His lips were parted, and he was staring up at her, as though he were entranced, and she vaguely wondered why she didn't feel self-conscious.

But she didn't.

She never had with Noah, for all her inexperience and uncertainty. Somehow, when they were together, she had been sure of herself—sure of him, and how he felt about her.

"Come in," he beckoned, and she hesitated only a moment, looking down at Noah and the waiting water.

Then, without allowing herself another moment to think it over—another moment to consider changing her mind—she closed her eyes and dove in headfirst.

When Mariel surfaced a few feet from where he was, Noah's first impulse was to swim over to her and take her into his arms. He knew what it meant, that she had shed her clothes and joined him in the water, and it was all he could do to curb the ferocious desire that had overtaken him at the first glimpse of her naked body.

He forced himself to hold back, to let her get used to the water's chill and the inevitable outcome of her actions. He knew she had teetered on the brink of backing out only moments ago, and he wanted her too badly to risk losing her again.

Whatever lay beyond this night—this interlude—would be left to chance. But not this.

He watched her sweep her hands across her cheeks and eyes to wipe away the streaming water, and he saw her smooth her hair back from her face. She was lovely in the moonlight, with those huge eyes and creamy white shoulders rising inches above the water's surface. He thought about what lay below, and he wanted to groan. He ached for her. It had been so long . . .

Months since he had made love to Kelly, and years since it had meant anything. If he allowed himself to think about the instinctive physical urgency to sate himself, this would be over before it had begun, and that wasn't what he wanted.

He held his ground, so to speak, treading water though he wasn't in over his head.

It was Mariel who swam toward him.

She stopped, treading water inches away, her movements enveloping him in ripples of water that teased and tantalized his sensitive flesh.

"Mariel, if you come any closer," he gritted out.

She did. She swam into his arms as he reached to embrace her, and his feet hit bottom as he crushed her against him, kissing her.

He moaned when she opened her mouth and allowed him to taste her, to explore the soft inner rim of her lips and to stroke her tongue with his. As he clasped her against him she wrapped her legs around his waist just above his aching manhood, and he held her weightlessness in his arms, dipping his head to close his mouth over her breast. He coaxed one nipple to a puckered nub, then turned his attention to the other, and she sighed, her wrists tucked under his arms and her fingertips clutching his shoulders.

And when she squirmed the apex of her legs against his belly, he nearly went mad with desire.

"I can't . . . I can't . . ."

Her eyes flew open, and she searched his face. "You can't do this?"

"No, hell, Mariel, I can't wait any longer."

"Then don't," she whispered, and that was all the encouragement he needed.

Cupping her bottom, he lowered her around his hips, and then he plunged into her with a groan. He felt her welcoming warmth, and the contrasting chill of the water played around his rigid flesh each time he rhythmically withdrew. The sensation was like nothing he had ever experienced, and he dragged his lips from hers to bury his face in her wet hair, breathing the wet herbal scent of her shampoo as he neared release.

Just when he knew he could last no longer, he heard her whisper, "It's okay, Noah, go ahead," as she reached up to stroke his forehead.

And then he was driven over the edge, soaring, white hot, melting into her, panting into her shoulder as his body shuddered violently.

"I'm sorry," he said when he could speak again, though his breath was still coming in pants. "You didn't—"

"It's okay," she interrupted.

"It's been a long time," he said by way of explanation.

"Fifteen years, Noah."

That wasn't what he had meant. He had been referring to the time that had passed since he had last made love to a woman—not to her. And then he realized that it didn't matter. That even if he had made passionate love to a different woman every night in the past decade and a half, he would have wanted her this desperately, unable to restrain his need.

He looked at her and saw the faint smile on her face, and he kissed her lips tenderly. She was still smiling.

"What are you thinking?" he asked.

"How right now, nothing else matters," she told him, running a fingertip down his cheek, tracing the path a water droplet had just taken before she repeated, "Nothing else matters. It's as though there's nothing down that path in the woods—no other place in the universe but this swimming hole—and we're never going to leave, and the sun is never going to come up."

But it is, and we are, he thought hollowly, then pushed away the melancholy thought.

She was right.

Tonight was all that mattered.

They would worry about the rest of it—all of it—in the morning.

CHAPTER SEVEN

On Monday morning, Mariel woke to the sound of a ringing telephone.

Dazed, she rolled over—and found herself face-to-face with Noah.

With that, last night came rushing back at her. She remembered making love in the water, and getting dressed and making their way back to the inn, only to undress each other hungrily once again and tumble into bed.

Whose bed?

She looked past him and saw yellow roses and butter-colored curtains at the window.

His bed. This was his room. That meant it was his phone, and he should answer it, which he was now rolling over to do.

"Yeah?" he asked, lazily picking up the receiver as he stretched.

She watched him listen, noticing that his eyes narrowed and his hand gripped the receiver more tightly. And she knew, as she saw the changes in his demeanor, that morning was here and, with it, the reality that had shattered their idyllic time together as she had known it would.

"When?" he asked sharply into the receiver. Then he said, "That would be fine. There are a few things I'd like to ask you, too."

Silence again, as he listened. Then he said, "Don't bother. I'll tell her myself."

As he hung up, he got up, rising from the bed in one swift movement. He stood naked, looking down at her, and she felt desire stirring despite the change in mood.

"Who was that?" she asked him.

"That," he said, striding across the room and taking a T-shirt from the open suitcase on the floor, "was the private investigator the Steadmans have hired to find Amber."

She gaped at him. "What did he want with you?"

"It wasn't just me he was looking for. He wanted to talk to you, too. He said he was going to call your room, and I told him—"

"Not to bother. I know. I heard." She sat up, pulling the pale yellow sheet with her so that it draped across her breasts. "I also heard what sounded like a plan to meet him."

"It was. We're having breakfast with him at a diner down the street in an hour." He pulled on the T-shirt.

There. They were both sufficiently covered. No more naked skin to distract them from the matter at hand, or trick them into thinking that they were here together for any reason other than to find their missing daughter.

"What does he want?" Mariel asked, trying to keep her mind on the private investigator.

"What do you think he wants?" Noah picked up his shaving kit and took a clean, folded T-shirt, boxer shorts, and cutoffs from his suitcase. "I'm going to go down the hall and take a shower. I won't be long."

"I'll go to my room and get my stuff. Knock when you're out."

"I will."

With that, he was gone, leaving Mariel to lean back against the pillows, her mind whirling.

Mere hours ago, they had been lying in this very spot, cloaked in darkness and wrapped in each other's arms, making love over and over again until one time melded into the next. Nothing else mattered; not the unrelenting heat that made their bodies slick and dampened the sheets, and not the fact that they were stealing forbidden moments together, pretending this was somehow right and okay.

Now she could pretend no longer.

It was time to deal with what was happening. Time to allow a stranger to intrude, no doubt with probing questions about their connection to Amber Steadman.

The full implication of what Noah had said hit her for the first time, and Mariel pressed a trembling fist against her mouth.

The Steadmans had hired a private investigator.

Did that mean that they didn't believe the police assumption that their daughter was a runaway, and that they suspected a crime had been committed?

That Amber had most likely been abducted?

Numb with worry, Mariel chastised herself for getting sidetracked last night with Noah. She was here to find her daughter, period. Yet she had been dining out, having margaritas, romping in a swimming hole, making love, as though this were some kind of long-overdue vacation, and she had a future with the man she had never expected—never wanted—to see again.

Well, that was going to change.

She wouldn't let her focus waver again, she vowed as she slid out of bed, threw on her rumpled clothes, and made her way back down the hall to her room.

"I'm Henry Brando," the dark-haired, surprisingly young man said, rising from the table at the rear of the diner when he saw Mariel and Noah approach.

"And you know who we are," Noah said, giving the guy a quick once-over. He wasn't the rumpled, cigarette-smoking cliché he had expected. Henry Brando was clean-shaven and neatly pressed, and wore a dress shirt and slacks despite the near-hundred-degree heat outside.

Noah, on the other hand, wore a simple white short-sleeved pocket T-shirt and green khaki shorts, and Mariel had on a sleeveless red madras plaid dress with sandals. She had piled her hair on top of her head, and little tendrils spilled out of the clips. Every time Noah glanced at her, he found himself wanting to brush them back from her face.

He reached for a chair to pull out for her, but Henry Brando beat him to it. Noah fought back a twinge of jealousy as he watched the private investigator giving her an appreciative appraisal. Well, what did he expect? She looked incredibly appealing—so appealing Noah hadn't been able to resist her himself.

But he would from here on in, he reminded himself. He couldn't afford to get caught up in his emotions now, when he had finally detached himself from a draining mess of a marriage—and when his job was on the line besides, thanks to calling in sick this morning.

He didn't know whether his boss, David Grafton, had believed him or not when he claimed to have eaten some bad shellfish yesterday. Probably not. And even if he had believed the lie, he would expect Noah to be over the food poisoning within a reasonable time frame. Like tomorrow.

That wasn't going to happen. He should have come up with some illness that would take at least a few days' worth of recovery . . .

Or the truth.

Why hadn't he just told his boss the truth?

Because he had never discussed Amber's existence with anybody. Not even Kelly, or his mother. Neither of them knew he had had a daughter and given her up for adoption, and he certainly hadn't told any of his friends. Now he wondered why he hadn't. Talking about it might have helped over the years.

Or maybe it would only have made the ache even deeper, and the longing more profound.

In any case, he wasn't about to tell David that he was four hours away from New York City, searching for his missing teenaged daughter. Not unless he had to, to save his job. They didn't take calling in sick lightly at the agency—not with the tremendous workload and demanding clients breathing down everyone's neck twenty-four-seven. A few times, Noah had even been asked to postpone a vacation at the last minute.

Kelly had been understanding, given her own work

ethic and dedication to her career—and the fact that it was she who had more or less pushed Noah into the corporate world. The first two times, she had rearranged her own schedule so that they could take their vacation at a later date. But the last time it had happened, a little over a year ago, she had said she wouldn't be able to take time off later and that she was going to go alone. She had jetted off to St. Thomas solo, leaving Noah to work six straight days of overtime on a new last-minute campaign that the client ultimately decided wasn't going to work after all, opting to go back to the original a few hours before Kelly landed at La Guardia with a fabulous tan and her designer luggage packed with souvenirs.

Frustrating business, advertising.

"Have a seat, Noah," Henry Brando offered, and Noah realized he was the only one still standing.

He slid into the chair beside Mariel's and eyed the private investigator across the table. A cup of steaming black coffee sat in front of him, along with three menus. Did the guy expect him and Mariel to actually eat at a time like this? Noah had completely lost his appetite.

As if to contradict that thought, the waitress materialized beside him. She was a cliche, from her red teased hair to her pink uniform with a white apron and the pen tucked behind her ear, which she removed now and held poised over her order pad.

"What can I get you?" she asked.

"Just coffee," Mariel said.

"Same here."

The private investigator handed over all three menus and said, "That's it, then."

When the waitress had walked away, Noah got down

to business before Henry Brando had a chance to jump in first. "You said you're working for the Steadmans. When did they hire you?"

"The second day into the police investigation," Brando replied. "When they realized that the cops were treating this as a runaway case and operating on the assumption that their daughter had left willingly, and would probably turn up sooner rather than later on her own."

"You don't think that's going to happen?" Mariel asked, a waver in her voice as she spoke for the first time.

Brando shrugged. *"They* don't think it's going to happen. What do you think, Mr. Lyons?"

Noah looked him in the eye. "I think you'd better do everything you can to find their daughter, Mr. Brando."

"Which is exactly why I've asked the two of you to meet with me here this morning." The private investigator stirred his black coffee and took a sip, directing his attention at Mariel. "Ms. Rowan, you told the Steadmans that you got an e-mail from their daughter. Would you be able to access that e-mail so that I can take a look at it?"

She shook her head. "I deleted it."

There was a pause, and then Brando repeated, "You deleted it? You heard from the long-lost daughter you had given up for adoption when she was a newborn infant and you deleted the message?"

Mariel nodded, looking down at her hands for a moment. Noah wanted to put an arm around her slumping shoulders for support, but instinctively forced himself not to. The less this man saw of whatever it was that was going on between them, the better.

When Mariel looked up at the detective again, her gaze was unwavering. Almost defiant, Noah realized, and he couldn't help but admire her.

"I deleted it because I didn't want anybody in my family to stumble across it," she told Brando. "Nobody knew that I was pregnant and gave birth while I was away at college."

"You never told your parents?"

"My father was a minister. I was a freshman. No."

"So it's been a secret you've kept all these years? What about you, Mr. Lyons? Did you share this with anyone in your family?"

"There was only my mother," he said. "And no, I never told her."

"What about a spouse? Are either of you married?"

"I was," Noah said as Mariel shook her head. "But not anymore."

"And you never told your wife that you had a daughter?"

"No, never."

The detective gazed intently at him for a long time. Noah forced himself not to lower his own gaze. Then Brando asked, looking from Noah to Mariel, "Do either of you have any idea who could possibly have had a reason to want to abduct or harm your daughter?"

"She isn't our daughter," Mariel replied. "She hasn't been our daughter since we handed her over to the people from the adoption agency the day she was born."

"We don't know anything about her life," Noah added. "We haven't been in contact with her since we gave her up."

"And you've never tried to locate her, or check on her?" Brando asked.

They shook their heads.

"And she didn't contact you, Mr. Lyons? Only Ms. Rowan?"

"No, she didn't contact me." That stung. He couldn't help it. If only Amber Steadman had reached out to him, he would have . . .

What? Would he have done anything differently than Mariel had? Would he have been able to prevent whatever it was that had happened to her?

"What brought you two to Strasburg and Valley Falls?" Brando asked abruptly, changing the tone of the conversation after the waitress had unobtrusively arrived to pour coffee for Mariel and Noah.

Noah glanced at Mariel, waiting for her to answer the question. After all, it was she who had arrived here first, and summoned him.

Mariel told the detective what she had told Noah— that she had wanted to respond to their daughter's e-mail in person, knowing that the discovery of her birth mother was an emotional and possibly traumatic event.

"So you just happened to turn up here right around the time Amber disappeared, Ms. Rowan?"

"I turned up here more than a week later, Mr. Brando," Mariel said succinctly. "And I had nothing to do with her disappearance, if that's what you're implying."

Brando ignored that, turning to Noah, who was stirring creamer into his coffee. "How did you happen to be here, Mr. Lyons?"

"Mariel contacted me when she got here and found out what had happened."

"So the two of you maintain a relationship after all these years?"

"No, we don't," Noah said quickly, in unison with Mariel. "We haven't been in touch since we gave up the baby," Noah added.

"Why not?"

It was a simple question.

There was no simple answer.

Again, Noah left it to Mariel.

"I returned to the Midwest," she said with a shrug. "I got on with my life. Noah got on with his. We just . . . went our separate ways."

The investigator seemed to consider this. Then he asked, "What did you think of the Steadmans?"

Caught off guard, Noah asked, "What do you mean, what did we think of them?"

Brando shrugged. "Did you think they were fit parents? Were you happy with what you saw? Were they the kind of people you had envisioned raising your daughter when you gave her up years ago?"

How do you answer a question like that? Noah wondered. He could no longer remember what he had pictured when he thought about his daughter. Mostly, he supposed, he had pictured the lost dream of what might have been—Amber living happily ever after with him and Mariel as her parents.

"It was hard to judge them under the circumstances," Mariel spoke up. "They were under a tremendous amount of strain."

"That's true," Brando agreed. "Amber's disappearance and their separation have been extremely difficult for them—"

"Their separation?" Noah cut in, staring at the detective in disbelief. "They split up after their daughter disappeared?"

He looked at Mariel, who appeared just as startled as he was.

"Before," Brando corrected. "They separated about two months ago."

"Why?" Noah asked, remembering the clues that hadn't registered yesterday when he and Mariel had been at the Steadmans' house. He recalled the way they didn't seem to be leaning on each other for emotional support, the way they didn't touch each other and barely looked at each other. It was telling; he had been there himself, with Kelly. He knew all the signs of a marriage's breakdown, yet he hadn't even suspected.

"I don't know the details," the detective said.

Noah found that hard to believe. It would be this man's job to investigate all the angles, to find out all he could about the people who had hired him.

"What do you plan to do now that you didn't get what you came here for, Ms. Rowan?" Brando asked Mariel.

"My flight home was scheduled for tomorrow morning, but I plan to change that and stay as long as I can," she said simply. "Hopefully, I can stay long enough to see Amber come home safely."

"What kind of role do you expect to play in her life?"

Mariel hesitated. "I don't know that I expect to play a role in her life," she said. "I only want to make sure that she's okay."

"And you, Mr. Lyons?"

"I want the same thing," he said, wishing it were the whole truth. But it wasn't. He wanted the impossible. He wanted to change everything that had happened since that long-ago day in the dorm room. He wanted

Mariel as his wife and Amber as his daughter. He wanted the family he had always imagined.

The family that had actually existed for a split second in that hospital room before fate had erased it, swept it into oblivion.

The day was overcast, the air so dense with moisture that Mariel felt drenched until she had spent twenty minutes in the air-conditioned rental car. She had insisted on driving today because Noah's friend Danny's car lacked air-conditioning, and Noah had quickly given up the argument. She knew why he preferred to do the driving. It was because he had always been an old-fashioned kind of guy, even back in college, when he had opened doors for Mariel and walked on the curb edge of the sidewalk. He was used to taking care of his mother, and he had taken care of Mariel the same way, back then.

One would think that might have bothered her when she was an eighteen-year-old college freshman, given her independent streak and her fierce desire to take care of herself at last after a lifetime with doting parents.

But she had never minded Noah's gentlemanly ways—she had been charmed by them back then, and was charmed by them now.

That didn't mean she couldn't do the driving—or that she had changed her mind about not getting involved with Noah again. Her mind was made up about that—even if her body betrayed her every so often, when her gaze met his and her flesh tingled in remembrance of the way Noah had touched her last night.

"There it is," he said, breaking into her thoughts.

Through the windshield, she saw the red-brick, two-story Valley Falls High School building just ahead, on the right. She slowed the car and pulled up at the curb in front of it.

"Summer school is definitely in session," she said, observing a cluster of students and a teacher on the broad front lawn, sitting in a circle with textbooks in their laps.

"And there has to be somebody here who can tell us something about Amber," Noah said, his hand on the door handle as she shifted into park. "Let's go."

"But we can't just interrupt classes," Mariel pointed out, adjusting the nearest air-conditioning vent so that it blasted cool air directly into her face. Hopefully her hair would dry a little. "And I doubt that we can just stroll into the school building unannounced, either."

"Okay, so what do we do?"

"We need to wait until they're done, and then try to intercept one of the teachers or some of the students who look like they're around Amber's age."

"How long do you think we have to wait?" Noah asked, leaning back against the seat.

"Probably not long. Summer sessions are usually half day, and it's already past noon."

"I keep forgetting you're a teacher," Noah said, smiling. "But the more time I spend with you, the easier it's getting to picture you standing in front of a classroom holding a piece of chalk."

"I'm trying to figure out whether that's a compliment," she said.

"It is."

Their eyes met, and she quickly looked away. She turned on the radio, suddenly needing to banish the silence. She fiddled with the dial, switching from a romantic Mariah Carey ballad to an old rock classic. Steely Dan. Then she remembered that Noah loved Steely Dan, and that they had once made out in his dorm room with Steely Dan playing in the background.

Did he remember, too? Was he thinking of that now?

"Maybe we should wait outside," she suggested, tapping the steering wheel nervously.

"Are you kidding? We'll melt. It's horrible out there."

"Those kids don't seem to mind."

"It's probably hotter in the classroom," Noah said. "The windows are open, so the school isn't air-conditioned."

She nodded.

More silence.

"Is your school air-conditioned?" he asked.

She realized he was grasping at straws, trying to make conversation. The Steely Dan song had probably triggered the same memory in him that it had in her.

Or was she assuming too much?

It was impossible to know how he felt, or whether last night had been purely physical for him, rather than emotional, too, as it had been for her. They hadn't talked about what had happened while it was happening, and they certainly hadn't talked about it this morning during the awkward five-minute walk from the inn to the diner.

Nor did they discuss it now, even though there was little else to say.

She told him that her school wasn't air-conditioned, and they talked about the weather. Mariel caught herself on the verge of wistfully saying that it would feel good to dive into a swimming pool. That was what had gotten her into trouble last night.

It seemed no matter what she did, no matter how she tried to condition herself, she couldn't seem to avoid lustful thoughts of Noah. Making love to him last night hadn't sated the urge that had lain dormant for more than a decade; rather, it had awakened a voracious appetite that was impossible to ignore.

Finally, the students gathered on the lawn disappeared back into the school. Moments later, the front doors opened again, and teenagers began trickling out.

"They're done," Noah said, opening his door. "Come on."

Mariel stepped out of the car and was immediately struck by the oppressive heat and humidity. She glanced up at the gray sky. "It looks like it's going to rain," she commented.

"Not until tonight," Noah said.

"How do you know?"

"I was talking to Susan in the lobby of the inn this morning while I was waiting for you to come down."

Mariel was momentarily amused, remembering that the older woman had correctly forecast the heat wave the first night she had arrived. She must spend a lot of time sitting around watching the Weather Channel, she thought, before she forced her thoughts back to the matter at hand.

She was expecting some difficulty locating a teacher who would be willing to speak to them about Amber, but to her shock, they hit paydirt on the first try when they waylaid a middle-aged woman on her way down the front steps, clutching a familiar black teacher's planning binder. She had short, curly black hair and wore dangling earrings and a tank top over a long sarong-style skirt with sandals. Obviously, she wasn't one of the more conservative teachers in the place, which Mariel took as a good sign.

When they struck up a conversation, she told them that her name was Patricia Gray, that she did teach at the school, and that yes, she did know Amber Steadman.

Then her friendly expression turned wary. "Are you reporters?"

"No, actually, we're—"

"Family friends," Mariel interrupted Noah. She had no idea whether it was public knowledge that the Steadmans had adopted their daughter. In fact, she wondered belatedly whether Amber had been aware of it all her life, or if it had been something she recently discovered. If she had accidentally stumbled across adoption papers, she would undoubtedly have felt betrayed by her parents. Betrayed enough to run away?

"We're close friends of the Steadmans," Noah picked up where she had left off, "and we're concerned that the police might not be exploring every possible avenue in their investigation. We thought if we contacted people who knew Amber—and you said you did know her?"

"I do," the woman said, and her use of present tense jarred Mariel. She hadn't realized Noah had been using past tense, almost as if . . .

No. She didn't want to think about that.

"Have you taught her?" Mariel asked.

"Yes, she was in my English class this past year, and I directed her in the school musical last fall. She played Dolly Levi."

"In *Hello, Dolly,*?" Mariel asked, smiling. That was one of her favorite musicals. She had played Irene Malloy, not the title character, in her own high school production of the same show. She was struck by the realization that Amber might have inherited her musical talent from Mariel. Then she remembered the piano in the Steadmans' living room and wondered reluctantly if they had nurtured it.

It wasn't that she didn't want to think that they had encouraged Amber. . . .

No, she should be glad that they had been able to provide her with piano lessons and sheet music.

But she couldn't help wanting to take credit for something—wanting to believe that Amber carried a piece of Mariel, that it was genetic, a gift passed from mother to daughter.

The teacher said, "She's very talented. Funny, too. She had everyone laughing."

"That's wonderful," Mariel said.

"So she was—she is—a happy kid, then?" Noah asked.

Mrs. Gray paused, seeming to think that over. "She was happy as far as I could tell," she said. "But toward the end of the school year, she became subdued. I heard through the grapevine about her parents' separation, and I figured that Amber's behavior change went with the territory."

Mariel nodded. She had been thinking the same thing, ever since Henry Brando had told them about the Steadmans' split. The breakdown of her family might have been enough to cause Amber to run away. It might have also been the reason she had gone looking for her birth mother.

"Is there anything you can think of that might indicate that Amber was in some kind of trouble?" Noah asked. "Drugs, or running with a bad crowd . . . ?"

"No." The teacher shook her head. "The only vice she seemed to have was surfing the Internet. She spent a lot of time on-line, in chat rooms, and e-mailing her friends. I was aware of it because she spoke about it often. She was always mentioning something she'd seen or read on-line. She even wrote an essay for me about the therapeutic benefits of on-line shopping," she added with a smile.

Mariel smiled faintly, because she knew it was expected, but her mind was racing. The Internet was rampant with sexual predators who preyed on young teenaged girls. Could Amber have fallen victim to one of them?

"So she was just a normal kid, then?" Noah asked.

"Absolutely. I told the police the same thing. There was nothing I could see, aside from the fact that she had recently become more quiet and withdrawn in class. But with her parents' marriage breaking up, I don't think that was unusual. Then again, I'm just a teacher. Teachers only see what students allow them to see. I'm sure Amber's friends can provide more insight into what was happening in her life before her disappearance."

"That was going to be my next question." Noah said. "Who are her closest friends? We'd like to talk to them, too."

"Sherry Leaman is her closest friend. Sherry and Nicole Wise. The three of them ate lunch together every day this past year."

"How can we find them?" Mariel asked, remembering that both names had popped up in the research she and Noah had done at the library last night.

"Nicole works over at the ice cream parlor at the mall out on Route 182."

"What about Sherry?" Mariel asked.

"I'm not sure. One day when I was monitoring the lunchroom, I overheard her saying she'd be away this summer at camp in the Catskills, so I'm not sure if you'll even be able to find her. She wasn't one of my students, and I don't know much about her."

"Is there any way you could check the school records and give us her home address, Mrs. Gray? Hers and Nicole's?" Noah asked.

Mariel knew what the answer would be before the teacher responded.

"I'm sorry," she said, a little less friendly than before. "School records are confidential."

"We understand," Mariel assured her. "You've been really helpful."

"I just hope Amber turns up soon," the teacher said worriedly. "I don't have a good feeling about this. I've been troubled ever since I heard she was missing."

"So you don't think she ran away?" Mariel asked.

"I don't know what to believe," Mrs. Gray said. "Even if she did run away, there's no way of knowing that she's safe. My brother is a cop in Vegas. All sorts of terrible things happen to teenagers on the streets."

Mariel felt sick inside. "Thank you for your help, Mrs. Gray," she said, shaking the teacher's hand before she and Noah headed back to the rental car.

"Nicole doesn't come on until six o'clock—she's closing tonight," the uniformed, college-aged girl behind the counter told Noah and Mariel, pausing in her rigorous scooping from a tub of fudge ice cream.

Noah turned to Mariel. "That's more than two hours away," he said, checking his watch. "What do you want to do?"

"Have some ice cream, before anything else," she replied, watching the girl ladle hot fudge onto the ice cream she had just piled in a paper bowl. "Then I have to find a phone and reschedule my flight."

"Ice cream sounds good to me," Noah said, realizing he hadn't eaten anything yet today. He hadn't had an appetite until now. First the discussion with the private investigator, then with Mrs. Gray—and through it all, his growing worry about Amber laced with uneasiness about being with Mariel.

It was almost enough to make him wish he had never come here, that he had never heard from Mariel again or known that their daughter had disappeared. There was something appealing, in retrospect, about the limbo he had endured for all these years. Then he had been insulated from the emotions that battered him now, growing more intense with every moment that ticked by.

"How long are you going to stay?" he asked Mariel, as they studied the flavor board above the counter.

"Maybe through the weekend," she said. "Or maybe, since I wasn't planning to be here longer than a few days, I should fly home on Wednesday and make sure everything is okay at home. Then I can fly back here again for a longer stay."

"Why wouldn't everything be okay at home?"

She rolled her eyes. "My sister is in a tizzy because she's getting married, and I'm more or less playing the mother-of-the-bride role. And my dad—well, I just worry about him. Leslie's got her hands full with her wedding, and somebody needs to make sure he's doing all right."

"Doesn't he live on his own in Florida?"

"He lives in a retirement community. It's assisted living, more or less. And he has a bunch of cronies. They all look out for each other. When he's up north, it's up to Leslie and me."

"Does he spend his summers back in Missouri, then?"

"This year he's been there from the middle of May, and he's not going back until after Leslie's wedding in July."

"Excuse me, can I help you?" a voice cut in.

"I'll have a triple scoop—rum raisin, butter pecan and toffee crunch in a waffle cone," Mariel told the girl behind the counter. "With sprinkles."

"And what about you, sir?" the girl asked Noah.

"Triple scoop of vanilla," he said. "No sprinkles."

"Vanilla?" Mariel echoed as the girl stooped toward the glass-fronted freezer bin again, silver scoop in hand. "And no sprinkles? That's no fun."

"What can I say? I'm just not a fun guy," Noah said, throwing up his hands as if to say, *What are you gonna do?*

"Come on, Noah." She poked him playfully in the arm. "Live a little. At least get chocolate or rainbow sherbet or something."

He pretended to be hurt. "Are you saying I'm bland?"

"Absolutely." As the girl handed her the triple-decker, three-flavored cone she had ordered, she waved it under his nose. "Doesn't this look tempting?"

He made a face. "It looks about as tempting as pizza with pickles and clams."

They both laughed at that, and he realized that the teasing tone between them had broken the ice. All day, things had been tense. The ride over here from the school had been almost silent, aside from the few times he had given her directions on where to turn. He remembered this mall from his college days. He and his fraternity brothers used to come to the Multiplex to see movies once in a while. Back then, there had been only three screens. Now there were twelve.

"Hey, you want to kill some time in a movie?" he asked spontaneously.

She looked surprised, then nodded. "We might as well. I mean, we have to hang around here for a few hours anyway. And it's air-conditioned."

"Great." He took his vanilla cone and reached into his pocket for some money to pay for the ice cream.

Mariel was already standing by the register with a ten in her hand.

"I'll get the ice cream," he said, putting his own ten in front of hers.

She pushed it away. "That's okay, I've got it."

"Then, I'll get the movie," he said firmly.

She shrugged.

He hated this.

He hated the awkwardness of it, the fact that they weren't in a relationship, weren't even dating. There were no rules for whatever it was that they were doing— and there should be no expectations, either.

When they returned to the inn later, they would go to bed in separate rooms, and that would be that. Right?

Of course.

Except, he couldn't seem to drill that into his mind.

And even now, he found himself envisioning the few

movie dates they had had back in college, when they had gone to see films that were shown at the campus center. He remembered sitting arm in arm in the dark, with Mariel snuggling against him, and he reminded himself that it would be nothing like that now. They were going to go see a movie because there was nothing else to do from now until six-thirty. Then they were going to talk to Nicole. And after that . . .

Well, who knew?

"I should find a pay phone, too," he said as they walked side by side through the mall, licking their cones.

"Who do you have to call?"

"My roommate. I should let him know where I disappeared to," Noah said, stopping to consult a mall directory.

"You have a roommate? What's he like?"

"I don't know, actually," Noah said. "He hasn't lived with me for very long, and I found him through a classified ad."

"It must be odd, living with a stranger," Mariel said.

He shrugged. "You do it when you go away to college."

"True. But that's when you're young, and you're so happy to be away from home that you don't care who you live with, as long as it's not your family. This is different. You're a grown man. It must be hard."

"It is," he found himself admitting. "I wouldn't do it unless I had to."

"You can't afford your apartment on your own?" she asked.

"Nope." Why didn't he feel uncomfortable telling her that? How had they once again established this easy intimacy, this pseudofriendship, when a short time ago they were struggling to find anything to talk about?

"So what's he like?"

"My roommate? His name is Alan, and he's a musician and a bartender, and he's incredibly lazy as far as I can tell. And he's possibly a freeloader and maybe a snoop, too," he added, remembering the missing beer and his rifled drawers.

That seemed a lifetime ago. He pointed down the corridor. "There's a public phone down there, by the restrooms."

"Okay, let's go," she said, popping the last of her ice cream cone into her mouth and crunching it.

"How was your ice cream?" he asked, amused, watching her lick her fingers.

"It was delicious. How's yours?"

"Bland," he admitted with a laugh. "Maybe I'll get sprinkles next time after all."

She used the phone next to his, standing poised with a pen and paper to write down her flight information.

Meanwhile, he dialed his home number. It rang several times, and then the answering machine kicked on.

"Listen, Alan, I hope you get this message," Noah said. "I had to leave town for a few days. Just wanted to let you know that if there's any kind of emergency, you can reach me at the Sweet Briar Inn in Strasburg, New York. I don't have the number, but it's listed. And if my boss calls looking for me, don't give out any information. Thanks."

"Your boss doesn't know where you are?"

Startled, he turned to see Mariel standing behind him, obviously having overheard the last part of his one-way conversation.

"Nah, I called in sick," Noah said, replacing the receiver.

"You're going to call in again tomorrow?"

"I guess I'll have to," he said as they headed back to the main section of the mall, where the Multiplex was located. The place was getting more crowded—mostly mothers pushing baby carriages and school-aged children. "I'll go back to the office on Wednesday afternoon, when I get back into town."

"Will that be a problem for your boss?"

"Maybe." He shoved his hands into the pockets of his shorts. "And if it is, he'll just have to deal with it."

"What if he fires you?"

"Maybe that would be a blessing in disguise," Noah said. "Like I told you, advertising isn't exactly my all-time ambition. I landed in an agency for lack of anything else to do."

"Just like I landed in teaching," Mariel said.

"Exactly. Only you enjoy what you do. I don't."

"Then, why do you stay?"

He thought about that. "Until now, I stayed because of Kelly. Now that she's gone . . ."

"There's no reason to stay?" Mariel asked, sidestepping a teenaged couple walking with their hands in each other's back pockets. "You loved her that much? Enough that you would work at a career you hated, just to make her happy?"

"I thought I loved her that much," he said, looking at her just in time to see her flinch at his words.

So it hurt her to know that he had loved another woman. Did he dare tell her that what he had felt for Kelly was entirely different from what he had felt for her? That his feelings for Kelly were long dead and buried?

No, he couldn't tell her that. Not when his feelings for Mariel were supposedly dead and buried, too. Last night wasn't supposed to have changed anything. He was supposed to go on believing that they weren't meant to be together, that she was too selfish to be the kind of woman he had always wanted.

She had a life of her own, a life she had built and a life that seemed to make her happy. A life to which she would return any day now, just as he would return to his own world.

"So what went wrong in your marriage?" Mariel asked, so directly that he was caught off guard.

"Basically, I realized that my wife didn't want what I wanted." He decided to be completely honest, even knowing the implications of what he was going to say to her. "To be more specific, Kelly didn't want children. I did."

He heard Mariel's breath catch in her throat, but when she spoke there was no sign that his words had rattled her. "I can see how that would be a huge problem."

He nodded. "We both realized we were better off apart. For all I know, she's already found somebody new. Some wealthy lawyer who doesn't want children, either."

"Have you tried to find somebody new, Noah? Somebody who will give you children?"

He shook his head, unable to believe that they were having this conversation. They had spent the night making love and dozing in each other's arms, yet today, they were acting as though nothing had happened between them. As though there was no question of picking up where they had left off all those years ago—no question of staying together, getting married, having a family.

And of course, that wasn't going to happen.

Yet he couldn't help wishing they could pretend they were something other than what they were. He wasn't in the mood for a frank discussion of his love life—or lack thereof—with other women. Yet hadn't he already probed her for similar information about herself?

So it was established that neither of them had anyone in their lives—including each other, he thought wryly.

"What happened when you called the airline?" he asked, to change the subject.

"They said that there are no direct flights on Wednesday from Syracuse. I have to fly back through La Guardia."

"Good luck making your connection," he said, making a face. "La Guardia's insane, and air traffic there is always a mess."

"Actually, I have a three-hour layover there, so it'll probably be fine." She stopped short. "I forgot to call the car rental place to tell them I need to keep it for another day. They think I'm turning it in tomorrow."

"Don't bother to change that," Noah said. "I've got a car. I'll drive you to the airport in Syracuse on Wednesday morning before I head home."

"That's completely out of your way," she protested.

"I don't mind. I never get to drive, remember? I live in the city. It's a pleasure for me to hit the open highway."

They had arrived at the entrance to the Multiplex and were standing directly beneath a listing of films that were now playing. "What movie do you want to see?" Noah asked. "How about the new Jim Carrey one?"

She made a face. "No, thanks. It seems kind of . . . I don't know. Stupid."

"Now who's bland?" he asked with a grin.

"How about the Meryl Streep one?" she suggested. "I love her."

"Too heavy," he quickly decided, after glancing at the movie's poster on a nearby wall.

"Well, the Disney cartoon one is out—I see enough Disney to last me a lifetime during the school year," she said.

"You take the kids to the movies?"

"I have video day in school once a month," she said. "I make popcorn, and we all draw pictures of the characters and have a discussion afterward."

"You must be everyone's favorite teacher."

"I don't know about that, but I am pretty loved," she said with mock conceit.

"I'm sure you are," he said, turning away from her so that he wouldn't be looking right into her eyes. She was standing close to him because the place was crowded, and he found himself longing to lean down and kiss her.

But he couldn't do that.

He *could*, but he wouldn't.

"How about the Meg Ryan movie?" she suggested.

He nodded. "Fine." At this point, he would have agreed to see just about anything just for something else to do—something other than stand here and think about kissing her.

He got in line and bought tickets, and then he got

in line and bought astronomically priced popcorn and soda.

"You didn't have to do that," she said when he walked back over to where she was waiting by the theater entrance.

"I thought we might get hungry."

"Thanks," she said, grabbing a handful just as he reached into the bucket. Their hands brushed, and he was jolted by the contact with her skin. His unruly mind flashed back to last night, with her, in the water, and he put the popcorn into his mouth and chewed vigorously, trying to forget how she had looked, how she had felt in his arms.

"Let's go in," he said, and she agreed.

Together, they walked into the darkened theater, and found it utterly deserted.

"Where do you want to sit?" she asked.

"Looks like we have our choice," he said dryly. "This doesn't happen in Manhattan, that's for sure."

"I wonder if this movie's supposed to be any good?"

"It's too late to leave now," he said, as the lights grew dimmer and the screen lit up with a preview notice.

They slid into seats halfway down the aisle, and Noah balanced the popcorn on the armrest between them. He let out a silent sigh of relief that for the next two hours at least, he wouldn't have to think about anything but the movie.

Choosing this movie had been a big mistake. Why on earth had Mariel suggested the Meg Ryan film, of all the features that were playing?

She knew Meg Ryan usually did romantic comedies,

and this had turned out to be no exception. The plot revolved around reunited lovers, and there were a couple of steamy love scenes along with a tear-jerking finale in which the heroine, clad in her wedding gown, was delivering the hero's baby.

When the lights came up, Mariel didn't even want to look at Noah. Nor did he look at her as they made their way back up the aisle past the only other occupant, a lone senior citizen sitting in an aisle seat, watching the credits roll.

"What did you think?" Noah asked, when they were out in the mall again.

"It was pretty good," she said. And it had been good. It had also been totally unrealistic. Nobody who had been through what the movie's hero and heroine had been through ever could have lived happily ever after as easily as they had.

Or maybe other people could.

Maybe it was just Mariel and Noah who couldn't.

"Did you like it?" she asked cautiously.

"It was okay," he said cryptically, and they turned in the direction of the ice cream parlor. The mall was a little less crowded now that dinnertime had rolled around.

The ice cream shop was as empty as the movie theater had been, and she knew right away that the girl behind the counter was Amber's friend Nicole. She was young and pretty, her long dark hair pulled back into a ponytail held in place by the visor cap of her uniform. She looked completely bored, leaning against the counter staring off into space until she saw that she had customers. Then she jumped to attention, obviously eager for something to do.

"Can I help you?" she asked from across the counter.

"You're Nicole, right?" Noah asked.

She nodded.

"We're wondering if you might be able to help us," Mariel said, noticing that she had gone from friendly and expectant to apprehensive. "We're investigating Amber's disappearance."

Now Nicole looked downright sullen. "I don't know anything about that."

"You and Amber are close friends," Noah said. "You must be concerned that she's missing."

The girl said nothing.

"Look, we're private investigators hired by her parents to find out what happened to her, Nicole," Noah said. "If you don't tell us what we want to know, we'll just question other people connected to her until we find out."

"What is it that you want to know?" Nicole asked. "Because trust me, I don't know anything about where she went."

Mariel noticed that she had said "where she went" rather than "what happened to her." That seemed to suggest that Amber had been in control, rather than that she had been abducted. Or was Mariel reading too much into the girl's wording?

"We're operating on the assumption that she's been kidnaped," Noah said. "That means this case might go to the FBI. They're not very receptive to witnesses who don't cooperate with them."

"Are you with the FBI?" Nicole asked.

"No, we're not," Mariel said, worried that Noah was going to dig them in even deeper. She hated to have him lie about who they were and what they were doing.

Then again, they were doing this for Amber's own good, and if it meant lying to her friends, then so be it.

"But the FBI will be called in if this does turn out to be a kidnaping," Noah said. "Do you expect it to come to that?"

"I don't know," the girl said, not looking at him.

"What about your friend Sherry?" Mariel asked. "She's still away at Camp Wannabuck, right?"

"Camp Drake," Nicole corrected.

"Are you sure? Because we were told it was Camp Wannabuck, in the Catskills."

"It's not. It's Camp Drake, in Clearwater Corners," Nicole said. "Believe me, I write to her there. I know which camp it is."

"Maybe you're right, but . . ." Mariel pasted a doubtful look on her face, inwardly giving herself a high five.

"If you think of anything we should know, you can reach us at the Sweet Briar Inn, Nicole," Noah said. He took a napkin from the dispenser on the counter and scribbled his name and Mariel's on it. "Just call and ask for us. We're really concerned about your friend."

"So am I," Nicole said. "If I knew anything, I would tell you. But I don't."

With that, she turned away.

Mariel could see her hands trembling as, with her back to them, she busied herself refilling the straw dispenser. *She knows something,* she thought. *She knows something, and she has no intention of telling us what it is.*

Out in the mall again, Noah turned to her. "Way to go, Mariel. That was excellent, the way you got the name of Sherry's camp out of her. How the heck did you come up with 'Wannabuck'?"

She grinned. "Sounds realistic, doesn't it? It just

popped into my head. What do you think? Do we head to Clearwater Corners?''

"Definitely tomorrow. But not tonight. I'm beat. How about you?''

She hadn't thought about it, but now she realized that her shoulders were aching and her eyes felt as though somebody had poured rubbing alcohol into them. "I guess I'm tired, too. But I hate to let another night go by, Noah, knowing that she's out there some- place . . . maybe in some kind of danger."

"I feel the same way. And we're going to help her, Mariel. But we'll be a lot more effective if we get a good night's sleep before we drive up into the mountains looking for Camp Drake. Besides, it's supposed to storm tonight."

"Looks that way," she said. They had arrived at the main entrance of the mall. Beyond the row of tall glass doors, the sky hung ominously low and dark over the sprawling parking lot.

"We'd better head back to Strasburg," Noah said. "We can get dinner in town."

Mariel nodded. As they headed out into the dense evening air, she realized he had assumed that they would be eating together tonight. They had officially become a team—a team with a mission. But what would happen once the mission was accomplished and their daughter was safely back where she belonged? Would she and Noah go their separate ways once more, never to see each other again?

The thought stung her, but she knew that it was realis- tic. What other option did they have? Yes, they were attracted to each other, but they couldn't rekindle a relationship that wouldn't work.

But how do you know it won't work this time? a nagging voice asked.

Because she and Noah were two different people, both with baggage. She couldn't leave behind the life she had built to try and start over now, with him. And he was just coming out of a marriage—a marriage that hadn't succeeded, from what she could tell, because his wife hadn't been willing to become the impossible ideal Noah had in mind.

Mariel knew what he was looking for, and he wasn't going to find it with her. He wanted the perfect family— the kind of life he had never had growing up. He wanted a woman who would devote herself to him, a woman who would bear his children and make his home and promise to stay by his side forever.

She couldn't be that woman. She couldn't let him smother her with his impossible expectations. And she couldn't have children. Not now. Not again. She had given up their first child because she knew her emotional limits.

She sighed.

Noah looked at her. They had almost reached the car.

"What's wrong?" he asked.

"Nothing," she said quickly. "I'm just worried about Amber."

"Don't worry," he said. "We'll find her."

"But what if, when we do, it turns out that she did run away? Will she be forced to go back to the Steadmans even if she's been miserable there?"

He shook his head. "I'll take her in myself before I let that happen."

"You can't take her yourself, Noah!" she said. There

he went again, creating an impossible fantasy. "How would you do that?"

"She's my own flesh and blood," he retorted, his jaw set stubbornly. "Do you think I can sit by and let her live with people who aren't taking care of her?"

"Who says they aren't taking care of her? From what I could see, they love her. And I'm not sure I believe the runaway scenario at this point. They've hired a private investigator to find her."

"That doesn't mean she didn't run away, and it doesn't make them decent parents. Besides, you heard what Brando said. They're splitting up."

"That doesn't mean they don't love her and won't take care of her."

"This isn't what we wanted for her, Mariel. If we wanted her to come from a broken home, we could have gotten married and raised her ourselves."

His words exploded between them like thunder, and she stopped walking, standing absolutely still, just a few feet away from the rental car.

"What are you saying, Noah?" she asked tightly. "Are you saying I made the wrong decision? Are you blaming me for this? Because I did what I thought was best for her."

And for yourself. Admit it. You also did what you thought was best for you. She tried to push that thought aside, but it wouldn't budge.

Yes, giving Amber up had been what was best for herself, too. But if raising the baby on her own had been a viable option, she would have taken it even if it meant tremendous self-sacrifice. Wouldn't she?

She didn't know.

Desolate, she realized that it didn't matter whether

Noah blamed her for this. There was a part of her that blamed herself—a well of guilt that she hadn't realized lay deep within her for all these years. Now it had swelled and overflowed, flooding her with doubts.

Should have.

Could have.

Shouldn't have.

Couldn't have.

She felt dizzy from going over and over it all in her head, reliving that dark, awful time in her life.

"What's done is done," Noah said, and she realized that she had been staring at him unseeingly, mulling over his words. "All we can do now is go forward."

She nodded silently, unable to speak.

It would have been easier if he had taken her bait. If he had lashed out at her so that she could release the emotion that choked her throat. Now there was nothing to do but force it back, swallow it, and, like he said, go forward.

They were silent all the way back to the inn, where they picked up his car. He followed her to the nearest car rental drop-off place and waited, parked out front, while she returned the keys and filled out the paperwork. Then they silently rode together back to the inn again.

The first raindrops splashed onto the windshield as they pulled into a diagonal parking spot in front of the inn again.

"Should we go get dinner now?" Noah asked, motioning at the row of restaurants and cafes on Main Street.

"I'm not hungry," she said. "I think I'll just go to my room."

"No, don't," Noah said, turning off the engine. "I'm sorry, Mariel."

Her heart skipped a beat. Whatever she had been expecting from him, it hadn't been this.

"Why are you sorry?"

"I didn't mean to make you feel bad about . . . what happened. Everything that happened. I'm just upset, that's all. You chose the people you thought would give her a wonderful life. They looked great on paper. And I backed your choice."

She had shown him the file on the Steadmans only after she had made up her mind. It was hard enough to choose the future parents of their unborn child, let alone struggle with Noah over the decision of whom they should select. Luckily, he hadn't argued with that. Nor, as he said, had he argued with her verdict. She remembered the day she had handed him the file, remembered how thoroughly he had gone through the background information before he finally looked up at her and said simply, "They look fine."

"Neither of us could have predicted that the Steadmans' marriage wouldn't last," he went on now. "And for all we know, they have absolutely nothing to do with what's happened to Amber."

She nodded. She couldn't look at him.

"Forgive me, Mariel." He cleared his throat, his voice smoky. "I didn't mean to hurt you more."

Tears stung her eyes, but she couldn't cry. Not in front of him.

"Have dinner with me," he said softly. "Please. We can eat right here in the dining room of the inn. You have to eat, and so do I. It would be ridiculous not to eat together."

"Okay," she heard herself say.

He nodded, satisfied. She saw him out of the corner of her eye, but she couldn't turn her head toward him. She was afraid of what she would see if her gaze met his.

She hadn't expected this. She hadn't *wanted* this; she had wanted an argument. She had wanted to clear her head and clear the air, once and for all.

She had wanted a strong, solid reason to believe that Noah Lyons could never be the man for her, a reason to turn her back on him and walk away for the second— and final—time in her life.

CHAPTER EIGHT

The dining room of the inn was all but deserted when Noah and Mariel descended the stairs to the lobby again. They had both gone to their rooms to change, and Noah had heard Mariel go into the bathroom across the hall for a long time.

Now she once again smelled of that captivating, clean herbal scent, and she looked refreshed. Her hair was pulled back into a high ponytail again, tied with a pink ribbon. Her face was obviously scrubbed, though he noticed that her eyes were red and slightly swollen. So she had been crying. He couldn't decide whether he was surprised about that or not. He still didn't know how to read her, after all this time.

Then again, was it surprising? Their relationship hadn't encompassed the past fifteen years; they had actually known each other for a brief interlude—if they had ever really known each other at all. Sometimes he wondered.

He glanced at her as they stood in the wide doorway leading to the dining room. Without make-up, she looked younger and more vulnerable than she had this afternoon. She wore a pale pink, sleeveless blouse tucked into a full floral print skirt, and her feet were clad in pale pink flats. She looked as though she had popped out of a 1950s teen fashion magazine. For some reason he found that more appealing than if she were clad head to toe in sexy, slinky black.

"Two for dinner?" asked the hostess, coming to the lamp-lit podium.

"Yes," Noah replied.

"It's quiet tonight. Most of the weekend guests have checked out, and nobody wants to come out in this weather." Her words were punctuated by a deafening boom of thunder.

"Guess you can't blame them," Mariel said.

"No, you certainly can't. Anyway, you have your choice of tables, as you can see." The hostess was middle-aged and overweight but attractive, with shoulder-length dark hair and round cheeks. She wore a wedding band and engagement ring, and a charm bracelet jangled on her wrist—the kind of gift a husband would get a wife for Mother's Day, and then add to each year as their lives grew richer.

She looked comfortable and motherly, Noah thought. Motherly in a way that his own mother would never look. Mariel either, he thought automatically, and then glanced at her and reconsidered. If he really concentrated, he could almost imagine her face softened by time and excess padding. He almost could see her in glasses and sweatpants, curled up on a couch with a toddler on her lap or a baby nursing in her arms.

Almost.

"So where would you like to sit?" the hostess asked, gesturing at the dining room. A family was just rising from a large round table near the row of windows overlooking the porch. Only one other table was occupied, by two couples, one in their fifties or sixties and the other in their twenties or thirties. All but the younger woman were sipping from champagne flutes.

"We can sit over there," Mariel said, gesturing at a table for two not far from the other group, and directly in front of a brick fireplace. A large dried flower arrangement occupied the hearth.

"That's fine," Noah agreed, and the hostess led the way.

The dining room was decorated in shades of green and rose in a style similar to the guest rooms, with floral print wallpaper, white lace curtains, and a Victorian-style patterned carpet. There were potted ferns everywhere, and whirling ceiling fans with frosted glass fixtures, and candles burned inside glass globes on every table.

Tonight was one of the longest days of the year, Noah realized, and if the sun had been out it would have more than an hour left before setting. But gloomy mist and rain were all that was visible beyond the rain-spattered glass on the two walls of the room that were lined with windows. He heard thunder rumbling ominously as he pulled out Mariel's chair for her.

The hostess cocked her head, listening to it, and commented, "We're going to get one heck of a storm tonight, I hear."

"Sounds that way," Noah said. "Glad we decided to dine in."

"You folks are staying here, then?" she asked. "I wish I didn't have far to drive, but I'm almost a half hour away. My husband doesn't like it when I'm on the roads in bad weather. I hope he doesn't send one of our boys for me."

"How many boys do you have?" Mariel asked conversationally.

"Three—two in college and one a senior in high school. And my older daughter's grown and married with my first grandchild on the way in two months, and the youngest is a high school sophomore."

"Congratulations on the grandchild," Noah said, thinking he had been right about her being motherly. He realized that he envied this stranger her big family and cozy life, driving to work at a small-town inn, the kind of job that didn't come home with you when the day was over. Yes, she was worried about driving, but she had a husband and children to look out for her.

Noah had no one. There was nobody he would even bother to call if he was going to be home late from work; nobody would be waiting, looking at the clock, hoping he was all right.

Even when he had been married, he hadn't lived that kind of life. Kelly had stayed more and more frequently at her office long after he had left his, even when he worked overtime. And even in the old days, when she occasionally beat him home, she wasn't waiting for him. There was no dinner in the oven warming the apartment with a mouth-watering aroma, no welcoming kiss at the door unless she was in the mood to make love, which hadn't been often once they were past their newlywed stage.

"We found out the other day that my daughter is expecting a little girl," the hostess said proudly. She added hastily, "It wouldn't have mattered either way, but I have all of Cindy's baby dresses and her christening gown ready to hand down to her own daughter now."

Noah glanced at Mariel, who was murmuring something polite in response. Her smile was tight, and he knew that she was thinking about her own daughter, who had never worn her mother's baby dresses.

The hostess said, lowering her voice, "That other group right over there is here celebrating because the younger couple is expecting their first baby. The older couple are his parents. They just found out tonight, and they had a toast with champagne."

"That's terrific," Noah said, glancing at the other table, where an animated conversation was in progress.

"Do you two have children?" the hostess asked then.

Noah's insides lurched. "No," he said quickly, and glanced at Mariel, who looked stricken.

"Honeymooners, then, right? I thought you—"

"We're not together," Mariel blurted.

The woman was immediately flustered. "I'm sorry, the Sweet Briar is popular with honeymooners so I just assumed—"

"It's okay," Noah said quickly.

"Here are your menus," the woman said, thrusting two leather-bound folders at them before she hurried away.

Noah looked at Mariel across the table with its dancing candlelight. "Boy is her face red," he said, trying to break the ice.

For a moment, Mariel didn't respond. Then she said, "I guess I can't cringe and shrink away every time somebody asks whether I have children. It's just that it doesn't happen to me often because everyone in Rockton knows me. It just caught me off guard, being here with you and having somebody assume that we—"

"I know. But it's a natural assumption. Like she said, this place is popular with honeymooners."

"Where did you go?" Mariel asked, picking up her cloth napkin, which had been folded in a fan shape, and placing it neatly in her lap.

"Where did I . . . ?" He didn't get it, and waited for her to clarify.

"For your honeymoon?" she asked. "Where did you go?"

"On a European whirlwind tour," he said, remembering how exhausting it had been. It had been Kelly's idea, and completely her style—but not his. He would have been content to lie on a beach someplace.

"That must have been amazing," Mariel said wistfully.

He remembered how she had once longed to travel abroad, how she had even talked of living in Paris or London.

"Have you ever been to Europe?" Noah asked.

She shook her head. "Someday, maybe."

"Well, here's some advice for you. When you go, make sure it isn't on your honeymoon," he said, forcing back the little voice inside that protested that her honeymoon should be with him. Of course it wouldn't be—and of course it was logical to presume that sooner or later she was going to find someone and settle down.

"Why not on my honeymoon?" she asked, sounding amused.

"Trust me, a wedding—especially the kind I had, with all the trimmings—is emotional and draining and stressful enough without following it up with a week overseas, traipsing all over Europe by boat, plane, train, rental car. . . ."

"So you didn't enjoy your honeymoon?" she said, looking surprised.

"Europe was just more my ex-wife's idea than mine. I'd have preferred something more laid back. Like this place."

Mariel looked around the cozy dining room. "I guess it is romantic."

He smiled. "And quiet. These days, I crave quiet. I guess I always have. And you crave action, right?"

"Maybe *crave* isn't the right word," she said, "but a little action is nice from time to time. You don't get much, living in Rockton. And I guess you get more than your share in New York."

Before he could answer, the waiter appeared and introduced himself, telling them about the specials. "Can I get you something to drink? Or are you ready to order?"

They hadn't even glanced at the menus yet.

Still, Mariel looked at Noah. "I know what I'm having, if you do."

He shrugged. "The filet special sounds good. I'll go with that."

She smiled. "That's what I decided, too."

They placed their order, and the waiter brought them their goblets of red wine.

As they sipped, he told her about Europe, carefully leaving out any details about Kelly. Why tell Mariel that even as soon as that first week, he had realized that he might have made a mistake marrying her? He still remembered the twinges of misgiving that had jarred him from time to time, and how he had tried to reassure himself that all newlyweds must feel that way. That it was a continuation of what he had, in the weeks leading up to the wedding, convinced himself was merely cold feet.

Now, in retrospect, of course, he knew better. He knew that he should have listened to his instincts. But he would certainly never ignore them again.

Their salads arrived, served on delicate Royal Albert bone china. Noah devoured the bed of mesclun greens flavored with a tangy balsamic vinaigrette and dotted with roasted eggplant, sun dried tomatoes and creamy white flecks of goat cheese.

The rain had intensified outside, and the staff hurried around the dining room, closing the screened windows as the curtains blew wildly. From his position facing the lobby, Noah spotted the hostess hurrying toward the front door wearing a rain slicker, a set of keys clutched in her hand as she called a farewell over her shoulder to Susan, who was at the desk.

"It's really nasty out there," Mariel said, casting worried eyes toward the window.

He followed her gaze just in time to see the sky light up.

"We're safe and sound in here," he pointed out. "Do you get storms like this back home in Missouri?"

"Oh, yeah," she said, nodding. "Worse, even. A twister went through Rockton a few years ago. Luckily, nobody was killed, but it took out a few trailers."

"We don't have twisters in Manhattan," Noah said,

"but we have subways, which are kind of the same thing, depending on the motorman's mood."

She chuckled.

He was glad.

He wanted—*needed*—her to be comfortable with him. It seemed that every time they reached a point where they could both relax, something happened to put the strain between them again.

Outside, thunder rumbled.

Inside, the lights flickered.

Noah and Mariel looked at each other.

"Think we'll lose power?" she asked him.

"Maybe."

The lights glimmered again.

"We lose power a lot back home," she said. "And the television cable goes out every time we have a storm. It used to drive Daddy crazy."

"Used to?" Noah echoed, wondering if she had lost her father as well as her mother. He recalled she had said her mother passed away two years ago from Alzheimer's, but was certain she had told him her father was still alive.

"Daddy lives in Florida now. He retired there after Mom died, and he got himself a big satellite dish. Now the cable never goes out."

Noah smiled. "It's hard to imagine a minister with a satellite dish. I thought he was a real straight arrow, and for some reason I didn't picture him watching much television."

"Daddy loves his TV," she said. "But only game shows and sports. He's a big Chiefs fan and an even bigger Royals fan, and he needs to follow his teams even though he lives on the other end of the country now."

"I can relate to that," Noah said. "I need my Yankees fix just about every night during the season. In fact, I'm going through withdrawal being up here. I've missed two games now."

"I didn't know you were a Yankees fan."

You didn't know a lot of things about me, he thought.

Aloud, he said, "Yeah, I've always been loyal to the Yankees, even though I was raised in Queens, which is where the Mets play. The Yankees play in the Bronx," he added, realizing she probably hadn't understood the significance of his unexpected allegiance.

But she nodded knowingly. "Daddy watches all teams, not just the Royals. I used to watch with him."

"You did?" He searched his memory. "That's funny. I don't remember us having any conversations about baseball back in the old days."

"Oh, that's because I was too busy being an *artiste* back then," she said, her tone and her expression self-mocking. Then her wry smile faded, and she added, "Actually, I never paid much attention to sports until I moved back home. I started watching with my father after my mother's illness started to progress and she couldn't follow the games anymore. It had always been something they did together—you know, sit down and watch a ball game. And after she got sick, he seemed so . . . I don't know, so lonely, sitting there by himself. So I started watching with him, just to keep him company. And I realized I liked it." She sipped her wine.

"It must have been excruciating, watching your mother fade away like that," he said gently.

She looked up at him and nodded. "Excruciating is exactly the word I would choose to describe what it was like. Especially knowing that things were only going to get worse, never better. The day she didn't recognize me was . . ." She trailed off, swallowing hard, and he saw tears in her eyes.

"It must have been the hardest thing you've ever gone through," he supplied.

She considered that, then shrugged. "It was one of the hardest."

And he realized, seeing the look on her face, what the hardest thing had been. He had all but forgotten about their child, and why they were here.

Impulsively, he reached across the table and squeezed her hand.

Her fingers were warm and solid in his, and she seemed to cling to his hand for a moment. He saw that the tears in her eyes had spilled over and rolled down her cheeks.

"I'm sorry," she said, using her other hand to reach up quickly and dab at her face with her linen napkin, glancing furtively around to make sure nobody had noticed.

"Don't be sorry, Mariel. Are you okay?"

She nodded. "I don't know what happened. I guess my emotions are just too close to the surface right now."

"That's understandable. So are mine," he said, feeling intimately connected to her just because he was holding her hand, and she wasn't letting go. "Do you want to stay here and eat, or should we leave?"

"We can stay," she said, composed again. "I'll be fine. Really. It's just that sometimes memories can be overwhelming."

He nodded. He didn't know whether she was talking about memories of her mother, or memories of giving up their daughter for adoption. Probably both. She had been through a lot since those first carefree days they had spent together as naive college freshmen. She was an entirely different person from the girl he had met, and from the girl he had later left behind.

Of course she was, but for some reason, acknowledging that basic fact took him almost by surprise. It was as if he didn't want to believe that she was different—that she had grown and changed—because that would mean things between them could be different.

Different as in better.

And he knew that would only be buying into false hope. Mariel might have changed, but what couldn't change was the tremendous amount of pain in their past as a couple. They couldn't change what had happened between them. Nor could they change the fact that they lived in completely different worlds, and they wanted completely different things out of life.

The lights blinked.

She jumped, and he squeezed her hand reassuringly.

As he opened his mouth to tell her not to worry, there was a deafening bang.

Then the room was plunged into silence, lit only by the flickering candlelight.

"What time do you want to leave tomorrow morning?" Mariel asked Noah as they mounted the stairs to the third floor, guided by the beam of the flashlight he held behind her.

"Early," he said. "Just as soon as we can get up and get on the road. I'll have to call my office first."

They had reached the third-floor hallway. The sound of the storm was much louder up here. She could hear tree branches creaking in the wind, and the rain pattered deafeningly on the roof directly overhead.

"I'll walk you down to your room," Noah said, holding the flashlight beam high to illuminate the hallway. Their bodies cast weird, long shadows on the walls. "And I'll make sure there are candles lit there, like they said there would be."

"Thanks," Mariel said.

After the power had gone out, Susan had come to the dining room to tell them that she would go up and light votive lanterns in both their rooms. She had been apologetic about the power loss and had told them there was no telling when the lights would be back on again—there was no telling in a storm like this.

Luckily, their meals had been cooked and were on the verge of being delivered to their table when the power was knocked out, so they had at least been able to eat. But the dining room had been warm and uncomfortable with the windows closed and the ceiling fans not working.

Now, though it wasn't much past nine o'clock, there seemed nothing to do but go to bed.

Mariel knew she should be satisfied with that, and that she should be exhausted.

But for some reason, she didn't want to go to bed yet, and—inexplicably, given last night's nocturnal activity—she wasn't exhausted.

She wanted to spend more time with Noah, whose presence had once again gone from disconcerting to comforting. When he had grabbed her hand across the table, she had been as stunned by the unexpectedly tender gesture as by her own welcoming reaction. It had simply felt right to hold his hand. In that moment when he had touched her, she had been less alone.

Now she knew that he was going to deliver her to her room and go off down the hall to his, and she would be alone once again.

Alone in the dark on the top floor of a big, old house with a violent storm raging outside.

She told herself that was the real reason she didn't want him to leave her. That she was afraid.

And maybe on some level it was true.

So she wasn't lying when she said, as she unlocked her door and opened it, "Would you mind coming in for a few minutes? I'm a little freaked out by this weather and the power being out."

"No problem," he said, so readily that she wondered if he had been hoping she would ask him to come in, or if he might have been on the verge of suggesting it himself.

Yet she noticed, even as they stepped over the threshold, that the thunder seemed to be growing more distant; the rain less urgent; the wind less ferocious.

She didn't want the storm to be over.

Not yet.

She didn't want him to have an excuse to go back to his room.

A candle glowed on the dresser top, just as Susan had promised, flittering shadows on the walls.

Noah closed the door behind them.

Mariel was suddenly aware of the silence in the room. The storm still raged outside, yes; but the windows were closed, and the room felt insulated from its ebbing fury. They were safe inside, alone together.

"My mother always said never to leave a burning candle unattended," Mariel commented nervously, just for something to say.

"I guess Susan just wanted to make sure we had some light when we got upstairs," was his somewhat inane reply.

She realized he, too, was acutely aware of the sudden intimacy, and that he, too, was unsure of how to handle it. After what had happened last night . . .

But he had made it pretty clear that it wouldn't happen again.

Why had they decided it shouldn't happen again? Now, for the life of her, she couldn't remember. The only memory that sprang readily to mind was what it had been like to lie naked in his strong arms, to feel his hot mouth on her lips, her neck, her . . .

"It's so hot in here," she murmured, moving to the window and tugging on the sash. It didn't budge.

"Here, I'll help you," he said, and he was instantly beside her, reaching past her. "Sometimes this happens in old houses. The frat house was an old Victorian, and the windows were always sticking. I remember that you had to push out on the bottom of the window first, like this," he grunted slightly, "and then pull. . . ."

The window raised slowly upward with a drawn-out groan.

"There," Noah said, brushing his hands against each other in a satisfied way. "Done."

"Thank you."

"No problem."

Now there was absolutely nothing to say.

His face was inches from hers.

She swallowed hard. "The breeze feels good," she

said, as the curtains stirred, brushing against her bare arm.

She focused her gaze on the wet darkness just beyond the screen, though there was nothing to see. The other night, there had been streetlights visible below, and shop windows, and restaurants. Now the street was dark.

The rain still fell steadily, pinging against a drainpipe or a gutter somewhere above.

"Yeah, it does," he said.

"But it hasn't cooled off."

"No, it hasn't."

Their voices were hushed.

He hadn't stepped away, and she couldn't step away; she was blocked by the chair beside the window and by Noah on her other side. The only way around him was to sidestep him, and that would feel too awkwardly deliberate.

Besides, it felt nice to stand here, close to him, listening to the summer rain.

A rumble of thunder sounded, far off, unthreatening.

"The storm is moving away," he observed.

Her heart sank. "I know."

"Do you want me to stay anyway?" he asked in a low voice.

For a moment, she couldn't reply. She wanted him to stay with all her heart—but her heart didn't know what was best. She should be thinking this through, not going on instinct. Look where instinct had landed her in the past.

"I want you to stay," she replied, reaching for him.

She tiptoed up, her lips expectant, and was swiftly gratified by his kiss as he swept her against him.

"Oh, hell, can we do this?" he asked, breaking away, his heart racing against hers.

"We can't *not* do this," she answered, knowing that if he stopped now, she would die.

But he didn't stop; he pulled her toward him as he backed across the room, and they fell onto the bed together. His mouth rained hot kisses on her throat. She undid the buttons on her blouse and writhed out of it, and he fumbled with the front clasp on her bra. When it opened he buried his face in her breasts with a groan, and then she felt his tongue swirling over her nipples, stroking the sensitive peaks as heat pooled between her legs, tickling and tantalizing, begging his manhood.

He changed his position, and she felt his taut bulge graze her thigh. She twisted her hips, squirmed, pressed herself against it, gasping, "Noah, please, now."

"Now?"

"Yes. I can't wait any longer. Now," she said ardently, slipping her hands beneath his shirt and hauling the hem past his shoulders. She ran her fingers over his skin, breathing his masculine essence. She heard him unzip his shorts, and he raised himself in one quick movement to ease them down over his thighs. She heard the swoosh of heavy cotton as they tumbled over the edge of the bed to the floor.

Then his hands moved to her waist, and she felt him pulling on the hook-and-eye fastener of her skirt. He tugged, then growled, frustrated. She reached up to help him, but he was already pulling the folds of fabric up to her navel, then pulling her lace panties down. She realized that he wasn't even going to bother to undress her all the way, and his urgency sparked her own. She opened herself to him, and he sank into her. She gasped; he moaned. They moved in an exquisite, age-old rhythm, once, twice, three times, and then she clenched around him as everything exploded in a storm more forceful than the one that had roared overhead. She saw flashes of light against her tightly closed eyelids as wave after trembling wave rumbled through her, and Noah, panting her name, gushed silken, white-hot liquid into her.

When the storm had waned, and they lay spent in each other's arms, Mariel kissed the top of his head as he burrowed his face against her breast, nuzzling her with his lips.

"Promise me that in the morning you won't run away," she said softly.

"I won't run away," he whispered. "Not until you want me to."

She couldn't imagine ever wanting him to leave her again.

But she noticed that he hadn't said *unless*.

He had said *until*.

And she realized that he believed it was inevitable, and that he was probably right.

But she shoved the thought away.

They had waited fifteen years to make love again.

Reality could wait another day or two.

CHAPTER NINE

"Katie Beth?"

"Is that you, Mariel?" her friend asked, across the long-distance wire.

Clutching the telephone receiver tightly, Mariel sank onto the edge of her bed, relieved to hear the familiar voice in her ear. "It's me."

"Hang on a second," Katie Beth said to Mariel, who could hear children chattering and cartoons blasting in the background. "Guys, Mommy's going to take this call in the kitchen. Olivia, keep an eye on T.J., will you? Don't let him tip over his Exer-saucer."

Mariel found herself smiling, imagining the early morning chaos in the Mulligan household.

"I'm back," Katie Beth said a moment later. "What's going on? Did you meet her?"

Mariel took a deep breath. "Not only did I not meet

her, Katie Beth, but she's vanished off the face of the earth."

Katie Bell cried out in dismay on the other end of the line. "Sweetie, are you serious? What on earth happened? Start from the beginning."

Mariel did, filling her in on Amber's disappearance. It felt good to pour out the whole story, and to hear Katie Beth's words of sympathy and comfort. "You must be just beside yourself, sweetie. Is there anything I can do to help? You're so far away, dealing with this all alone . . ."

"Not exactly," Mariel said.

"What do you mean?"

"Noah's here, Katie Beth."

She heard the gasp on the other end of the line. Quickly, she told Katie Beth what had been going on between them.

"I can't believe all this," Katie Beth said. "What are you going to do?"

"I'm going to deal with this one step at a time," Mariel said. "The most important thing is finding Amber. Whatever is happening with Noah is just a result of both of us being emotionally frazzled. It won't last. I'm flying home tomorrow, and he's going back to New York."

"What about Amber?"

"I'm going to come back here in a few days if she still hasn't turned up."

"Why don't you just stay there now?"

"Because I'm worried about Leslie, and Daddy—"

"Don't you say another word about them, Mariel," Katie Beth said with a snort. "They'll be fine on their own. It might even do your sister some good not to have you here taking care of everything for once."

"But Daddy—"

"Is fine, Mariel. He's perfectly capable of taking care of himself, but if you're worried, I'll check in on him when I bring Olivia to her play date later."

"But there are so many things Leslie needs to do for the wed—"

"Listen, I ran into Jed's mother in the supermarket yesterday, and she was on her way to pick up Leslie to take her to a dress fitting. Everything is under control. You don't need to be here."

"Yes, I do, Katie Beth," Mariel said, and bit her lip. "I need to be there, because I can't keep being here. Not with Noah. Not like this. I need to get away so that I can get some perspective. When I'm with him, I can't think straight."

"Yeah, but your feelings for him are not going to go away just because you get on a plane, or just because you want them to. There are some things you can't fight, Mariel."

"And there are some things you have to fight, Katie Beth. This is wrong, with Noah. He wants a certain kind of woman, and I'm not her. My heart broke once because of him, and I can't go through that again."

"Maybe you won't have to," Katie Beth said. "Who says you're not his kind of woman? Who says your heart is going to break this time?"

"I say so," Mariel said. "Because I know it. There's no other possibility. But for the next twenty-four hours, I'm not going to think about that. I'm going to live in the moment for a change."

"You do that, sweetie," Katie Beth told her. "And you might be surprised at what happens."

"This is David Grafton."

Noah cursed silently, clutching the phone against his ear. He had been hoping to get his boss's voice mail at this hour. It wasn't even seven-thirty yet.

He didn't have to force a distressed note into his voice; it came naturally. "David, it's Noah. I'm still not feeling well."

"I'm sorry to hear that, Noah." There was no sympathy in his boss's words. He was a cold human being under the best of circumstances. Noah could just imagine, if David was in the office this early, what kind of a deadline the client had imposed upon the group this time. His boss definitely wouldn't be thrilled to bestow another sick day on Noah.

"I'm not going to make it to the office today," Noah said, trying to will away the surge of guilt. He reminded himself that he wasn't doing anything *illegal*, for Christ's sake. He was taking a sick day, one of the ten sick and personal days that were allotted to him by the company for each calendar year. Granted, so far this year he had used more than half of them, but he had been forced to use several during the divorce proceedings.

"I would strongly urge you to rethink that, Noah," David said crisply.

"What do you mean?"

"I mean that unless you're on the brink of death, you'd better get in here. The story boards for the new Douglas campaign are missing. I tried to call you several times yesterday to see if you knew where you had put them.''

Noah fumbled for something to say, his mind careening.

He had better get in there today? Impossible.

Where were the story boards? Lord only knew.

David had tried to call him yesterday? Terrific.

He braced himself for the inevitable: for David to say that he had spoken to Alan and Alan had told him that Noah hadn't been home in a few days. A lie formulated quickly: he could say that he had been away for the weekend when he had fallen ill from eating the bad shellfish, and that he was too sick to travel back to the city. He had never told David he was at home when he called yesterday, had he? Damn, he couldn't remember.

"I was under the impression that you were at home, sick," David went on. "But when I called, there was no answer. The machine kept picking up."

Noah wanted to say that the machine had picked up because he hadn't been home.

That, in fact, he had been called to a tiny town in the central part of the state because his daughter was missing.

He wanted to say it . . .

And he did.

It wasn't his intent. Some part of him knew he would be a fool to dig himself in deeper with the food poisoning tale now, but an even bigger fool to opt for honesty.

Yet even as his mind was formulating a lie about how he had been too sick to get out of bed and answer the phone, his mouth began spewing the truth.

Not the whole truth.

It was none of David Grafton's business that Noah's

daughter had been given up for adoption, or that he hadn't seen her since the day she was born.

His boss was silent for a moment.

Noah half expected him to dig for more information, to ask for proof that the tale was true, or perhaps to chide him for lying about having food poisoning. Or maybe even for his boss to express his concern for the teenager who had vanished from a small-town street without a trace.

David did none of the above.

He merely asked, in a tone that was impossible to read over the telephone line, "When do you expect to be back in the office?"

"It might be tomorrow," Noah said. "Or Thursday. Or it might not be for a while. I can't leave without knowing where she is, and that she's all right."

"I would strongly advise you to make it tomorrow," David said. "And Noah?"

"Yes?"

"We need those story boards. What the hell did you do with them?"

Bastard.

Noah tried to remember where he had put them and gave his boss a few possible places to look.

He had screwed up, he thought grimly as he hung up the phone. He knew he had absolutely screwed up. First he had misplaced the damned story boards, and then he had admitted to lying about being sick. He would be lucky not to get fired over one or the other of those actions. Considering he had both strikes against him, he probably wouldn't have a job when he got home.

Funny . . .

For some reason, that didn't seem to matter.

Even though the July rent was due in a week and he had no savings account and no wife's salary to fall back on if he lost his job.

Right now, all that mattered was finding his daughter. And being with Mariel.

He had told her he would meet her downstairs in the lobby. By the time he left his room, descended the stairs and saw her standing there, David Grafton had all but vanished from his mind.

"I have an idea," he said spontaneously.

"Uh-oh," she said with a chuckle.

He wanted to kiss her, but he restrained himself. He relished this new easy rapport between them, and he wanted it to last. With any luck, it would hold out for their remaining time together . . . which brought him back around to the idea that had popped into his head when he saw her.

"Why don't we both pack our stuff now and check out? We can drive back to New York from the Catskills . . . after all, we'll already be halfway there. Then you can pick up your flight out of La Guardia on Wednesday, and I won't be late to work—not that that has anything to do with my plan. Anyway, depending on what we can find out from Sherry today, and depending on whether Amber turns up again before then—which God knows would be a blessing—then I'll meet you back in Strasburg for the weekend and we'll keep looking for her."

"Where would I stay tonight?" she asked, hesitant.

"Are you kidding? With me," he said, picking up her hand and squeezing it. "You'd stay with me."

"Are you sure that would be a good idea, Noah?"

"It's one night, Mariel," he said, his grip tightening

on her fingers. "It's only one night. What harm can it do?"

His words hung in the air between them, and he wished he could take them back.

They both knew what harm one night together could do. One night together was all it had taken to create a child they couldn't keep and destroy their relationship in the process.

One night.

Just one more night.

He didn't care. He couldn't pretend any longer. He wanted to hold on to this time with her and make it last a lifetime.

Clearwater Corners consisted of a combination gas station, mini-mart perched across a shady, winding road from a weathered, arrow-shaped wooden sign that read CAMP DRAKE, 1 MILE. This was truly God's country, Mariel thought as she glanced at the soaring, wooded mountaintops and majestic towering evergreens above them, and the lush undergrowth, dotted with purple wildflowers, that lined the road. Wisps of mist hung in the air, but not as heavily as it had earlier.

They had passed several closed ski resorts, some houses and campgrounds, and a few bustling tourist lodges on the way here, but the trip had been largely through the wilderness.

Last night's storm had cooled things off, and the morning temperatures were in the seventies in Strasburg, with a forecast high of the low eighties with less humidity. Here in the mountains, it was even cooler.

The sky was overcast again, but without the threat of rain that had permeated yesterday's clouds.

Mariel had spent most of the trip leaning back in the passenger's seat, staring out the window, admiring the majestic mountain scenery. Noah had been quiet, too, listening to an old Rolling Stones tape that his friend had left in the car.

This time, however, the silence between them wasn't moody or uncomfortable. Every time she had glanced Noah's way and seen him lost in thought, she had noticed a contented expression on his face. Was he thinking about her, and last night? She wanted to think so. Last night had been wonderful, and she had slept soundly in his arms for a full ten hours before he woke her.

This morning, there had been no awkwardness, no scrambling to leave each other.

Which ultimately left her wondering what this all meant. But she wasn't dwelling on it now. This wasn't the time to ponder their relationship or the fact that she was going to New York City with him. Now was the time to focus every effort on finding their daughter.

Now, as they bumped over the dirt road leading to the camp, Mariel saw that Noah's face had lost its peaceful expression and that he looked worried.

"You're thinking about Amber, aren't you?" she asked.

He nodded. "There are times when I can push the whole thing from my mind, if I try hard enough. But not now. We can't give up on finding her. Just because you're flying home tomorrow and I'm going back to work for a few days doesn't mean we aren't going to see this through."

"No, it doesn't," she said fervently. "I'm going to take care of a few things at home and get back to Strasburg as soon as I can."

"And I'll drive back up on Friday night after work." Then, after a pause, he said, "If she hasn't been found by then."

"Right," Mariel agreed, feeling hollow inside. She wanted nothing more than her daughter's safe return, yet she knew that if Amber showed up before she could fly back east, there would be no reason for her to meet Noah in Strasburg.

She hated herself for the implication of that, and for wanting an excuse to see him again—and she knew that if she had to choose between seeing him again and their daughter's safe, speedy return, she would opt for the latter. She couldn't stand the thought of Amber in danger somewhere, whether she had run away on her own, or been abducted. And that was what this trip was about, she reminded herself firmly.

It was about finding Amber.

Not about rediscovering Noah.

"Here we are," Noah said, pulling up in front of a rustic, two-story log building beside a sign that read CAMP DRAKE LODGE.

There were other, smaller buildings nestled on the downward-sloping incline beyond, and Mariel could see several children, all in red T-shirts and white shorts, standing on a pier jutting out into the gray waters of a lake. A teenaged boy was gesturing at several other children and another teenager who were pulling toward them in a canoe.

A middle-aged man in a red T-shirt and white pants stood expectantly on the narrow porch of the big building, obviously having heard their car crunching on the gravel.

Noah leaned out the window and called, "Hello. Can we park over here for a few minutes?"

The man nodded and pointed at a spot under a nearby tree. Noah pulled the car over there and turned off the engine.

"Do you want to do the talking, or should I?" he asked Mariel in a low voice.

"You can," she said, and they got out of the car.

The man had walked down the three steps and was waiting for them. "I'm Dean Drake," he said, shaking their hands. "I'm the camp director."

"I'm Noah Lyons and this is Mariel Rowan. We're here to talk to one of your employees, if it's possible to interrupt her for a few minutes."

"Which employee, and what is this regarding?" he asked warily.

Noah explained the situation, telling the camp director that they were investigating the disappearance of a teenaged girl from Valley Falls without letting him know that they were Amber's birth parents. Mariel half expected the man to ask if they were law enforcement officials and demand to see their badges, but he didn't.

"I'll go see where Sherry is and send her over," he said. "I heard from another counselor something about one of her friends being missing. I guess Sherry's pretty upset about it. I know she'll want to help you if she can."

He disappeared down the slope behind the lodge.

Mariel paced nervously while Noah perched on the bench of a nearby picnic table.

Then a teenaged girl appeared through the trees,

heading up from the lake. She was a pretty girl, slightly pudgy, with short, sun-streaked blond hair and sun-burned cheeks. She, too, wore what was obviously the camp uniform: a red T-shirt that bore the inscription CAMP DRAKE, and a pair of white shorts. On her feet were thick socks and low leather hiking boots.

Noah hopped off the bench when he saw her, and Mariel stopped pacing.

"Are you Sherry?" Noah asked.

She nodded and glanced cagily from him to Mariel. She bit her lip and said, "Dean told me you guys are investigators. But I already talked to the cops back home. I told them I don't know anything about where Amber is."

"We think you do, Sherry," Noah said.

The girl's blue eyes widened. "What makes you say that?"

"Because Amber told you everything, didn't she?"

"Almost everything," Sherry said, dragging the toe of her hiking boot along the grass, studying the path it made.

"So you knew that she was thinking about running away," Mariel jumped in, instinctively sensing that the best way to go about this was to take a chance and make an assumption.

"Yeah, but that doesn't mean she told me where she was going," Sherry said.

It was all Mariel could do not to sink to the bench behind her. Amber had run away. Sherrie had all but confirmed it. They weren't out of the woods yet—not by a long shot—but at least they knew that she hadn't been abducted by a stranger.

Mariel didn't dare look at Noah as he said, "We think

she did tell you. And we're not the only ones. A few of your teachers, as well as Amber's parents, have told the police that they suspect you know where she was headed.''

"Well, I don't.''

But she was lying. Mariel could tell. "Listen, Sherry, we know Amber spent a lot of time on the Internet, in chat rooms and sending e-mail. We're concerned that she might have been lured away from home by someone she met on-line—somebody who wanted to harm her.''

"Well, she wasn't,'' Sherry said, then clamped her mouth shut.

"What—or should I say *who*—did lure her away?'' Noah asked.

Sherry shrugged.

"Look, we know she was upset about her parents splitting up,'' Noah said.

"Yeah. Who wouldn't be?'' Sherry glowered at them, her arms folded.

"Where do you think Amber would have gone?'' Mariel asked. "Did she have money saved up? Or was somebody meeting her? Somebody who was going to take care of her?''

Something flashed in Sherry's eyes. Something that told Mariel that her question had hit home. That Amber wasn't on her own, wherever she was.

But the girl only shrugged. "I told the police everything I know,'' she said.

"Well, if you think of anything else, you can contact me at this number,'' Noah said, and handed her a slip of paper with his phone number scribbled on it.

"Where is this?'' Sherry asked, looking at it.

"Manhattan,'' he said. "Why?''

"We're not allowed to call long distance," she mumbled, scuffing her toe in the grass again.

"So call collect," Noah said. "I mean it, Sherry."

"Whatever." She looked over her shoulder. "I have to get back down to the lake. Dean's watching my campers, and he doesn't appreciate you two showing up here and dragging me away from my job."

"Really?" Noah asked. "I think Dean's fine with it. I think you're the one who doesn't want us here, Sherry. What are you afraid we're going to find out?"

"Don't you want to make sure your friend is safe?" Mariel asked, trying, and failing, to catch the girl's eye.

"She's safe," Sherry said, before spinning on her heel and walking away.

Noah and Mariel looked at each other.

"She ran away," Mariel breathed, and she realized she was crying.

Noah hugged her, pulling her against him and stroking her hair. "Are you crying because you're relieved?"

"I don't know," she admitted, sniffling. "I couldn't stand the thought of her being kidnaped, but just because she left willingly doesn't mean she's safe, no matter what Sherry thinks. Dammit, Noah, where is she?"

"We'll find out. We're not going to give up on this. Maybe we should scrap the New York idea and go back to Strasburg after all."

"No," she said quickly. "We can't do that. You have to get to work, and I have to fly home. We'll come back this weekend and pick up where we left off."

He nodded, looking at her with a strange expression.

"What?" she asked.

"Nothing," he said, and jangled the car keys. "Let's head to New York."

What if Mariel didn't come back?

The question had been on his mind back at the camp, when she had said they would meet back in Strasburg this weekend, but he hadn't felt comfortable voicing it aloud.

She had said she would come back. He should believe her. Why wouldn't he believe her? Her coming back to Strasburg had nothing to do with him. It was about finding Amber. That was the only reason she was coming back. That was the only reason he was coming back.

Right?

Wrong, he thought, staring grimly through the windshield at the heavy midafternoon traffic on Route 287 leading east through Rockland County toward the Tappan Zee Bridge just ahead. They couldn't keep pretending that they could come together as passionately as they had these past few days and then casually go their separate ways. Before she got on that plane tomorrow, they had to talk about what it had meant.

The trouble was, Noah didn't know what it had meant. He couldn't tell her how he felt because he had no idea how he felt. Maybe a few days away from her would give him the ability to think clearly—to see the situation for what it was, and not for what he wanted it to be.

What did he want it to be?

The impossible, he thought, vaguely noticing as the Bob Dylan tape that was playing came to an end.

He wanted this to be the beginning of the rest of their lives. He wanted her to be the woman who would fill the aching need inside of him, the woman who would make him a home and bear his children and stay by his side until they were old and gray. He wanted her to give him now what she hadn't been willing to give him fifteen years ago.

Which was insane, he thought, barely registering a yellow flashing LANE ENDS, CONSTRUCTION AHEAD sign in the left lane.

She might have changed in some ways, but she was still the same person. Yes, she was an adult now, where she had been a kid before—but she was still Mariel. She hadn't morphed into some happy homemaker, willing to spend the rest of her life making meatloaf and changing diapers and growing old with the same man. If that was what she wanted, she could have had it long before now.

Besides, if she really thought he could make her happy—if she really had changed that drastically—he would sense it. She wouldn't be skittish and frightened and hot one minute, cold the next.

Not that she had been cold to him since last night, when they had made love again, during the storm.

Promise me that in the morning, you won't run away.

He hadn't taken her words lightly, and he hadn't run away.

It meant a lot to him that she had been willing to ask him to be with her, just as it meant a lot that she hadn't held back physically. But emotionally, she was reticent. She was fighting whatever she felt for him, and he knew why, because he was doing the same thing.

She knew they weren't meant to last, just as he knew it.

But there were so many things he didn't know, he

thought, braking the car as an eighteen wheeler veered in front of him, having run out of left lane.

He didn't know what was going to happen when their daughter was found.

Amber had gone looking for Mariel, so it was likely that the two of them would meet. Would the girl want to meet Noah, too? Would the three of them face each other together, as a family? Or would Amber meet them one at a time? What if she had changed her mind about everything and no longer wanted any part of her birth parents? What if she didn't want Noah to be a part of her life?

He couldn't stand the thought of returning to his solitary life in New York after all this, without having made a connection to his lost daughter.

His life couldn't go on as usual now.

It couldn't, because now he had a name and a face to place with the child who had always lived in his mind.

And now there was Mariel.

For years, with her out of his life, he had kept his thoughts from dwelling on her as they had on his daughter. Yes, he had thought of her. Often, in fact. But it was with a sense of melancholy—and yes, of anger.

That was gone now.

If nothing else, they had healed the rift between them. He had forgiven her at last, he realized, as the vast bridge span appeared before him, three miles long, the far portion rising high above the Hudson River to meet the elevated bank on the Westchester side.

"It's beautiful," Mariel said, startling him out of his thoughts.

He glanced at her and saw that she was staring out the window at the smoke-colored sky and water, and the house-dotted shores on both sides. A single sailboat was on the water below, and there was an enormous barge slowly drifting downriver.

"If the weather was nicer today, you'd be able to see the Manhattan skyline straight out your window," he told Mariel.

"We're that close?"

He nodded. "Less than an hour away, with any luck."

She smiled. "I can't wait to be in the city again."

"When was the last time?" he asked, surprised.

"When I was in high school," she admitted. "I went on a trip with my choir, and I never forgot it. That was when I decided that I wanted to live there, and have a career in musical theater."

She had told him about that trip, years ago, when they were together. He had been enchanted by the image of a small-town Midwestern girl coming to the big city with stars in her eyes.

"You never came back again?"

"No," she said. "I always wanted to, but . . ."

"Well, in that case," he said, banishing unsettling thoughts of the past, "we'd better hurry up and get there."

He pulled into the passing lane, picking up speed.

"Why?" she asked, laughing.

"Because you've got a lot to see, and we don't have much time."

"You don't have to take me sightseeing, Noah," she protested.

"I know. But I want to," he said truthfully. "It'll be a pleasure to see the city through your eyes, Mariel. Maybe you can help me fall in love with it again, because lately, I can't seem to remember why I live there. Do you ever feel that way about Rockton?"

"Not anymore," she said after thinking about it for a moment.

And for an instant, he imagined himself there, in her small Midwestern town.

That's a crazy, totally insane thought, he told himself. Yet maybe it wasn't. Hadn't he been toying with the idea of pulling up his roots and starting over again, someplace affordable, someplace where the living was easier than it was in Manhattan?

Oh, come on. There are hundreds of thousands of places like that—sleepy American towns where getting through each day, once you venture past your own door, isn't a challenge.

Yes, but only one place had Mariel in it.

Well, he couldn't just move to Rockton, Missouri, because she lived there.

The bridge traffic had come to a standstill in front of the toll booths, and Noah kept his foot on the brake, creeping forward every time the traffic in front of him moved.

"What's it like?" he asked Mariel.

She looked at him blankly.

"Rockton," he said, realizing she had lost track of the conversation.

"Oh, Rockton." She shrugged. "It's small. The people are kind and caring, and pretty conservative, which used to bother me. But now I don't mind as much, maybe because I'm a teacher. I guess traditional values are a good thing, especially when children are involved. Let's see, what else can I tell you? Everybody knows everybody else. There's a barbershop with an old-fashioned striped pole out front. There are two super-markets, and both of them carry only iceberg lettuce."

"No mesclun?" he asked with a grin.

"Not even romaine," she said with a sigh. "And like I said, there aren't many places to shop for clothes—or anything else. Although we do have a big feed store and a couple of places to buy farm equipment. Oh, and there's a new restaurant that's supposed to be pretty good, out on the highway. I think it's called . . . hmm, what was it? Oh, yeah. Pizza Hut."

He burst out laughing.

She joined in. "The sad thing is, I'm serious, Noah."

"That's not sad," he said. "I think it sounds charming."

"It is." She fell silent.

He eased the car forward.

He wanted her to invite him to visit her in Rockton sometime.

But she didn't.

She merely leaned over to the tape deck and pressed the Play button. The cassette whirred, and then Bob Dylan's voice filled the car once again.

"What the hell . . . ?"

"What's the matter?" Mariel asked Noah, who stood in the vestibule of his building, staring into the metal mailbox he had just unlocked.

"My roommate hasn't picked up the mail," he grumbled, pulling envelopes and flyers from the crammed box. "It looks like this is yesterday's mail, and today's. I left him a message asking him to get it for me. That's the least he could do."

Mariel shrugged, thinking that Leslie probably hadn't gotten their mail, either, and Daddy probably wouldn't think to, now that he no longer lived with them. It wasn't that big a deal. She would be home tomorrow.

The thought wasn't comforting, though.

Now that she was in New York, she wasn't in any hurry to leave. She wondered if she could ever get her fill of the sprawling city, with its fleet of bright yellow cabs and teeming sidewalks and dazzling store windows. She had stared out the window, fascinated, as Noah drove the car around block after block, cursing as he looked for a parking space. When they finally found one and he complained because it was a long distance back to his building, she had assured him that she didn't mind. It was a thrill to stroll along the sidewalk with him, taking in the sights. He had insisted on carrying both her bag and his, so all she had to worry about was keeping up with his long-legged pace and making sure she stopped on the curb whenever a sign said DON'T WALK.

"Okay, let's go," Noah said, hoisting his duffle bag over his shoulder once again and picking up her suitcase in one hand as he clutched the mail in the other. "It's a walk-up, so get ready to exercise."

He wasn't kidding. When they finally reached the top floor, she was out of breath, and she wasn't even the one hauling the luggage. He led the way to his door and handed her the stack of mail to hold while he fished for his keychain in his pocket.

"I can't believe I'm about to see the inside of a real New York City apartment," she said as Noah inserted his key into the top lock on the battered gray door.

"Don't expect too much," he said, turning the key.

The lock clicked, but instead of pushing the door open, he put a different key into a different lock below the first one.

"Is this a safe neighborhood?" she asked, noticing that there was a third lock, and that there was a peephole on the door, too.

"Yeah, it's pretty safe," Noah said, jangling his keys, searching for the next one. "I should warn you—my roommate will probably be here. He usually is at this time of day."

"That's okay."

"You say that now," he said with a snort.

Mariel looked around the hallway, wondering what it would be like to live in a place like this. She supposed it could be difficult, climbing all those steps every time you wanted to come or go.

She glanced at the dingy, mustard-colored paint on the walls and the row of closed, numbered doors along the corridor. She thought about her house back home, perched in the middle of a tree-shaded block lined with clapboard houses with shutters and yards, some with picket fences. She thought about how the neighbors always waved as she came and went, and how the whole street got together for a block party every September, and how at this time of year the air was scented with freshly mown grass and roses.

She wondered if she ever could be happy living as Noah did. He certainly didn't seem to be content here in New York. She realized that he would probably be willing to leave, if he had a good reason. A reason like—

"There we go, come on in," he said, throwing the door open at last, calling, "Alan?"

There was no reply.

She stepped over the threshold, glad to be distracted from the thought that had been on the verge of materializing.

She found herself in a tiny hallway. It could have been nice, she supposed, if it weren't so—dark. There were no windows. And there was no furniture, only an exercise bike that had several coats and jackets draped over it.

"Alan?" Noah called again, poised, listening.

The apartment was silent.

Mariel couldn't think of anything to say as she looked around.

Noah laughed at her. "You're speechless, huh? This is what we call a foyer here in New York City," he said. "Anywhere else, it would be a closet."

She laughed, too, and followed him through the nearest doorway. There were three—one obviously leading to a kitchen and the second to the bathroom. The third, which they crossed, led to a living room. Here there were windows, and she wondered if the room might have been brighter if it were a sunny day. But when she crossed the room and looked out, she saw that any sunlight would be blocked by the tall buildings across the street.

She looked at the piles of books and papers, the stacks of CDs, the few forlorn-looking pieces of furniture. She saw the bare nails on the walls and the exposed cords stretched along the floors, and the dust and the crumbs. The place desperately craved a good cleaning. And a woman's touch.

There was no evidence of Noah's ex-wife here. She had feared that there might be, but now she found it almost disconcerting that there wasn't. This was clearly a bachelor pad; nothing about it was soft or warm or welcoming. It spoke of loneliness—of a solitary life.

"It's a dump," Noah said flatly.

"No, it isn't," Mariel protested.

"Yes, it is," he said, crossing the room and dropping to the couch. "It's as though I'm seeing it for the first time. You get kind of used to it when you're living in it, but now—after the Sweet Briar—I mean, look at this place. What made me think this apartment was so wonderful that I couldn't move out of it after Kelly left?"

Mariel went to sit beside him, following his incredulous gaze around the room. "Noah, you can't compare it to the Sweet Briar. That's an inn."

"It's a house, too. A house—not an apartment. Maybe I'm ready to live in a house." He looked at her.

His face was close. She fought the urge to reach up and brush a stray lock of dark hair from his eyes. "Maybe you should live in a house."

"It won't be here. There are no houses here in Manhattan, unless you're a multimillionaire."

"You can always move."

"To where?" The two words were loaded with suggestion, begging a reply. And not just any reply.

She shrugged and dragged her eyes away from his gaze. He put a finger under her chin and turned her face back to him, forcing her to look up at him.

"Mariel," he said softly, "where can I go? I'm looking for a small town. The kind of place where I can breathe easily. Maybe the kind of place that has an old-fashioned barbershop with a pole . . . and a Pizza Hut."

Her breath caught in her throat. "Noah—"

"Shh, wait, just let me say this. I want us to start over.

I want us to be together, Mariel. I'm not asking you to drop everything, pick up your whole life, and change it to suit me. All I want—"

"Is for you to do exactly that to suit me," she cut in, her mind spinning. "You're telling me that you want to move to Rockton to be with me, Noah? That makes no sense."

"It makes perfect sense."

She shook her head, desperately wishing it were true. But it wasn't. This didn't make sense.

It was just like before, she thought, trying to fight back the wave of panic that rose within her. Just like that long-ago day in the dorm room, when he had gotten down on his knee and proposed marriage.

Once again, Noah was caught up in the moment without seeing the big picture. Once again, he was rushing to an idealistic conclusion, assuming that just because he wanted something, he could make it happen.

She bristled at the thought of him swooping into her world, the isolated, safe little world that had harbored her after the tempestuous year she had spent with him. If Noah came to Rockton, there would be no escape. There would be nowhere to retreat to protect her heart from being shattered again.

This wasn't fair.

It wasn't what she wanted.

She felt trapped.

"We can just try it, Mariel," he said fervently. "We can see if we can make it work."

"It'll never work, Noah," she said, her gaze focused on his, though she realized he wasn't even seeing her.

He was seeing what he wanted to see.

"You don't know that," he shot back, his voice half-pleading, half-contradictory. It was the plea that made her uncomfortable.

He wanted so badly for this to work.

She recognized that, because some part of her wanted the same thing.

But she couldn't take another chance on him. She had lost too much the first time. More than she was willing to lose again.

Then she had been a teenager. Teenagers were supposed to have a few false starts as they tried to find their way through life. Adults were supposed to be settled. They were supposed to know where they were headed. Hell, they were supposed to be there, at their destination. And she had thought she was.

The first time her life had been shattered, she had scrambled to pick herself up, losing herself in school, and her family and friends.

She was no longer in school. Her mother was dead; her father, aged and living in Florida most of the time; her sister, about to marry Jed and leave home. Katie Beth was married and had a family of her own.

Everything that had sustained her the first time she had been nearly destroyed was no longer there for her. If they tried once more to make a go of it together, and they failed, she wouldn't survive.

But what if you don't fail? a faint, hopeful voice asked. *What if this is your one chance at true happiness, and you're about to blow it?*

No. She couldn't take the risk.

"I'm sorry, Noah," she said, shaking her head, her voice hoarse with emotion. "If we were meant to be together, we would have found a way to make it work the first time. Instead, we both walked away."

"That was different. We were kids. We'd been through hell."

She shook her head, not wanting to let him talk her out of it. She had to stand her ground.

"No," she said.

He looked at her in disbelief. "You're telling me that I can't move to Rockton, Missouri, if I feel like it?"

"That's exactly what I'm telling you," she said.

"You're telling me that you'd rather keep on living like you are, all alone, hiding out in this small town?"

"Hiding out?" she echoed angrily. "Who says I'm hiding out?"

He rose and strode across the room, then spun around to look at her. "What else are you doing if you're not hiding? You had big plans, Mariel. You took the easy way out."

"That's not true!"

"Then, why did you give up your dreams? You were going to be an actress, see the world, live in New York."

"You have no right to judge my life by what I said I wanted when I was eighteen," she retorted, leaping off the couch to confront him. "I love my life, Noah, no matter what you think of it. It makes me happy, just the way it is."

"Then, why are you alone?"

"Why are *you*?" she shot back.

They stared at each other. Her hands were trembling. Her whole body was trembling. She wanted to sob, to take it all back, to hurl herself into his arms and beg him to just hold her. She wanted to do anything but stand here looking at him, but she was frozen, consumed by a potent mixture of passionate rage and passionate need.

He spoke first. "I haven't been alone for the past fifteen years, Mariel. I was married. I took a chance. It didn't work out, but at least I'm not afraid to be with somebody else."

His words stung. "I'm not afraid to be with somebody else," she said, struggling to keep her voice level.

"No, you're afraid to be with me."

She chose to ignore that, saying instead, "You're the one who isn't happy with his life, Noah, not me. You're the one with a job you hate, living in a place you hate. You're the one who feels compelled to make changes. Not me."

"I didn't take the easy way out," he said again.

Her temper flared. "Didn't you? Wouldn't you rather be writing screenplays? Wouldn't you rather be living someplace else? Stop blaming your ex-wife for the things that are wrong in your life."

"I don't blame her."

"I think you do."

"Well, you're wrong," he said, but she could see in his eyes that she wasn't. Not entirely. He did blame his ex.

And he blamed her, she realized. Just as she blamed him.

"Maybe you're right," he said suddenly, and she blinked at the contradiction. "Not about me blaming Kelly, because that's not what this is about. What you're right about is that this wouldn't work between us."

"No, it wouldn't work," she said, deflating.

"I can't believe that for a minute there, I had convinced myself that things could be different."

She shrugged. So she had won the argument.

And she felt lousy.

"Look, I don't want this to change anything as far as Amber goes," he said. "We still have an obligation to find her."

"Maybe we should leave that to the Steadmans and the police and Henry Brando," she said. "Maybe we should call somebody and tell them what Sherry told us, and maybe we should just take ourselves out of this. Maybe we're only complicating matters for everyone involved."

He gaped at her. "Do you really think that?"

"Amber is a mixed-up girl, Noah. Mixed-up enough to have run away from home. Do you think that if we get involved it's going to help matters any?"

"She went looking for you because she needed you," Noah pointed out.

His words caused a pang in Mariel's heart, but she forced herself not to think about that. She had no business having maternal feelings for a child she had given to somebody else to raise. She had done that because she wanted what was best for Amber. Maybe staying out of her life now would also be what was best.

"And maybe I came here looking for her because I needed her," Mariel said around a lump in her throat. "But like you've said, I'm selfish."

"I didn't mean that," he said quickly.

"Yes, you did," she told him, "and it's true. I think we both want to find her partly for selfish reasons."

"How can you say that? She could be in danger."

"I know," Mariel said, flinching at the thought. "But she ran away, Noah. She wasn't abducted. Hopefully, she's taking care of herself, wherever she is, and she'll find her way home on her own if she isn't found first."

"I can't believe you're talking this way."

Mariel was suddenly bone-weary of the whole mess. "Maybe I'll feel different later, or in the morning, or even after I get back home," she said. "But for now, my instinct is to just let her be, Noah. We entrusted her to strangers fifteen years ago when she was born, believing they would take care of her. I think we need to follow through on that now, and believe that they still will. It's their place. Not ours."

He closed his mouth and exhaled heavily.

"Do you want me to go to a hotel?" she asked.

"A hotel?" He blinked. "No, come on, don't do that. I still want to show you New York. You can stay here, and I'll put you in a cab to La Guardia in the morning."

"Okay." She sighed shakily. "At least we've cleared the air."

"Yeah."

But they hadn't. Storm clouds hung over them still, the air heavy with tension.

Well, she had only to get through a few more hours with him. Then she would have the rest of her life to get over him—again.

CHAPTER TEN

It wasn't easy to show someone the view from the top of the Empire State Building for the first time and stay angry with them, Noah realized a few hours later.

Not that he was trying to stay angry with Mariel. But after the confrontation back at his apartment, he had felt distinctly unsettled, wondering why the hell he had put himself on the line that way, practically begging her to reject him.

"This is incredible," Mariel said, her elbows propped on the railing as she gazed out over the city.

"It is pretty incredible," he agreed.

The clouds had finally lifted, and the last traces of pinkish sun had vanished from the sky. Now the moon shone brightly amidst the stars that twinkled above them, seeming to reflect the lights of the city. The bridges glowed as though they were strung with Christmas lights across the dark ribbon of river, and the streets were strands of yellow headlights and red taillights draped in every direction.

"Queens is out that way," Noah said, pointing to the far side of the river. "That's where I grew up. Now there are office towers there, too, but it used to be mostly houses and schools—residential."

"Your mom is out there someplace, then?" Mariel asked.

He nodded.

He wanted to say that he would love to introduce them, but he kept the words clamped firmly inside. Mariel would never meet his mother.

She was leaving tomorrow, and now he knew that she was never coming back. They had pretty much agreed not to continue searching for Amber, and Noah had promised her that he would call Henry Brando in the morning to tell him what Sherry had said about Amber running away.

"Come on, let me show you the Bronx," he said, moving away from the railing and leading the way to the north end of the platform. "Let's see if we can find Yankee Stadium. It'll be all lit up if they're playing at home."

Apparently they weren't, because he couldn't find the familiar stadium lights, but he showed her the telltale dark rectangle that was Central Park—acres of wilderness in the middle of the city. He pointed out the unique spire of the Chrysler Building and the diagonal top of the Citicorp building.

Then they rode the elevator back down to the street, and he took her down the block to Macy's, where she bought perfume for her sister and one of her friends, and shirts for her father and her future brother-in-law.

At a tourist trap shop around the corner, she bought twenty postcards for her students, taking her time choosing them, making sure they all showed different views of the city.

He watched her, bemused, trying not to find her incredibly appealing, standing there in her sleeveless coral-colored blouse and khaki shorts with a beige sweater tied around her shoulders, looking as though she had stepped out of . . .

Well, out of the Midwest.

Which she had.

And she would be going back there as soon as the sun came up.

"I'm starved," she told him as they walked down Fifth Avenue, Noah holding one of her Macy's shopping bags. "Can we eat now?"

He nodded. "I thought we could go to Little Italy, if you like Italian."

"I love Italian," she said. "Pizza Hut, remember?"

Her eyes were twinkling at him.

Struggling to quell a surge of sadness, he smiled at her. "I'll try to find a place that measures up."

"Do you think your roommate will be here now?" Mariel asked Noah, lifting one of her aching feet to rest it against the opposite ankle as she once again watched him go through the series of keys and locks necessary to gain access to the apartment.

"Trust me, he's always here," Noah said. "Last time was a fluke."

But when they stepped into the apartment, it was dark and silent.

Damn. She had been counting on the supposedly ever present Alan to diffuse any tension that might arise between them now that bedtime had arrived.

She couldn't help thinking about last night—had it only been last night?—when they had gone together to her room at the Sweet Briar and made love.

"Looks like he's out," Mariel commented as Noah walked across the living room and switched on a lamp.

"Looks like he is," Noah said, frowning. He walked over to the answering machine.

Mariel could see the red light blinking from where she stood and knew what it meant. There were messages. Before they had left earlier, he had played them back. The first five had been hang-up calls that Mariel realized were probably the calls she herself had placed to Noah on Saturday night.

Now Noah pressed a button, and the machine rewound noisily. "Maybe it's Sherry or Nicole telling us something new about Amber," he said.

"Maybe." She walked over to a chair and sat, her attention focused on the machine.

"Noah, it's Rick. Kelly has some additional concerns about the pension issue that need to be ironed out before we draw up the final papers. Call me as soon as you can."

Two beeps after the message told them that was it. Nobody else had called.

"Rick is my divorce attorney," Noah said flatly.

"And Kelly was your wife," Mariel said.

"Exactly. Apparently she's worried that it's not clear enough that not only will I not be entitled to any of the millions she already has, but to any of the millions she'll get when she's seventy-five or eighty or whenever the hell she decides to retire. If she ever does," he added, his voice laced with bitterness.

Mariel only nodded, uncertain how to react. His divorce was certainly none of her business, but she couldn't help wondering, if his wife had millions, how it was that he had come to be living in this small apartment with no decent furniture. Then she recalled what he had told her—that by New York standards, this was a big apartment. And, over dinner, he had mentioned that he and Kelly had been saving to buy a co-op uptown, which Kelly had apparently done without him right after they split.

"I wonder where Alan is," Noah said, striding across the room to a closed door. He knocked on it and called, "Alan?"

No reply.

"I thought maybe he was here, asleep or something," Noah told Mariel. "But it looks like he really is out. Which is odd. I'm starting to wonder if I should worry."

"Why?"

"What if something happened to him? From what I can see, he leads a fairly footloose life. I mean, I'm probably the only one who would notice if he suddenly disappeared."

She nodded, her thoughts flashing back to Amber. Their daughter was out there in the night somewhere, on her own—or worse. Mariel wondered if she was doing the right thing, going back home to Rockton when Amber was still missing.

But what else could she do?

You could stay, she reminded herself. *You could go on trying to find her.*

But that could take weeks. Months. Years. If Amber

had run away, she might have no intention of ever going home. And when she did go home, it wouldn't be to Mariel. It would be to the Steadmans, the parents who had raised her. There was no way of knowing when or if Amber would ever want to get in touch with Mariel again, let alone make her a part of her life.

All Mariel needed to know, then, was that her daughter was safe.

The police were investigating, as was Henry Brando, and the Steadmans themselves. There seemed little Mariel could do that wasn't already being done. It made no sense for her to stay on the East Coast any longer—and even less sense for her to fly back again anytime in the near future.

She should leave.

It made sense.

She had already made her decision that she was going to do just that. . . .

So why was she going over and over it again in her mind? Why was she trying to convince herself that she wasn't turning her back on her daughter?

The only person she was turning her back on was Noah.

That thought rose unbidden, and she tried to crush it back down again, but it refused to exit. It was, after all, the truth. She was leaving, in part, because of Noah. Because something that had started out to be so straightforward and logical had grown far too complicated.

It was one thing to investigate their daughter's disappearance together.

It was quite another for them to rekindle their relationship after all these years.

"You can sleep in my bed," Noah said, startling her.

Her jaw dropped. Hadn't they already decided that this last night together was to be platonic? A part of her was stunned by his assumption, but another part of her welcomed it. She could feel her body's betrayal as it stirred in anticipation of lying naked with him again.

She recovered her senses. "Noah, I thought we—"

"I'll take the couch," he went on, as though she hadn't interrupted. "It's really comfortable. At least, it must be, given the amount of time Alan spends sprawled there."

She clamped her mouth shut, grateful he had cut her off.

She had misunderstood completely.

"I just want to grab one of the pillows from my bed and some pajamas from my drawer," he said, opening the door beside the one that obviously led to his roommate's room.

"I can take the couch," Mariel offered, her voice sounding weak to her own ears. "I don't want to put you out of your bed."

"No, I don't mind," he said, and she could hear him opening and closing drawers. "That way, if Alan shows up in the middle of the night, you won't have to deal with him."

"He really sounds like a character," Mariel said, trying to keep things light. "I think you should consider getting another roommate."

Wrong thing to say, she realized.

He had already considered getting another roommate. Namely, Mariel. At least, that was what he had implied when he had talked about moving to Rockton.

The very idea of Noah moving into her house—of not having to spend the rest of her life there, alone—

was enough to send shivers of anticipation through her. She imagined what it would be like to wake beside him every morning, to share coffee and the morning paper, to go off to teach school knowing that when she returned, he would be there, waiting to welcome her.

It was a tantalizing fantasy, but it could never be more than that.

Which was why it was a good thing that she would be leaving in the morning.

Noah emerged from his room with a pair of pajamas rolled up under one arm, clutching a pillow beneath the other. "The bedroom's all yours," he said. "You can have the bathroom first if you want. I'm going to try to stay up a little while and catch a score on the Yankee game."

He didn't invite her to stay up with him, she noticed with a pang.

But as she walked toward the bathroom, she reminded herself that it was better that way. Safer. With him in one room and her in the other, there was no chance that they would accidentally land in each other's arms.

In the bathroom, she washed and brushed her teeth. She decided to change into her nightgown in the bedroom, not wanting to walk past him in it. Not that she thought it would tempt him, but . . .

Well, maybe she did think it would tempt him.

And maybe she thought that if he made the slightest move toward her, she would cave in. Not just on her resolve not to let anything physical happen further between them, but on the rest of it, too. The part about him coming to live in Rockton, just to see how he liked it.

After all, it was a free country.

He could live wherever he liked.

Who was she to stop him?

"Did you find the toothpaste?" Noah asked, glancing up when she came out of the bathroom and crossed through the living room again. He was sitting on the couch holding the remote control, and a late newscast was on the television screen.

"I had brought my own," she told him.

"That's good."

"Well . . . good night," she said awkwardly.

"Good night." He shifted his gaze back to the TV. Then, as she stepped over the threshold into the bedroom, he called, "Oh, I set the alarm for tomorrow morning. I'll put you in a cab to the airport before I leave for the office."

"All right."

It was so final, she thought as she closed the door behind her with a click.

This was it.

She was leaving.

For a moment, she fought the crazy impulse to open the door, to rush back into the living room and hurl herself into his arms.

Then it subsided, and she exhaled shakily, feeling as though she had survived a close call.

She changed into her nightgown and slid between the sheets. His scent wafted around her, and a wave of longing swept over her.

She lay awake for a long time, thinking about Amber, wherever she was. And about Noah. And about the life that lay waiting for her back in Rockton.

They could have been a family.

And maybe . . .

Maybe they should have been a family.

Maybe, if they had married and raised their daughter, it would have been okay. After all, not every teenaged shotgun marriage ended in divorce.

Maybe they would still be together, and their daughter would be safe and sound, secure in the love that her birth parents had for her—and for each other.

Maybe.

"Did you remember to get all your stuff from the bathroom?" Noah asked Mariel as they rushed out into the hallway. He stopped to swiftly lock the door.

"I think so. If I forgot anything, it isn't important," she told him, putting on an earring as they hurried toward the stairs.

"Or I can send it to you." He shifted her bag to his other shoulder.

But he didn't have her address. If she pointed it out, it would seem as if she should give it to him. She could hardly refuse to do that, yet giving him her address would imply that they would stay in touch. And of course they wouldn't.

She needed to change the subject, and she seized the first thing that came to mind.

"I can carry that," she offered, gesturing at her bag, though she had already asked and been refused twice since he picked up the bag back in his bedroom.

"It's fine," he said, as they reached the landing and continued down the next flight. "Do you have your plane ticket?"

"I have the old one. I had to change the flight, remember?"

"Oh, Lord. That means you have to go to the ticket counter when you get there, and the line is always long." He checked his watch. "I can't believe the alarm didn't go off. I could have sworn I set it."

"It's okay," she said, trying not to notice how handsome he looked in his business suit and tie. She had never seen him dressed like this. It gave him a whole new aura of masculinity. An appealing aura of masculinity. Thank God she was leaving. All she had to do was get into a cab headed to the airport, and it would be over at last.

"I'll call Henry Brando from the office," Noah said, a bit breathless from the stairs.

She nodded, huffing herself. "We probably should have done it yesterday."

Noah shrugged. "He's probably already talked to both Sherry and Nicole. We probably don't know anything he didn't already know. Listen, when you get into the cab make sure the driver heads back uptown and takes the Queens Midtown tunnel or the Queensborough Bridge. We're on Broadway, which runs downtown, so he should go around the block to head over to the FDR."

"Won't he know how to get to La Guardia?" she asked, alarmed.

"Sure, but sometimes, if they think you're a tourist, they'll try to take the long way. And whatever you do, don't tell him to hurry."

"Why not? I'm in a hurry." Her flight was leaving in a little over an hour.

"Because New York cab drivers always hurry. If you give one permission to really take off, you'll be in for a thrill ride. You might never get there in one piece."

"Are you sure I'm going to make my flight?"

"If you don't, you can always take the next one."

She nodded, trying not to feel disappointed. She had thought he was going to say that if she didn't, she could always come back here. But that was ridiculous, of course. Why would she?

She was on her way home.

They had reached the first floor. Noah threw open the door and held it for her, then followed her out to the street.

"Sometimes it takes a few minutes to get a cab," he muttered, looking around.

She blinked in the bright sunlight after the dim vestibule. It was a glorious day, the sun burning brightly in a clear blue sky without a hint of a cloud.

Again, she felt a flicker of disappointment. Her flight wouldn't be canceled because of weather. An hour from now, she would be on the plane, and there would be no turning back.

Not that she wanted to turn back. This had been her idea.

And it was the right idea.

"There's a cab," Noah said, bolting out into the street with his arm raised, shouting, "Taxi!"

He certainly was eager to be rid of her, she thought as she watched the yellow cab screech to a stop.

"Come on, before the light changes," he said, hurrying across Broadway as the DON'T WALK sign flashed its orange warning.

On the opposite curb, the cab driver waited, having popped open the trunk of the car when he saw that Noah was carrying luggage. Noah put the bag into the trunk and spoke to the driver, who nodded and got behind the wheel."

"Okay, you're all set," Noah said, opening the back door for her.

She felt as though somebody had snatched her breath and her voice away.

This was it.

She was leaving.

"I'm sorry about the alarm," he said again. "It's too bad we had to be in such a rush this morning. You didn't even get a chance to have coffee."

"It's okay," she said, thinking that it had probably been better this way. They had been too harried for awkward moments back at the apartment. Now, in the broad light of day, with traffic careening by and the sidewalk crammed with pedestrians, there was no opportunity for any last moment of intimacy.

There was only time for a quick, public good-bye.

"Have a safe trip," Noah said, his eyes concealed behind sunglasses. When had he put them on?

Mariel nodded, wishing she could hide her own eyes, afraid he would see that they were on the verge of swimming with tears.

"Don't forget your bag in the trunk," Noah said. "If he drives off with it, you'll never see it again."

"I'll remember," she managed to say, clinging to the top of the open car door for support, her knees feeling weak. She couldn't believe this was happening.

"Okay, then," he said. "I'll call Henry Brando. If there's any news, I'll call you."

"You don't have my number."

"How many Rowans are in Rockton? I'll find you if I need to."

She nodded. He would find her—if he needed to.

"If you hear from Amber again . . ." His words were hurried, yet tinged with concern. "Look, you have my number," he said. "Please, if you hear anything, just let me know."

"I will. And you do the same."

So they would probably talk again, she thought, feeling a pinprick of irrational hope. Then she was furious with herself. What the hell was she doing? She had made her decision. She had to stick to it. This was what she had wanted. To leave.

And she had better do it now, dammit.

"I've got to go," she said.

He nodded, looking hesitant. Then he leaned toward her.

She braced herself for one of his soul-searing kisses, knowing that it would be her undoing.

It didn't happen.

His lips brushed her cheek softly, fleetingly, and he whispered, "Have a good life, Mariel."

A sob caught in her throat. She got into the cab, and he closed the door after her.

The light had changed again. The cab immediately merged into traffic, swooping along Broadway as Mariel stared out the window unable to see, her eyes blinded by tears.

Damn.

Damn, he was crying.

Noah swallowed hard, his throat aching with the effort of holding back the emotion that threatened to burst forward in a soul-encompassing flood. He swiped at a tear that had trickled down his cheek, past the protective barrier of his sunglasses, and sniffled.

He felt in the pockets of his suit for a tissue and found none.

He would go back upstairs, just to blow his nose and calm himself. He couldn't get on the subway with tears streaming down his face.

He crossed Broadway again and made his way up the stairs, amazed that only moments earlier, she had been here with him.

Now she was gone, and she would never be here again.

He would go off to work in a few minutes as though nothing had changed, when everything had changed. His world had been rocked these past few days, and it was impossible to digest all that had happened. Getting caught up in Mariel's spell again had only been a part of it.

His heart ached for the daughter who, for all he knew, had hitchhiked across the country to meet some pedophile she had met on the Internet. He longed for the news that Amber had returned safely to Valley Falls as deeply as he longed to get into a cab, chase Mariel to the airport, and beg her to stay.

He had done practically that last night, and she had turned him down flat, he thought, reaching his floor and searching for his keys in his pocket.

No, actually, he had offered to move to Rockton to be with her.

Would it have made any difference if he had asked her to move to New York to be with him?

Tired as he was of the hassles of living in the city, he knew he could survive here if she was with him. Last night had been almost magical, eating sweet, icy gelatto as they strolled along bustling Mulberry Street past the lively shops and restaurants, some of them lit by strings of white Christmas lights. It was a part of the city he rarely visited, and he had seen it appreciatively through her eyes. He imagined taking her on the ferry boat into the harbor to Ellis Island, or on the Roosevelt Island tram, with its open-air view of the skyline, or on a carriage ride through Central Park this fall, when the brilliant foliage turned the place into a Monet painting.

No, it wouldn't be so bad living here if she were with him.

What if he had suggested that?

It wouldn't have made any difference. He knew it in his heart. She had left because she knew it couldn't work between them.

He walked into his apartment just as the phone rang, and he thought, with a complete lack of logic, that it might be her.

He rushed to pick it up, and an unfamiliar female voice answered his hello. A wave of disappointment swept over him, and for a moment he couldn't grasp who it was or what she was saying.

Then he realized, and his blood ran cold.

All thoughts of going to the office had left his brain. All he could think of was that he had to stop Mariel. He had to tell her.

A minute later, he was out on the street, frantically trying to flag a cab.

Miraculously, he got one. "La Guardia airport," he shouted at the driver. "And step on it."

The cab lurched away from the curb, roaring through traffic, weaving wildly from lane to lane as it maneuvered toward the next corner. The driver swung around the turn on two wheels with a screech of tires, then raced to the entrance for the northbound FDR highway.

Noah's heart was pounding, his mind whirling with the incredible news he had just received. There had been no time to even stop and verify it. He had to catch Mariel before she got on that plane.

It was rush hour. Traffic on the FDR crawled. Despite the driver's best reckless efforts to skirt around the jam, it was taking far too long to get to the airport. Noah told himself that Mariel, too, had been stuck in this traffic. That she probably hadn't made the flight.

Finally, he was at La Guardia. Checking his watch, he shouldered his way through the crowd, racing to the nearest monitor that listed flight information. He frantically scanned the glowing blue lettering, searching for her flight, praying that it had been delayed.

He found what he was looking for—and groaned in despair.

The plane had just taken off.

Mariel emerged from the ladies' room into the terminal, her back aching from the weight of her luggage. When Noah had carried it, he had made it look effortless, as though it were filled with foam peanuts. But then, Noah was a man whose tall, lean stature belied the muscular upper body that lay beneath his clothes. Mariel felt an unsettling flurry of desire at the memory of how he had looked bare-chested, all rippling muscle and firm flesh.

She firmly put the thought out of her mind and focused on the matter at hand, which was finding a flight out of La Guardia.

Thanks to a savvy cab driver who knew his way through the streets of Queens and managed to avoid the rush-hour traffic snarls on the main roadway, she had arrived at the airport in time to catch her plane. But when she made it through the line to the ticket counter to check in, the agent informed her that her seat had been given away.

Apparently, passengers couldn't assume that they would be able to pick up a connecting flight without taking the first leg of the journey. When a traveler didn't board at the original starting point, this particular airline's computer automatically canceled the rest of that trip.

There was no other available flight to Mariel's destination until later this evening. At least, not from La Guardia. The ticket agent had informed her that there were seats on a noon flight from Newark airport in New Jersey, which was only about two hours from here. She had advised Mariel to take a cab back to Manhattan, then take a bus from the Port Authority to Newark.

What Mariel wanted to do was take a cab back to Manhattan, find Noah, and tell him that she should never have left—not without him.

But that was out of the question. She would only be setting herself up for the potent brand of heartbreak that had nearly destroyed her once in her life.

They weren't meant to be.

If they were meant to be, she would know it, without doubt, deep in her heart.

But, she wondered, what if she was trying so hard not to allow herself to fall for him that she was ignoring what she really felt? If they weren't meant to be, why was she so irrevocably drawn to him for the second time in her life?

Was it because she was lonely? Or perhaps just starved for a physical relationship?

She didn't believe that. Yes, she was lonely—yes, she was a red-blooded woman with a woman's needs—but there had been other men in her life since Noah. No one else had ever made her feel the way he did.

Yet no one else had ever made her hurt the way he had.

If only there were some way of knowing what fate held in store for her. If only she could be given a sign that they were meant to be. That, in accepting him into her life, she would be enriching her future and not jeopardizing everything she had worked so hard to create.

With a sigh, Mariel shifted the weight of her bag to the other shoulder and made her way to the exit, following the signs for ground transportation.

The airport was teeming with activity this morning, bustling and bright with sunlight that flooded through the skylights above. Mariel gazed at the businessmen and businesswomen who strode past wearing stylish suits, briefcases and laptops and carry-ons in tow. There were elderly retirees embarking on vacations, and college-aged students traveling in groups, and families with toddlers and babies and mountains of luggage.

Everybody was in a hurry.

Everybody except Mariel, she realized, as she approached the outdoor taxi stand. The line snaked along the curb and then made an about face and wove through a rope-defined path. At the head, a harried dispatcher blew his whistle and shouted at the cab drivers, lining them up and funneling the passengers into them. The pace and the commotion of steady departures was dizzying, and Mariel rested her bag on the sidewalk at her feet, watching the strangely orderly confusion in idle fascination as she advanced slowly through the line, her thoughts still centered on leaving Noah.

Then, to her amazement, she heard her name on his lips.

It had to be her imagination, she realized. She wanted so badly to be with him that she had conjured the sound of his voice.

"Mariel?"

Hearing it a second time, she froze. Then, realizing that it was real, she turned slowly and found herself face-to-face with him. He stood on the other side of the rope barrier, at the end of the line, yet directly beside her because of the way it doubled back on itself.

She gasped. "Noah!"

For a moment, all she could think was that she had wished for him, and somehow, he was here. Then she reached up and put her arms around him, pulling him close. "I don't know what you're doing here," she said raggedly, "but I've never been so happy to see anyone."

"I was looking for you," he said, his voice close to her ear as he held her.

And in that instant, she knew it was meant to be. This was her sign. He had come to the airport looking for her, unwilling to let her go. She had been a fool not to believe they had a chance. He obviously believed it. Why shouldn't she throw caution to the wind for the first time in more than a decade?

"Your plane left," he said, "and I was sure you were on it. Why weren't you?"

She saw the hope in his eyes, and she hesitated, wishing the truth were more romantic—that she could tell him what he so obviously wanted to hear: that she hadn't taken the flight because she couldn't bear to leave him behind.

But it would be a lie.

She opened her mouth to tell him the truth, but before she could speak, he cut her off. "Mariel, I have to tell you what happened. Why I'm here. I stopped back in my apartment right after you left because I had, um, forgotten something, and I was just in time to answer my phone. It was Sherry—Amber's friend."

She gaped at him as it dawned on her that he hadn't come here because he wanted her to stay, after all. He had come because of a phone call.

Then, dread mingling with hope at the realization that he must have some kind of news about their daughter, she asked, "What did she say?"

"Excuse me," a brash voice cut in. Somebody jostled her from behind. "The line is moving, and you're not, lady."

Mariel turned, vaguely seeing the irked expression on the face of the man who had spoken. "Go ahead of me," she said absently, stepping closer to the rope, and Noah, to let him pass.

"Can I go ahead of you, too?" asked a peeved-looking businesswoman behind him. "I've got a ten o'clock meeting in midtown."

"Go ahead of me," Mariel said impatiently, lifting the rope. "You can all go ahead of me, I don't care."

She ducked under the rope to stand beside Noah, who held her arm to steady her, then bent and pulled her bag across the concrete to rest at their feet.

"What did Sherry want?" she asked Noah.

"She wanted to tell me that something had been bothering her ever since we spoke to her. She's worried about Amber. At first, she had figured Amber wasn't in danger, because she had run away, and she had said she was definitely coming back. She just had to take care of something. But Sherry realized that Amber had said she would be back within a few days, and now that she hasn't shown up, something might be wrong."

A chill slid over Mariel.

Noah had removed his sunglasses when they first came face-to-face. Now, looking up into his dark eyes, she saw the stark fear there, and felt the same emotion surge within her. Her first instincts, upon learning that their daughter was missing, had been correct. Amber was in danger, runaway or not.

"Did Sherry know anything at all about where Amber might have gone, or what she had to take care of?" Mariel asked Noah.

He nodded. "That's why I had to stop you. I just—I can't believe this is happening."

She stared at him uneasily. "What? What's happening?"

"Sherry said that she had come to New York, Mariel. She was looking for her birth father. She was looking for me."

Mariel's jaw fell open. She tried to collect her thoughts. "She's here? In New York? She's looking for you?"

He nodded grimly. "There's more. And it's not good."

"What is it, Noah? For God's sake, tell me before I assume the worst."

"Sherry said that she had found her birth father and had been corresponding with him by e-mail for a few weeks before she ran away. She said that Amber had planned to meet him in Manhattan."

"But you're her birth father." Perplexed, Mariel's thoughts whirled.

Again, he nodded. "Apparently, she made contact with my computer, Mariel. But not with me. Somebody else answered the e-mail she sent. And I have a sick feeling that I know who it was."

CHAPTER ELEVEN

"What do we do first?" Mariel asked Noah as they entered his apartment forty-five minutes later.

"We check the computer," he said, depositing her bag on the floor just inside the hallway, then striding to the living room without bothering to close the door behind him.

He heard Mariel close and lock it before she caught up with him just as he was sitting at his desk. He turned on the computer and waited for it to boot up, wondering why he hadn't done this before dashing off to the airport when he first got Sherry's call.

Because his first thought, his first impulse, had been to stop Mariel.

He needed her.

Yes, he needed her in the long run—needed her in his life, needed her by his side, needed her in his arms.

She had made it clear that wasn't going to happen, and he had no choice other than to accept that.

But, just as desperately, he needed her now, in the wake of this latest development. He needed her support as he sought to confirm his suspicions, and he needed her help in tracking down his bastard of a roommate if those suspicions proved to be correct.

Which they should know any moment now.

The desktop appeared, and he clicked on the Internet icon.

"So you think that Alan actually snooped through your e-mail?" Mariel asked, watching over his shoulder as the computer rumbled into action.

"I'm sure of it," Noah said. "I've suspected him of snooping through my things in the past, and now that I think about it, there are messages I've never gotten from the answering machine, and magazines that I usually get in the mail that have never arrived—at least, not since he moved in."

"But how could he intercept your e-mail?" Mariel asked. "Wouldn't he need a code word to sign on and check your mailbox?"

"No," Noah said shortly, as the sign-on screen came up. He gestured at it. "See? If you sign on from your home computer, you have the option of entering the password with your screen name just once so that it automatically goes in every time."

"So there was no security."

"Why would I need it? I never had anything to hide when I lived with Kelly, so that was how I set it up. I never changed it when Alan moved in. I never dreamed the guy would invade my privacy this way."

Fury stormed through Noah's gut—fury at himself,

for being a trusting fool, and fury at Alan for violating his privacy, and perhaps committing a far worse crime.

"Maybe he didn't," Mariel said, laying a hand on Noah's shoulder. "Maybe you're jumping to conclusions."

"I doubt it," Noah said, logging on, then thumping his fingers on the desktop impatiently as the computer whirred, preparing to bring up the Internet server. "Sherry said that Mariel had sent her birth father the same note and photograph that she had sent to her birth mother. She said that she had been receiving e-mail from her birth father ever since—and that sometimes, they sent instant messages back and forth. She said it was always in the late afternoon hours, when Amber had just arrived home from school, and that sometimes she was with Amber when she corresponded with him. She said Amber was always careful to delete the messages because she didn't want her parents to know what she was up to. I guess she thought that it would make them uncomfortable."

"But maybe she had the wrong person," Mariel told him.

He shook his head. "She told me the screen name, Mariel. It was my screen name. It had to be Alan, posing as me."

"But why would he do it?"

"Who the hell knows? Because Amber is a vulnerable teenager, and he's some kind of twisted pervert. Because she's a beautiful young girl who unwittingly broadcast her picture over the Internet without realizing that it might fall into the wrong hands."

The sign-on screen came up, and an electronic voice announced, "You've got mail."

"Her screen name is *Indegrl*, Noah," Mariel said quietly, and she spelled it for him. "Just so you know what to look for."

Noah nodded. *Indegrl*.

Her birthday was Independence Day. A lump rose in his throat, and he forced it back. He couldn't afford to get sidetracked by his emotions now. He had to find out what the hell was going on.

He clicked on the mailbox icon and saw a long list of incoming messages. He glanced over them disinterestedly, noting that there was nothing out of the ordinary. Then he checked in the file that held his recent incoming and outgoing mail. There was nothing unusual there, either.

"He probably would have deleted the messages," he realized desolately, shoving the mouse away from him in disgust. "There's no way to know whether he corresponded with her."

"Yes there is," Mariel said, reaching past him for the mouse. Her herbal scent enveloped him, comforting him somehow, despite his distress. "I use the same server, Noah. Even if you delete a message from the incoming mailbox, it stays in your personal electronic filing cabinet unless you delete it from there, too. Alan might not have known that you have to delete it from both places."

"I didn't know that either," Noah said. He sat up straighter in his chair, staring at the screen as Mariel clicked on the file cabinet icon.

It opened, revealing a list of incoming mail. Noah recognized some of it as junk mail that he had deleted from his mailbox without even reading. He had assumed it would vanish from his system, but Mariel was right.

There was a back-up copy of everything that had ever come in, right here in the file cabinet.

Mariel gasped and pointed at the screen.

"My God, there it is," Noah said, his heart bolting in his chest. "There it is. The bastard. What the hell has he done with her?"

"Stay calm, Noah," Mariel said. "I think we're about to find out."

Then she asked, her voice laced with trepidation, "You don't think he's capable of . . . of . . ."

"I don't know," Noah said bleakly. "He's a stranger to me, Mariel. For all I know, he's capable of anything at all."

Mariel picked up another sheet of paper as it shot out of Noah's ancient dot-matrix printer, glanced at it to make sure it was legible, and added it to the growing pile on the desk beside the computer.

Noah stretched and tried to rub the back of his neck, looking weary, and she fought the urge to reach out and knead his muscles for him.

"We're almost done," she noticed, checking the screen. They had almost reached the bottom of the list of outgoing messages that had been sent to *Indegrl* from Noah's computer over a period lasting from Memorial Day weekend—the same time Mariel had received her message from Amber—through the second week of June, when the messages had suddenly stopped.

They had read through all of them before deciding to print them out as hard evidence.

So.

Now they knew.

Posing as Noah, Alan had indeed corresponded with Amber Steadman. It had sickened Mariel to read his e-mails to their daughter. All were brief, and most contained spelling and punctuation errors. Apparently, written correspondence wasn't Alan's strong suit.

Mostly, the letters were small talk. There was a lot of discussion of popular music and television shows and sports. Mariel's fears had subsided a bit now that she had read the letters, yet she hadn't entirely rid herself of the nagging worry that Alan had harmed Amber in some way after luring her to New York.

That, of course, was exactly what had happened. He had extended an invitation for Amber to come visit, and naturally, she had pounced on the offer, assuming she was going to be meeting her birth father at last.

Her e-mails were far more detailed than Alan's, and Mariel's heart ached as her daughter's personality emerged in letter after letter. Amber was creative, speaking passionately about music and art and her love of playing the piano and performing. She was a bright student who got good grades, and she seemed to have a typical social life with a large circle of friends.

She was also deeply troubled over her parents' separation. She spoke sparingly about the situation, yet her pain came through loudly and clearly. She was an adolescent only child whose world had been rocked, and she was desperately seeking some kind of stability.

Clearly, Alan had preyed upon her vulnerability, offering to have her come visit—and, if it worked out, to have her move in with him. He had painted a false picture of Noah's life, portraying himself as a wealthy businessman who had much to offer his long-lost daughter. He had asked her to call him Daddy, which Amber had done, obviously having jumped at the chance to make herself a part of his life.

According to the plainly outlined e-mail plan, Amber had left home using baby-sitting money she had been saving all winter, hoping to buy herself a car when she turned sixteen.

She had taken a bus to the Port Authority on the day she had disappeared from Valley Falls, unrecognized later by those who were questioned by police because she had possessed the foresight to disguise herself. She had told Alan—lovingly referred to as "Daddy"—that she would wear make-up and one of the blond wigs she still had from a performance in last fall's class play.

She had acknowledged that her parents would be worried about her disappearance, but had written that the anxiety over her whereabouts might do them good. *At least it will bring them together again,* she had written, and wistfully added, *maybe even for good. After all, they're only separated, and you never know.*

Clearly, hurt as she was by their separation, she cared about her parents.

"We should call the Steadmans," Noah said to Mariel, as if he had read her thoughts. He clicked on the Print icon, sending another letter to the printer. "Detective Brando, too. Or the police."

She shook her head, an image flashing in her mind. She saw Henry Brando's skeptical face, and heard an echo of his doubtful tone as he questioned them that day in the diner about Amber's disappearance.

"Not yet, Noah," she said firmly.

"Why not?" he asked, looking up at her with a surprised expression. "They need to know what's going on. Her parents are worried sick. They deserve to know what we've found."

"All we've found are e-mails written on your computer, outlining a plan to meet. Who's to say you didn't write these letters yourself? Who's to say you're not involved?"

"But I'm not. It was Alan."

"You say it was Alan. I believe it was Alan. Why should the police? This doesn't look good for you, Noah. Until we know more about what's going on with Alan, I don't think we should go to the police. Let's try to find him first."

Noah stared at her. "You want to withhold this information from her parents and the police just because it might implicate me?"

"Not forever. Just until we know more about what we're dealing with. It sounds to me as though Alan was planning to spend some time with her here in New York."

"How do we know he's not a serial killer who lured her here to murder her?" Noah demanded, slamming his hand down on the desk. The top papers on the pile lifted in the draft, and Mariel caught one as it flew into the air.

She set it back on top of the pile and said firmly, unable to quite believe her own assuredness, "I doubt that Alan meant to kill her, Noah. I get the sense that he's just a slacker who saw the chance to take advantage of a trusting teenaged girl. And don't get me wrong," she said, cutting him off with an abruptly raised hand as he started to speak, "it makes me sick to think of what he might have been planning. But we have to believe that she's still alive, and that she's someplace here in New York. That's what I choose to believe. And I think we can find her if we start looking."

He shrugged, brooding.

"Who are Alan's friends?" she prodded. "Come on, Noah. We can talk to people who know him and see if anybody can give us a lead."

"For all I know he has no friends," Noah said. "He seems like a loner."

"Then, let's go through his room and see what we can find," Mariel said, as the last letter came out of the printer. She put it on top of the sheaf on the desk, then headed for the closed door that led to Alan's room.

Noah remained seated.

"Are you coming?" she asked him.

"I don't think it's right for me to protect myself, maybe at Amber's expense."

"That's not what this is about, Noah. We just need a few hours, or maybe longer, to see if we can come up with anything on our own. If we don't, we'll go to her parents and the police, and we'll pray that they believe us when we say you're not involved."

He sat for a moment longer, and she watched him, aching to hold him, to comfort him. Somehow she had regained her strength, finding hope in the information they had gleaned, even as Noah had become desolate, convinced that Amber had met dire trouble.

Mariel just couldn't believe the worst.

And this time, she wasn't going to give up and go home.

She was going to stay here and see it through until they found their daughter.

Only then would she allow herself to leave . . .

Or to seriously consider the alternative.

"Are you coming?" she asked Noah again.

This time, he nodded and stood, walking toward her.

The phone rang.

They looked at each other.

Then Noah bolted toward it, snatching up the receiver with a breathless, "Hello?"

Mariel saw his eyes narrow.

"David," he said tersely. "Yes, I'm back in town."

David, she knew, was his boss. For a few moments Noah only listened, his back to Mariel. But when he finally spoke, he turned so that she could see the stony expression on his face, and she realized what was coming.

"I understand, but I can't possibly be there," Noah said evenly. "I'm involved in a family crisis."

There was another pause.

"I don't think that's any of your business, David. Whether or not she lived with me—whether or not I've even seen her in the past fifteen years—she's still my daughter, and I'm going to find her."

He was silent again, listening.

Mariel stood watching him, seeing the way the muscle in his jaw clenched before he spoke again.

"I'm sorry you feel that way, David. But I'm going to do what I have to do. I guess you'll just have to do the same."

Another pause.

Then Noah said abruptly, "I see. That's what I expected. I'll come by when this is over to pick up my things."

With that, he hung up.

Mariel stared at him, waiting.

"I just got fired," he informed her.

"I figured," she said, and asked cautiously, "Are you okay?"

"I'm free," Noah said with a shrug. "Right now, that's all that matters. Maybe it'll sink in later that I'm flat broke and unemployed. At the moment, I just don't give a damn about anything but finding Amber."

"Then, that's what we'll do," she said, holding out her hand.

He took it.

She squeezed his fingers. "Everything's going to be okay," she said.

"Maybe," he said.

And together, they went into his roommate's room to begin searching for clues.

"This is it," Noah realized, stopping short in front of a decrepit-looking building just off Lenox Avenue. It was a plain, ugly brick rectangle with crumbling cement steps, and unlike some of the other buildings on the block—faded brownstone-types whose glory days had ended a century ago—this one had clearly never been anything more than what it currently was: a rundown tenement in a rough neighborhood. The street was ominously deserted, and hip-hop music blasted from an open window somewhere above. The smell of rotting garbage permeated the warm summer day.

"Are you sure this is the right place?" Mariel asked, standing close at Noah's side. "This place looks like a hell hole."

"I'm not surprised," Noah said, leading the way up the steps.

"Careful," he said, pointing to a syringe just beside

his foot. He sidestepped it and reached back to take Mariel's hand, muttering, "This is dangerous. I should have come alone."

"That makes a lot of sense," she said sarcastically.

"No, you shouldn't be in a place like this, Mariel," he said, as a beat-up car raced down the street behind them, then screeched around the corner.

"Neither should you. And I hope to God Amber isn't here," she said heavily as they stepped into the dingy, smelly vestibule.

"I doubt it." Noah consulted the notes he had scribbled on a yellow Post-it note back home, then shoved it back into his pocket. He had changed from his suit to jeans, and for that, he was grateful. He definitely didn't want to be caught in this neighborhood looking like a yuppie.

"Alan lived in apartment 2B," he informed Mariel.

"Then, let's go."

He put his foot on the bottom step of a steep flight that led upward, into cavernous darkness, and his sneaker crunched on broken glass. "Be careful," he warned Mariel, hating that she was here with him.

"I'm fine," she said brightly. Too brightly.

Together, they made their way to the second floor.

The hip-hop music was even more deafening here, but it wasn't coming from apartment 2B. Noah knocked on the battered door, and a voice called from inside, "Yeah? Who's there?"

He was startled by the instant response. He supposed he hadn't really been expecting to find Alan's former roommate at home—if, in fact, that was who had answered the knock. He had found the address, and Chas's name, on the application he had asked Alan to fill out when he had answered Noah's ad. At least something good had come from being married to a nitpicky lawyer for all those years. Not that he had bothered to confirm the information Alan had supplied before inviting him to move in.

The application had been something Kelly would have thought of. And thank goodness Noah had, because Alan's room had yielded nothing by way of clues to his lifestyle.

"Chas Brown?" he called. "I need to talk to you a minute. About your friend Alan Henning."

The door was flung open. A surprisingly normal-looking guy stood there, wearing jeans and a T-shirt. He was barefoot and unshaven, and his blondish hair was long and straggly, but he could have stepped off a stage at a rock concert, Kurt Cobain resurrected. Nothing menacing about him.

"I'm Chas," he said, and took a drag from the lit cigarette in his hand before saying, "If you're talking about the asshole who just moved out of here, he's no friend of mine."

That didn't bode well, Noah thought, as he quickly corrected himself. "I'm sorry, I meant to say your roommate. Alan Henning was your roommate, right?"

Chas nodded and regarded them warily. "What do you want? Are you cops?"

"No."

"Are you sure? Because it wouldn't surprise me if the cops showed up looking for him."

Uh-oh.

"No, I'm just his roommate," Noah said.

"Yeah, well, you have my sympathy, dude. He rip you off, too?"

"What do you mean?" Noah asked.

"Look, you want to come in?" Chas asked, holding the door open wider. "The place isn't great, but it's the best I can do on my salary."

As he stepped over the threshold and saw the dingy surroundings, Noah remembered that he no longer had a salary. He thought about his apartment downtown, comparing it to this place, then constrained the panic that tried to push its way into his consciousness. One thing at a time.

"What do you do?" Mariel asked politely, as though they were at a cocktail party instead of in this cramped, rundown, sparsely furnished apartment.

"I'm a social worker," Chas said, leaning forward and flicking the ash from his cigarette onto the floor in the hallway before closing the door. "I work with Harlem kids who have been abused. Figured I might as well live in the neighborhood, you know?"

Out of the corner of his eye, Noah saw something scurry down the wall beside the door. He turned his head just in time to see the biggest cockroach he had ever encountered before it disappeared into a crack near the baseboard.

Suppressing a shudder, he asked, "Did you say Alan ripped you off?"

"Among other things. I never realized he was helping himself to the change from my pockets until I caught him red-handed. That was when I threw him out."

"What else did he do?" Mariel asked. "You said there were other things."

"The guy was a snoop. He opened my mail a couple of times, then said he had done it by accident—that he thought it was addressed to him. And I know he went through a box of letters from my girlfriend—she's living abroad right now, so we write a lot—because I could tell it had been disturbed, and nobody else could have had access."

"Yeah, I don't doubt that he'd do something like that," Noah said flatly, thinking that it was mild compared to the way he had violated Noah's privacy.

"Don't trust him, dude," Chas said. "He has no conscience. He's pathological. I can't believe I didn't see it. I work with kids like that. They don't care who they hurt with their actions."

"Do you think he's capable of worse than just snooping or stealing?" Mariel asked worriedly.

Chas shrugged. "Do you mean, is he violent? Hard to tell, but having lived with the guy for a few months, my gut instinct is that he's just deeply screwed up, and not dangerous."

Relieved, Noah asked, "How did you meet him?"

"Placed an ad in the paper for a roommate. He showed up. He was the most normal dude of the bunch, so I picked him. Now I'm working two jobs to pay the rent on this place until my girlfriend comes back and moves in. Anything's better than living with some guy off the street again."

"I know what you mean," Noah said. "Look, Chas, I need to track down Alan, and I don't know where to look. He said he tends bar, but I never bothered to find out where."

"What'd he do? Take off with some of your stuff?" Chas asked. "I was surprised it never got that far with me. Then again, it's not like I've got anything anyone would want," he added ruefully, gazing around at the meager contents of the apartment.

"No, he's just taken off, period," Noah said, not wanting to go into the details. "I need to find him."

"Well, he does tend bar. I know that for a fact because I went out with him a few times when he first moved in, and we stopped by the place where he works so we could get some free drinks. It's a real dive bar, over in the meat-packing district."

"Do you know the name of it, or where it was?"

"I don't know what the place was called, but I remember the block it was on," Chas said. "And you can't miss it—it's right next door to some gay leather bar that has a whole dungeon thing going on."

"Sounds charming," Mariel said. "Listen, Chas, do you know anything about Alan's, uh, love life?"

"You mean, was he straight? Because I can tell you that he definitely wasn't gay. He was into women."

"Did he have a girlfriend?"

"Nah. Not that I know of. He talked big talk, but I think that was all it was. The guy knew a lot of people wherever we went, but he seemed pretty insecure around women, from what I saw when we went out."

Insecure. That would explain why he might be drawn to a teenaged girl. *Sick bastard,* Noah thought in disgust.

"Okay, Chas, you've got to tell me how to find that bar," he said, pulling out the Post-it note and a pen he had remembered to put into his pocket.

A minute later, he and Mariel were on the street again, breathing fresh air and heading for Lenox Avenue to look for a cab.

"Let me guess—we're headed for the meat-packing district," Mariel said, and Noah nodded.

"Shouldn't we wait until at least after dark?" she

asked, checking her watch. "I mean, isn't that when most bartenders work?"

Noah glanced at her wrist and saw that it wasn't even four o'clock yet. "I don't want to waste any time," he said. "Even if Alan isn't there, the place might be open. And maybe somebody can tell us something about the lowlife. When I find him . . ." He clenched his fists in fury. "He's going to pay for what he did."

"Noah, you're not going to do anything stupid, are you?" Mariel asked worriedly, laying a hand on his bare arm. "He could be dangerous."

"If he hurt Amber—"

"Don't even think about it," Mariel said, and he allowed himself to be soothed by her voice, and her touch. He let her take his hand as they walked, and he entwined her fingers in his, taking strength from the contact.

Maybe it was wrong.

Maybe he should be keeping his distance from her, knowing that if she hadn't missed her flight, and if he hadn't caught her at the airport, she would be halfway across the country by now.

He knew that when this was over, whatever the outcome, they would inevitably say good-bye again.

How many times could they put themselves through that?

As many times as it took before they were out of each other's lives for good, he thought grimly.

But he didn't let go of her hand.

*   *   *

The bar was just as Chas had described it—a dive, located beside a strange-looking place that had a false stone facade and bars across the windows.

"Bet you don't have places like that in Rockton," Noah said, and Mariel shook her head with a faint smile.

As they approached the door of the place where Alan worked, she commented that this neighborhood was even scarier than the last.

To her surprise, Noah said, "Don't let appearances fool you. This is one of the trendiest sections of town. There are a lot of hot clubs here, and some of the biggest celebrities in New York hang out here after dark. A few even live here."

Her eyes widened in disbelief as she looked over her shoulder at the dismal-looking row of warehouse-type buildings on the opposite side of the street.

"New York is a strange place," she commented.

"And it's filled with strange people," Noah said dryly as a man walked by wearing a bird cage on his head.

They laughed, and it helped to relieve the tension.

But not for long.

They entered the dimly lit interior. It was nothing more than a hole in the wall, really—a long bar lined with stools along one side of the narrow room, and a few neon-lit beer signs on the wall. There was a füssball table and a dart board, both in a dark corner, looking as though nobody had bothered with them in ages.

There were a few men seated at the bar, all of them hunched over their mugs in a way that told Mariel they had absolutely nothing better to do on this beautiful Wednesday afternoon in June. It was incredibly depressing.

Behind the bar, a youngish man with a shaved head eyed them with abstract curiosity. "Can I help you?"

"Sure," Noah said, and he slid onto one of the stools.

Fighting the impulse to wipe it off before she sat on it, Mariel hopped up on the one beside his, trying to look as though she wasn't squeamish.

"I'll have a bottle of Bud," Noah told the bartender, who nodded and looked expectantly at Mariel.

Normally, she would order wine, but she didn't. For one thing, she was skeptical about the caliber of Merlot in this place, and for another, she figured it would be best not to drink out of a glass. Even from here she could see the smudges on the row of mugs and glasses that lined a shelf behind the bar.

"I'll have a bottle of Bud, too," Mariel said.

"No problem." The bartender turned away and moments later was plunking two open beers on the bar in front of them.

The men at the far end of the bar had gone back to their brooding conversation.

"Hey, buddy, can I ask you something?" Noah asked the bartender, handing him a twenty-dollar bill.

"Got anything smaller?" the bartender asked, ignoring the question.

Noah shook his head. "Keep it," he said pointedly, and sipped his beer.

Mariel almost cringed. Noah had just lost his job. He didn't have money to throw around. But she knew what he was up to.

"Can I ask you something?" Noah repeated.

The bartender's gaze slid from the bill in his hand to Noah's face. "What is it?" he asked warily.

"You know a guy named Alan who works here?"

"What about him?"

"I'm trying to find him."

"Yeah? What for?"

"He's my roommate. Hasn't been around in a few days. I'm worried that something might have happened to him. I know he doesn't travel in the best circles."

"Alan's all right," the bartender said. "He worked just last night."

"Yeah? Do you know where he's been staying?"

"Nah. Why don't you ask him yourself? He'll be here at eleven."

"I don't want to wait that long," Noah said. "I need to find him sooner."

"How come?"

"Like he said, he's worried," Mariel told the bartender. "Do you know where he is now?"

The bartender shrugged. "Maybe."

"Where?"

The guy just looked at Noah. "Why should I tell you? How do I know you're not looking to cause him trouble?"

"What is he, a friend of yours?" Noah asked, and Mariel marveled at how he had altered his usual manner of speaking to fit into this place. There was a regional inflection in his voice, the kind of accent she had heard in mob movies set in New York. The kind of accent the bartender himself had.

"Nah, he just works here. But I don't know if I should go telling a couple of strangers where he is."

Before Noah could make a move, Mariel felt in the pocket of her jeans and pulled out some folded bills she had stashed there. She handed him a twenty. "Tell us."

The bartender stuffed the bill into the front pocket of his black jeans. "He's staying at a friend's apartment. A friend who bartends here on weekends sometimes. The guy's away right now, on an out-of-town gig with his band for a few more days. So Alan's keeping an eye on his place."

"He staying there alone?" Noah asked.

The bartender threw up his hands and said, "I don't know anything more than that, man. That's all I can tell you."

"You know where this friend lives, though. Right?"

"It's way out in Brooklyn. I don't know where."

He was lying, Mariel realized. She could see it in his eyes. He saw her watching him and turned away, picking up a grimy rag and going down to wipe off the other end of the bar.

"He knows where the apartment is," Mariel told Noah.

"Yeah, I'm sure he does, but we're not going to get it out of him," Noah replied in a low voice. "We'll just have to come back here late tonight when Alan's here."

"But then we won't be able to catch him off guard. This guy's going to tell him that we're looking for him."

"There's nothing else we can do," Noah said. "We're at a dead end. At least we know Alan's still in New York, still coming to work."

"What if he did something to Amber?" Mariel asked, despair suddenly welling up inside of her again. "Or what if he's keeping her prisoner somewhere? She could be terrified, and desperate. We have to try to get to her, Noah. We owe her that much."

He stared at her, taken aback by her outburst.

"I'm sorry," she said, realizing she was on the verge

of tears. And here she had been the one holding it together all day, while Noah seemed to be teetering on the brink of losing it altogether. The tables had turned. Her nerves were frazzled; her emotions were shot. She had been living in a state of high anxiety for five days now, and the stress had taken its toll.

"It's okay," Noah said, reaching out to touch her hand.

"I just keep picturing her somewhere, alone and afraid. I feel like we've let her down, Noah. Not just because we haven't found her yet, but because . . ."

She couldn't say it.

She had convinced herself repeatedly that giving up the baby had been the right thing to do. She didn't really believe that it hadn't been. And yet, if she and Noah had kept Amber and raised her themselves, this wouldn't have happened. Amber wouldn't have fallen into the clutches of . . .

Well, of whatever Alan was.

She felt hot tears sliding down her face, and she wiped her cheek against her shoulder, sniffling.

"Here," Noah said, reaching into his pocket and offering her a crumpled tissue. "It's clean."

She let out a laugh that sounded more like a choking sob. "Look at this place. It's the only thing in here that is clean."

He laughed, too.

And then she really did sob—a shuddering sound that escaped her and set off more tears. "I'm sorry, Noah," she wailed into her tissue. "I just can't help it. I can't take this anymore. We have to know what happened to her."

"Is everything okay?" a voice asked behind her.

She turned to see that the bartender had come back to their end of the bar and was watching her.

She wiped her eyes.

Noah said shortly, "She's fine."

The guy just watched them for a moment.

Then he reached for a cocktail napkin behind the bar, grabbed a pencil, and scribbled something on it. He handed it over to Noah, saying, "Here. This is where you'll find Alan. Good luck."

"Guess you're really getting to know a part of New York most tourists don't get to see," Noah commented as they ascended the subway steps and emerged on a Brooklyn street corner. Traffic whizzed by, and pedestrians hurried past them.

"Yeah, lucky me," Mariel replied. "Do you even know where we are?"

"I've never been to this part of the city, but it's pretty safe, from what I know," he said. They started down the block, passing several men in hats and beards, with curly locks falling past their ears and long black coats flapping around their calves. Most had prayer books tucked under their arms. He noticed the way Mariel gaped at them, and then at the women who trailed behind, wearing prim dresses and stiff wigs.

"They're Hasidic Jews," he explained in a low voice. "There are a lot of them in this neighborhood."

She nodded, and sniffed the air. "Something smells wonderful."

He saw that they were passing a kosher restaurant. "Are you hungry?"

"I'm too nervous to be hungry. But it smells good."

"When this is all over, I'll take you to a place like that," he said without thinking.

"That would be great."

But he heard the awkwardness in her voice. Dammit, he had crossed the line again. He had acted as though they had a future, even the slightest future, once they found their daughter.

"What kind of food do they serve?" she asked as they walked on.

"In a kosher restaurant?"

She nodded.

Grateful for something to say—something that couldn't get him into trouble—he said, "They have bagels and lox, and soup—mushroom barley and matzoh ball. And chopped liver and whitefish salad. And knishes, and kasha, and blintzes, and the best sandwiches you've ever tasted. Piles of pastrami and corned beef, with real pickles."

She laughed. "As opposed to fake pickles?"

"As opposed to those limp, murky green slices that come in a jar from a supermarket shelf."

"There goes my taste for deli food," she said as they rounded a corner.

Noah looked up at the street sign and saw that this was the block they were looking for. So did she, and her grin faded.

"What are we going to do when we find him?" Mariel asked, hanging back a little as they approached the address, an aluminum-sided, two-family row house. All the houses on the block looked the same, fronted by chain-link fences and concrete stoops.

"We're going to ask him what the hell he did with Amber," Noah replied, his gut clenching in anticipation of the confrontation that with any luck, was about to unfold. All the way down here on the subway, he had prayed that Alan would be at home. Knowing his roommate, there was a good chance of that.

"What if he tries something?" Mariel asked. "What if he pulls a gun on us, Noah?"

"He won't," Noah said with a confidence he didn't feel.

They made their way up the steps. Noah rang the bell for the upper apartment.

They waited.

Then they heard footsteps on the other side of the door.

Noah shouldered his body in front of Mariel, instinctively shielding her from whatever was about to happen.

Then the door opened and Alan stood there.

"Noah! What the hell . . . ?"

"Where's my daughter, you S.O.B.?" Noah asked, pushing past him, pulling Mariel along.

Looking dazed, Alan protested, "I don't know what you're talking about. What are you doing?"

"I'm looking for my daughter," Noah said, taking the narrow flight of stairs two at a time, Mariel keeping up with him.

Alan had managed to compose himself and hurried up the steps behind them, sputtering, "What are you talking about?"

"You know," Noah said, storming through the open apartment door and looking around the small living room. The television was tuned to MTV, and the pillows were propped on the couch in a way that indicated that Alan had been sprawled there before he answered the door.

With Mariel on his heels, Noah strode into the next room, and then into the next, looking around, finding no sign of another person in the small kitchenette or bedroom with its pullout futon.

He returned to the living room and faced Alan, who stood there wearing a bemused expression. "Where is Amber?" he demanded. "And don't pretend that you don't know who or what I'm talking about, because we read your e-mails. The ones where you pretended to be me and lured Amber Steadman to New York. Where is she?"

Alan smirked.

Noah wanted to haul off and hit him, and he would have if he wasn't so desperate to hear the answer to his question.

"I have no idea where she is," Alan said. He stepped backward and held up a hand when Noah growled and reached toward him. "Hang on, I'm not saying I didn't see her when she got to town. She thought I was you, man. She got here thinking she was going to meet her old man. So I let her think it."

"What the hell were you doing?" Mariel asked shrilly, in Alan's face, glaring at him. "Was that your idea of a joke?"

"Actually, it was," Alan said with a shrug, not appearing the least bit perturbed by her outburst. "I mean, it was her idea to come to New York. When I offered to meet her and let her stay at my place, she was into it."

"She thought you were her father," Noah bit out.

"Yeah, well, she would have found out soon enough that you were her father. I was going to surprise you with her."

Noah stared at him in disbelief.

"I was, man. I figured I would get her to New York, have some fun with her, show her around, and introduce her to you."

"What did you do with her?" Noah ground out. "Where is she?"

"She took off the day she got here," Alan said. "I swear to God, man. She got all spooked on me when she thought her old man was trying to put the moves on her. I told her I wasn't really you before I tried anything, but she didn't believe me. She thought I was lying and that it was incest or something, and she freaked out. She took off and I haven't seen her since."

"Why should I believe you?" Noah asked, looking Alan in the eye, trying to decide whether he was telling the truth.

"I don't care if you believe me. That's what happened."

"She took off."

Alan nodded.

"And you didn't go after her?"

"Why would I?"

"Because she was a teenaged girl alone in New York City," Mariel shrieked, grabbing Alan's upper arms and shaking him. "Because you betrayed her trust. What the hell is wrong with you? What kind of an animal are you?"

Alan pushed her away, cringing back. "Hey, get your girlfriend off of me, Noah. Speaking of animals, has she had her shots?"

"You're pathetic," Noah said, and slapped Alan in the face, hard. "Don't bother coming back to my place for your stuff. The locks have been changed."

"You can't do that."

"I already did. Come on, Mariel. Let's go."

Together, they left the apartment, with Alan standing there, speechless, looking after them.

"Do you believe him?" Mariel asked shakily.

Noah nodded. "I think he was telling the truth."

"So she's out on the streets somewhere," Mariel said.

"Probably traumatized, believing that her own father tried to seduce her," Noah said, his insides recoiling at the very thought of what Alan had put Amber through.

For a moment, they walked in silence, heading toward the subway.

"You have to change your locks," Mariel said.

He nodded. "I'll call a locksmith when we get home. At least I'm rid of him."

"Now all we have to do is find Amber." Mariel sighed. "How impossible is that going to be?"

"You don't want to know," Noah said wearily.

"Do you think she's all right?"

"There are hundreds of runaways here," Noah told her. "They find a way to survive."

He didn't want to tell her that the vast majority fell into drugs and prostitution along the way. But when he looked at her, he could see by the glum expression on her face that she knew exactly what he was thinking.

"Where do we start looking?"

"At the Port Authority," Noah said. "That's the bus terminal on Forty-second Street, just off Times Square. A lot of runaways congregate in that neighborhood."

"Should we go there now?"

He hesitated. They had almost reached the kosher restaurant again. Suddenly, he wanted nothing more than to sit down in a quiet place with a hot bowl of soup.

"Let's get something to eat," he suggested to Mariel. "And we'll figure out our strategy from there, okay?"

"Okay," she said easily, surprising him.

He held the door open for her, and together, they went into the small neighborhood restaurant with its savory aroma.

And for a little while, at least, they sat and ate and forgot the dark clouds that hung over them. They talked about pickles and New York and the Yankees.

When they were done and waiting on the subway platform, Noah said, "Why don't we go back to my place and get a good night's sleep, Mariel?"

He saw her hesitate.

"You can have Alan's bed," he offered, thinking that was why she looked so indecisive. "I'll change the sheets for you, and I'll move his stuff out of the room."

"That's okay," she said. "It's just that I feel like we need to keep looking for Amber. I feel guilty taking time off to rest, and to eat . . . We don't know if she has food, or a place to sleep. It just doesn't seem right."

"Mariel, stop beating yourself up over this," Noah said. "You can't carry this guilt with you. It's going to eat you alive."

She shrugged, tears glistening in her eyes again.

"What is it?" Noah asked, stepping closer to her. "Are you still thinking that none of this would have happened if we hadn't given her up? Because you have to stop doing that. You have to stop wondering what if, and accept what is."

She nodded mutely, but he could tell that she was torn inside. Only days ago, he had wanted to hurt her because of the decision she had made. Now it seemed impossible that he had ever felt that way. He wanted only to ease her pain, to make her see that what was done was done. There was no changing things, no going back.

"Mariel, we did the right thing," he said, reaching for her, pulling her into his arms. He held her against his chest, stroking her hair.

"You don't really believe that, Noah," she said. "There's a part of you that still isn't sure. And sometimes I think that that part of you still resents me for the choice I made."

"That isn't true," he protested.

"Yes, it is," she said, and pulled back to look at him as the train roared into the station, shaking the platform. "You still haven't forgiven me. You might want to, but you won't. Or maybe you can't."

He turned away, unable to maintain eye contact with her, knowing that she was right.

CHAPTER TWELVE

Mariel turned onto her side, bunching the pillow beneath her cheek, willing herself to drift off to sleep again.

But slumber refused to take over, just as it had for the past—she lifted her head and glanced at the clock—thirty-five minutes.

It was past three A.M. now. Six hours ago, she had climbed into this bed, exhausted, her body aching from the exertion of walking all over New York City. She had fallen into a deep sleep the moment her head hit the pillow, only to find herself wide awake now, in the wee hours.

Her mind just wouldn't stop working.

The unfamiliar bed and the sounds of the city didn't help. Especially the sirens. There were always sirens, she had come to realize. Some were nearby, some racing just below the window, and some off in the distance.

Here in Manhattan, sirens were as omnipresent a night sound as the cicadas were back home.

She couldn't stop thinking about Amber being out on the streets somewhere, perhaps only blocks away from where Mariel was now.

She wanted desperately to hold her daughter in her arms and tell her that she loved her—that everything was going to be all right. She wanted to bring her home to Rockton and to hell with everyone else and what they thought. So what if her secret was exposed now, fifteen years later. Bearing a child out of wedlock no longer had the stigma it had carried even as recently as a decade ago. Everybody did it these days—celebrities, royalty, regular people.

But there was more to it than just bringing Amber back to Rockton to live and shrugging off the scandal.

Mariel knew in her heart that even if she found her daughter, it was unlikely that they would spend the future under the same roof. Amber already had a mother who loved her. A mother, and a father, and they weren't Mariel and Noah.

The Steadmans deserved to know what they had discovered. Noah had told her as much on the subway ride home. But Mariel was still reluctant to have him call them to reveal what had happened. She still feared that Noah might somehow be dragged into this—that there might be suspicion that he had been involved. She couldn't bear to think that anyone would suspect him of playing a role in Amber's disappearance. She couldn't bear to think of anyone hurting Noah.

So why had she?

Every instinct she possessed told her to protect Noah. To trust him. To believe in him.

Why couldn't she allow herself to love him?

Why did she feel as though the two of them living happily ever after in Rockton was about as likely as Mariel bringing Amber home with her to live happily ever after?

Why didn't she believe in happily ever after, dammit?

How long was she going to punish herself for what she had done fifteen years ago?

She heard a muffled sound and instantly went still, listening.

There was a thump in the next room.

Her heart started pounding.

Had Alan come back?

Noah hadn't changed the locks. He had called a twenty-four-hour locksmith upon their return and was told that there was a three-day waiting list for non-emergencies. This wasn't considered an emergency.

It had to be Alan, Mariel thought, slipping silently out of bed and moving across the room to the door. She reached for the knob, telling herself that she would open the door a crack and peek into the next room to see what he was up to.

She slowly turned the knob, wincing when it clicked softly. She waited a long time before pulling it toward her, and she realized that there was silence in the next room now.

Had it been her imagination? Maybe there was nobody there.

But when she pulled the door open a crack and peered through, she saw the outline of a man in front of the living room window.

She gasped involuntarily, and he jerked toward her.

"Noah!" she said, recognizing him in the shadowy room. "You scared me!"

"You scared me, too," he said. "What are you doing up?"

"I couldn't sleep." She stepped into the living room. "I heard something, and I thought it was Alan prowling around. What are you doing?"

"I couldn't sleep either," he said, standing beside the window. Silvery moonlight spilled over the sill, illuminating him.

Mariel tried not to notice that he was bare-chested, wearing only a pair of thin cotton shorts. The night air was pleasantly cool. She felt goose bumps prickling the bare flesh that was exposed by her summer nightgown, yet she knew that they weren't a reaction to the temperature, but to Noah.

A familiar craving took hold somewhere deep inside of her as she remembered what it had been like to be held in those masculine arms.

"I keep thinking that she's out there somewhere," Noah said, looking out over the street five stories below.

Mariel came up behind him and looked over his shoulder.

Even at this hour, there were lights in the apartments across the way. Traffic zoomed by, more traffic than Main Street in Rockton had ever seen. Somewhere in the distance, there were sirens, of course, and a car alarm bleated its incessant rhythm.

Mariel wondered if she would ever get used to the commotion outside her window if she lived here.

She wondered if Amber was as thrown by it as she was.

"Do you think she's sleeping on the street somewhere?" she asked Noah.

"Maybe. Or in a shelter. There are shelters for kids like her. We'll start searching them tomorrow."

She nodded.

He turned to her. "I keep thinking about what you said earlier."

"What did I say?" she asked, though she knew, instinctively, what he meant.

"The thing you said about me still resenting you after all these years. You were right. I do still resent you for the decision that you made."

She shrugged, feeling a pang in the vicinity of her heart.

Well, what did she expect?

For him to gather her into his arms and tell her that he loved her? He had never done that, not even when it would have mattered most. When it could have made a difference.

"I'm not surprised," she said quietly. "And you certainly have a right to your feelings."

"The thing is, I don't know what to do about my feelings," he told her. "I'm wondering why it is that I can't let go of that last little bit of anger. Lord knows I've tried these past few days. But I think that I have an idea about what's holding me back."

"What's that?" she asked dully.

"You are."

She blinked. "I am? I'm holding you back?"

He nodded. "You don't want my forgiveness, Mariel. You're afraid of it."

"I am not," she said, about to take a step back, away

from him, when he turned and put his hands on her shoulders.

"You're afraid of what might take its place," he said softly.

"I'm not afraid, Noah. I just don't—"

Her words were snatched away by his mouth as he swooped down and kissed her hungrily.

"You don't what?" he asked, lifting his head, running his hands over her hips, positioning her against him so that she could feel his straining arousal against the most intimate part of her own body.

"I don't . . ."

"You don't what?" he asked, raining kisses down her throat.

She moaned, at first in protest, and then in helpless ecstasy when he pulled her nightgown over her head, tossing it aside, and she felt him suckling her breast. She squirmed in his arms, but he held her fast, his hands stroking her naked body, his gentle touch everywhere at once. They sank to the floor, and she willingly leaned back, writhing as his wet mouth moved lower, across her belly, and then lower still. She felt his tongue graze her tender flesh that yearned for him most, and she gasped at the electric sensation.

She squirmed, aching for him to do it again, a ticklish need building rapidly inside of her, and when he obliged, positioning himself between her quivering thighs, she quickly reached the brink.

"Noah," she gasped, and then she was shuddering, violently exquisite ripples coursing through her. When she thought it was over, he continued to nuzzle her, pleasuring her with his mouth and then with his hands, and finally, with his manhood. She opened herself to him, and he sank into her, breathing her name. They moved in perfect unison, panting in rhythm until they exploded together, rocking back and forth in each other's arms until the spasms subsided.

"That's what you're afraid of," he whispered softly when it was over.

"I'm not afraid of that."

"Then, what is it? What's holding you back?"

"Do we have to talk about it now?" she asked, tracing his jaw with a fingertip, her cheek resting against his chest. "Why can't we just be? Why can't we just let things happen?"

"We just did." He leaned back to look down into her eyes. "You can let go physically, Mariel. Why can't you let go with the rest of you? The part that's holding back?"

She was silent.

"It's okay," he said, pulling away from her. "I'm going to go take a shower. This is a good time to head over to the Port Authority and see what I can find out."

"It's three thirty in the morning."

"Exactly." He looked over his shoulder at her. "Are you coming with me?"

"Definitely," she said, scrambling to her feet.

"Okay." His eyes gleamed. "Come on."

"I thought you said you were going to take a shower."

"I am," he said, and repeated, "Come on. Why waste water?"

She broke into a slow grin and followed him.

* * *

The next three days passed in a blur.

A blur of seedy streets and unfamiliar faces and making love to Mariel in his apartment.

Noah didn't know whether to be grateful that she had given him this—this last chance to fulfill himself, or this last chance to try to capture her heart, or whatever it was that she had given him. All he knew was that they seemed to have reached an understanding. As long as they were in this state of limbo, searching for their daughter on the streets of New York, they would be together, physically. In every way.

He was free to put his arm around her as they sat together on the subway, or to hold her hand as they walked down the street, or to start kissing her the moment he had closed the apartment door behind them in the twilight of each day.

They were sleeping together in his bed, making love until they fell asleep in each other's arms, exhausted, and then waking in the wee hours to hit the streets again. The early morning hours were the most rewarding time they searched, because it was then that the streets were alive with the nocturnal inhabitants who saw things and knew things that escaped the others—the commuters, the old-timers, the mothers, the nannies, the businessmen.

With Mariel in tow, Noah talked to prostitutes and pimps, to drug dealers and undercover cops and homeless people and those who tried to help them. They had printed out Amber's photograph and carried it everywhere they went, showing it to everyone they met. A few times, she was recognized by somebody they questioned, but those sightings never led to anything concrete. Several people vaguely said that they had seen her around; that it had been recently; that she hadn't been turning tricks or dazed on drugs.

Noah and Mariel were grateful for that information, but they yearned for something more concrete.

They got it at dusk on Saturday, when, on Eleventh Avenue, they approached two multipierced, tattooed girls who couldn't have been older than fourteen or fifteen. Both wore too much make-up and skirts that in another neighborhood might have been considered fashionable, but here only pegged them as hookers.

Teenaged hookers, probably runaways, Noah thought, looking into their surprisingly focused eyes. He had gotten used to seeing the bleary expressions of junkies, and he immediately recognized that these two kids were straight. That they weren't selling themselves to support a drug habit was somehow more unsettling than it would have been if they were, he thought illogically.

"Whassup?" the smaller of the two girls asked, looking curiously from Noah to Mariel. Her hair was blond and unevenly shorn—again, in a style that would have been trendy anywhere else, but was a whole different story here on Eleventh Avenue.

"We were wondering if you've seen this girl," Mariel said, showing her the picture of Amber.

They both leaned in to look at it, then at each other.

"You've seen her." It was a statement, not a question, and Noah tried hard to keep the nervous anticipation from his voice. He had spoken to enough skittish street kids these past few days to sense that these two girls knew something, and the last thing he wanted was to scare them off.

"Yeah, we've seen her," said the other girl, a pretty mulatto with dark, flashing eyes. "That's Amber."

Noah felt Mariel stir beside him, and he reached out to squeeze her hand, warning her to play it cool.

"Any idea where we could find her?"

"She hangs down in the park with a bunch of friends," the blonde said.

"Central Park?" Mariel asked urgently.

Noah nudged her, reminding her to hold back. She had made a mistake. Central Park was uptown from here. They wouldn't have said "down."

The girls looked at each other.

The rapport was broken.

"Whatever," the blonde said, and Noah's hopes slid.

"Any idea who her friends are?" he asked casually, to keep the conversation going.

"Just some guys. They keep the pimps away from her. She's not into that."

Noah felt his knees go weak with relief at those words.

"Who are these friends?" Mariel asked, and he could hear the quiver of excitement in her voice. He willed her not to ask too many questions or put her foot into her mouth again. They had to tread carefully.

The darker girl shrugged. "Just kids like her."

"You mean, other runaways?" Noah asked.

"Pretty much," the girl said.

"Do any of them have names?" Noah asked lightly.

"Yeah, there's Blinky and—"

The blonde nudged the darker girl into abrupt silence, giving her a look.

"Listen, we're just concerned about Amber's well-being," Noah said. "You don't have to worry about what you tell us."

"Yeah, right," the blonde said. "You're her parents, right?"

Noah and Mariel looked at each other, then shook their heads.

"Uh huh, sure. She looks just like you."

"Look, can you just tell us which park?" Noah asked. "Washington Square, or—"

"Nope, we've got to go now. See ya."

With that, the two girls took off, leaving Noah and Mariel to stare helplessly after them.

Or maybe not so helplessly, Noah realized.

"Let's go," he said abruptly, and started walking east.

"But where are we going? This city must have dozens of parks."

"Not all of them are downtown."

"How do you know it's downtown?"

"They said, 'down in the park,' remember? I'm thinking it could be Washington Square, or Tompkins Square—a lot of kids hang out there. And there are others. Union Square. Madison Square . . ."

"Yeah, and now we have a name to go on," Mariel said, keeping up breathlessly with his long strides. "Blinky."

He laughed. "Blinky. There can't be too many guys named Blinky around, even in this crazy city. I have a good feeling about this, Mariel."

She stopped walking and clutched his arm. "You mean you feel like we're going to find her?"

He thought about it, then nodded. "Maybe not tonight. But soon."

"Do you think it's time to call the police?" Mariel asked slowly, searching his eyes.

He considered that. He had thought that they should call the police, and the Steadmans, long ago, but she wouldn't let him. One more night wouldn't make a difference, he told himself.

"We'll call tomorrow," he said aloud. "If we don't find her, we'll call tomorrow. And we'll tell them what we know. Okay?"

"Okay."

Then, in silent contemplation of what might happen when they called, they walked toward the subway.

It was almost midnight when they reached Tompkins Square park. They had spent hours in the other parks Noah had mentioned, especially Washington Square, because it was particularly busy on this warm June night, filled with dog walkers and street musicians and crowds of kids hanging out. They asked everyone they saw whether they had ever heard of anyone named Blinky, and whether they had ever seen Amber. So far, they had run up against another brick wall.

They had decided that Tompkins Square would be their last effort tonight. Mariel was exhausted and could tell that Noah felt the same way. He kept yawning, and he was limping thanks to a blister on his left heel.

She, too, had blisters, and she ached all over. There was a hollow pit in her stomach, and she vaguely knew that it had been too long since they had last eaten; she couldn't remember when or where it had been.

This park wasn't far from Noah's apartment, she thought as they crossed First Avenue to get to it. They could spend an hour or so talking to people here, and then they would be back in the apartment. Back in each other's arms.

She had come to relish the moments they spent alone

together, now allowing herself to give in to the intense sensual need she had instinctively suppressed since she had first seen him a week ago tonight.

Had it only been that long ago?

In a sense, their time at the Sweet Briar Inn now seemed as though it was as ancient as their college affair. Both had been marked by furtive, desperate, guilt-tainted encounters, drastically unlike what they now shared. When they were together now there was nothing held back; they were living in the moment, savoring each other without contemplating the past or the future.

Mariel wouldn't allow herself to look beyond this stolen interlude.

And now that they were fairly certain that Amber was going to be all right, wherever she was, it was almost tempting to slow the pace of their search. To make it last, because it was all they had. When it was over, they were over.

"Stay close," Noah said, tucking her arm beneath his as they walked into the park.

The mood here was faintly menacing, she thought as they headed along the path, approaching a group of kids gathered on a bench beneath a tall stand of trees. There were plenty of cops patrolling the streets nearby, but here in the park, there was a sense of isolation.

Mariel glanced at the cluster of teenagers as they walked toward them. They had stopped their conversation and had turned toward the interlopers, all of them watchful and silent. She scanned the faces, and then her heart went still.

Noah stopped short, and she knew that he, too, had seen it.

Amber's face.

She was there, in front of them, her features a mask of apprehension. Not because she sensed who they were, Mariel realized, but simply because she trusted no one. She was living on the streets. She feared for her safety.

For her life.

She couldn't know that the two strangers who approached had given her that life . . . .

Or that they intended to save it.

A lump rose in Mariel's throat, and she quivered, fighting back the emotion that threatened to spill over as she stared into her daughter's eyes—eyes that were familiar, yet not. These were Mariel's own eyes, and they were set in a face that belonged to someone else. They were no longer frozen in a photograph, but alive with suspicion, and focused on Mariel herself.

"Don't," Noah said in a low voice, as though he sensed that Mariel was about to lose control.

She didn't know what was going to happen—whether she was going to burst into tears, or rush forward and grab her daughter, or even drop to the ground in a faint. But whatever her reaction was going to be, she fought it off, heeding Noah's warning, understanding that this was the moment of truth. She couldn't make the wrong move now, when they had found her at last.

"What's up?" Noah called casually, walking toward them.

They mumbled various greetings, all of them shifting their gazes from Noah to Mariel, clearly sensing that something was up.

"Are you cops?" one of the boys asked.

They shook their heads. Mariel saw that the boy's cheeks were pitted with acne and that he wore braces. What had led this boy—somebody's child, somebody's son—to be here, in a deserted park in New York City in the middle of the night?

What were any of them doing here?

She turned her attention back to Amber, whose gaze still hadn't wavered.

She was staring at Mariel and Noah.

Staring at them intently.

And as she gaped, an expression of wonder and disbelief began to creep over her face.

She knows, Mariel realized, her attention now focused completely on her daughter.

"Are you Amber?" Noah asked gently, turning toward her.

She nodded mutely.

"I'm Noah," he said. "And this is Mariel."

The girl didn't speak.

She didn't move.

"We've been trying to find you for a long time," Mariel said, her voice trembling. "You have no idea, Amber. . . ."

With a sob, the girl suddenly moved forward, rushing toward her.

Mariel opened her arms, and then, for the second time in her life, she embraced her daughter and wished for the impossible.

That she would never have to let her go.

CHAPTER THIRTEEN

"Do you want some more soup?" Noah asked Amber, watching her set her mug carefully on the coffee table.

She shook her head. He saw her steal a glance at Mariel, who sat beside her on the couch, her hands folded in her lap. They were trembling still, he saw, though it had been almost an hour since they had found Amber in the park.

"More crackers?" Noah offered, picking up the box of saltines he had left on the table and waving it toward her.

"No, thank you," she said politely. She had consistently used good manners, and in some remote part of his consciousness, Noah acknowledged that her parents had raised her well.

"Did you eat enough, then? Because I have other stuff. Uh, granola bars and maybe some black olives. . . ."
He was chattering, needing to fill the silence.

Why didn't Mariel feel the need to do the same? She had barely said a word since they had arrived back here.

All she had done was sit on the couch beside Amber, almost protectively, while Noah bustled around heating canned chicken noodle soup and pouring orange juice—the only beverage in his bachelor fridge besides beer—and generally making himself nervous.

Why wasn't Mariel nervous?

He glanced again at her shaking hands and acknowledged that she obviously was. Yet her anxiety didn't manifest itself as his did.

Bustling in the tiny kitchen, he had cut his finger on the edge of the soup can, and he had clumsily toppled the first glass of orange juice all over the counter.

Now he sat in the uncomfortable fake Stickley chair across from the couch and regarded his daughter, trying not to be obvious about it.

But he couldn't help looking. She was a part of him, this human being. A part of him and Mariel. She had his mouth, Mariel's eyes; his coloring, and Mariel's faint dusting of freckles across her nose. She was a pretty girl, he could tell, despite the gaunt exhaustion that haunted her face. She was very thin, too, and he wondered how much of it was hereditary, and how much was due to living on the streets for more than a week.

She wore a pair of denim cutoffs and a grungy-looking T-shirt, and her feet were filthy in a pair of Teyva sandals.

"You can take a shower if you want," he said without thinking, and his voice was startling to his own ears.

"Oh . . . thank you," she said awkwardly. She looked faintly embarrassed, glancing down at her filthy clothes and skin.

"Whenever you want to," Mariel spoke up. "It doesn't

have to be now. I mean, we can talk first. Or . . . later. If you want to.''

Amber shrugged.

What was there to say? Noah wondered. During the walk to his apartment, he and Mariel had explained to her what had happened with Alan. He had been apologetic, and she had acted as though she understood. She had pretended to shrug it off, even making a faint joke about it, but he knew she was still spooked by the whole thing; and he didn't blame her.

He was almost surprised that she had come with them when they had asked her to come back to his apartment.

But then, what other choice did she have? To hang around in the park all night with a bunch of street waifs who looked like a ragtag cast of extras from *Les Miserables?* The hunger in Amber's eyes was plain to see when she looked at Noah and Mariel and accepted their invitation.

As the three of them walked away, one of her friends called after her, ''Hey, who are they, anyway?''

''They're my parents,'' Amber had replied over her shoulder. Then, to Noah and Mariel, she had said, ''You are, aren't you?''

Mariel had answered softly in the affirmative, but Noah had only nodded, unable to find his voice. Instead, too choked up for words, he had put an arm around her shoulders and kept it there all the way home.

Now, with the topic of Alan settled, there was something else they had to discuss. It couldn't be put off any longer.

''Amber,'' he said hesitantly, ''we were in touch with your parents about a week ago, and they were frantic.

They were going crazy looking for you, worried out of their minds.''

"They were?" She perked up at that, sitting up straighter on the couch. "How do you know? What did they say?"

"That they love you very much and they want you to come home."

"Were they together?" Amber asked in a tone that betrayed her true purpose for staying in New York even after the horrible experience with Alan. Clearly, Noah realized, she was hoping that if she remained missing, she could bring her mother and father back together.

"They were together when we visited them," Mariel said reluctantly, choosing her words carefully, and Noah sensed that she, too, was aware of Amber's motive. "But I do know that they had separated, and I don't know whether they're back together now or not."

"The separation is so stupid," Amber lashed out. "I don't know why they had to get so carried away. Just because Mom wants to go back to work now that I'm in high school, and Daddy doesn't think she should . . . It's such a stupid fight. They have it all the time. Finally, he said that if she was going to work, then she didn't need him to support her, and he would move out. And she said fine."

Her voice was tinged with anger and hurt, and she looked from Noah to Mariel, as though seeking support.

Noah wanted to tell her that her parents' argument probably went much deeper than that single issue. That the separation was undoubtedly the product of months or even years of discontent, and soul searching.

Yet he didn't want to be the one to dash her hopes. After all, he thought optimistically, it was possible her plan had worked. Carl Steadman had been in the house when he and Mariel had shown up there last Sunday morning.

"Maybe they've worked things out," he said. "Sometimes people who love each other get carried away, like you said. But then they realize that they can't live without each other, and they find a way to make each other happy."

"And sometimes," Mariel said, her voice strained, "they realize that they can't live with each other even though they really care about each other, and they have to go their separate ways."

Noah couldn't look at her. He knew she wasn't just talking about the Steadmans. His hands clenched the arms of the chair as he said, "Amber, the point is, your parents love you very much. There's no doubt about that. Whatever happens with their marriage, they're both going to be there for you."

"How do you know? You're a stranger." Amber's tone was derisive. For the first time, she sounded like a resentful adolescent.

And she had every right to feel that way.

Yet he felt as though she had hit him in the gut with a two-by-four.

Mariel recovered first. "You're right," she said quietly. "Noah is a stranger, and so am I. But that doesn't mean that we haven't thought about you every day of our lives since the day you were born."

"You didn't even answer my e-mail," Amber said accusingly, turning on her. "If you care so much, why didn't you at least write back to me?"

"I wanted to," Mariel said, and Noah saw her eyes glistening. He wanted to go to her, and comfort her, but he stayed where he was. The room was too charged with emotion; he was afraid that if he moved, he would crumple. It was all he could do to keep his composure.

"Instead of writing back to you, Amber, I went to visit you. It took me a few weeks to make the arrangements— I live in Missouri," she added. "Did you know that? A small town in Missouri, called Rockton."

"We went to Missouri once," Amber offered, some of the sullenness dissipated.

Mariel, looking startled, seized the tidbit of information. "Really? When? What did you do?"

"We went to St. Louis with Daddy on business two summers ago, and we went to Six Flags Amusement Park."

"That's . . . that's a lot of fun," Mariel murmured.

Noah knew what she was thinking: how strange it was that the daughter she had been wondering about for fifteen years had been so close to her, physically, and she hadn't even been aware of it.

"And you live here," Amber said, turning her attention to Noah. "I've never been to New York—until now. And I've seen pretty much all of it. Well, maybe not everything."

"Have you been to the top of the Empire State Building?" Mariel asked brightly. "Because Noah took me up there a few nights ago. It's incredibly . . . cool." The last word was forced, as though she had tried and failed to search for a word Amber might use. Here she was, Noah thought, doing what every mother had done in every generation, trying to relate to an adolescent daughter, doing her best to establish a bond through the use of what was undoubtedly outdated slang.

At least Amber didn't roll her eyes. 'What are you doing

here in New York?" she asked Mariel, as though something had just dawned on her. "Are you two . . . ?"

"We're not together, no," Noah said quickly, just in case she was thinking that the three of them could somehow be a family. "Mariel went to Valley Falls to meet you, and when she found out you were missing, she called me."

"So you guys never got married?"

Again, Noah felt as though she was swinging that two-by-four in a direct hit.

"Not to each other," Mariel told Amber, and hastily added, "but we're friends. We became friends again while we were looking for you."

Noah said nothing.

"You've been looking for me?" Amber contemplated that. "I guess that's why you were in Tompkins Square, huh? I mean, it's not the kind of place where you go for a stroll after dark unless you're looking for someone."

"Or looking for trouble," Noah said.

Amber flashed him a wry smile. "Yeah, some pretty skeevy things go down in this city after dark."

"You were lucky," Mariel said somberly. "You know that, don't you? Terrible things happen to girls like you on the streets, Amber. You could have been—"

"Don't remind me," Amber cut in. "I know. But it was okay. I had friends who looked out for me."

"And now I guess your adventure is over. I'm sure you've had enough," Mariel said, looking at Noah in a silent cue.

"It's time to call your parents," Noah said, standing and walking toward the phone on the desk.

"No!" Amber said sharply. "Not yet!"

"Why not?" He turned and looked back at her. "We

have to let them know you're all right, Amber. They've been through hell. They want you back home again, where you belong."

"But ... who says that's where I belong? In *their* home."

"We say it," Mariel told her firmly. Noah knew it was wrenching for her, but her expression betrayed only resolute assuredness.

"It's not just their home," Noah pointed out. "It's your home, too. That was obvious when we were there."

Amber glowered.

"We chose the Steadmans from lots of other people who wanted to give you a home," Mariel told her. "We knew they were right for you. It's time for you to go back to them."

"They're not even there," Amber said. "Not together, anyway. Now I'm going to be some kid whose parents are divorced. It's bad enough being some kid who was adopted."

Hearing her words, Noah froze. He didn't dare look at Mariel.

"It was bad?" Mariel asked softly after a long moment. "Being adopted?"

"Not so bad," Amber said in a small voice. "Not until they split up. Then it felt like I didn't belong anywhere."

Mariel put her arms around her. Noah walked over to them and sat on Amber's other side, reaching out to stroke her silky hair as she buried her head on Mariel's shoulder and sobbed. Mariel was sobbing, too, silently.

"I'm sorry," she wept into Amber's hair. "I'm so sorry. I never meant to hurt you. I only wanted what was best for you. And you," she said, turning her ravaged gaze on Noah. "I only wanted what was best for both of you."

And for you, he added silently, turning away. Because it was easier to believe that Mariel had acted selfishly.

That way, he couldn't allow himself . . .

To love her.

No, he thought, pushing that thought away as emotion welled within him. Not love. This had never been about love. It was about responsibility, and trust, and—

"I had just turned eighteen," Mariel said tearfully, turning a beseeching gaze on Amber. "I wasn't much older than you are, Amber. And I was convinced that I didn't know anything about being a parent. You didn't deserve me. You deserved so much better. The Steadmans . . . they were better. She was—she was like my own mother. Trying for so many years to have a child. When you try for that long, and you yearn for it so badly, you're the kind of mother . . . well, the kind of mother who will treasure her child."

Amber was crying, too, her shoulders quaking as she fumbled blindly for the napkin on the table beside her empty soup bowl. Noah handed it to her, and she blew her nose and wiped her eyes.

"When did they tell you that you were adopted?" Noah asked Amber hoarsely, needing to know more. Needing to know that she hadn't been tormented by the adoption. That it really had been okay.

"They never told me," Amber said.

Horrified, he started to ask her how she found out. Had she stumbled across the adoption papers?

Then, before he could speak, she clarified, "I mean, I guess it was always just common knowledge in our household. I always knew that I grew in somebody else's tummy because Mom couldn't grow me in her own. They said that I was special, and that they wanted me so badly they had to wait for years to have me. Just like you said."

Mariel nodded, wiping her eyes on the sleeve of her T-shirt. "That's the truth, Amber. They had wanted a baby for so long, and when they found out they were getting you, they were ecstatic. The adoption case worker told me that they rushed right out and bought a roomful of nursery furniture, and an entire baby wardrobe, and the biggest teddy bear they could find."

"Dunbar," Amber said solemnly. "That's what I used to call him. It was how I pronounced 'teddy bear.' I still have him in my room, and he is pretty big."

There was a wistful note in her voice.

Noah knew that it was time to call the Steadmans. They couldn't put it off any longer. It wasn't fair. They deserved to know.

He got up and picked up the cordless phone and walked back over to the couch. Amber, still in Mariel's embrace, looked at him.

"Do you want to call?" he asked. "Or should I?"

"I will," she said in a small voice, and took the phone. They watched her dial.

She stood up and said, "Can I talk to them in the other room? Just, you know, so that I won't feel . . ."

"Go ahead," Noah told her.

She walked toward the hall carrying the phone.

He looked at his watch. It was past midnight. He knew what they would think when the phone rang at this hour. Maybe they should have waited until morning to call, if only to spare her parents the heart-stopping moment of fear.

"Daddy?" Amber asked, and her voice broke. "You're there? You're at home?"

And then she was sobbing, taking the phone into the bathroom and closing the door behind her.

Noah looked at Mariel.

She stared back at him.

"So," she said softly, after a minute. "It's over."

He nodded. "It's over."

And he knew that they weren't talking about the search for their daughter.

The three of them passed the next four hours in the living room, on the couch. Noah made coffee, and even Amber drank some, saying that she wanted to be awake when her parents arrived.

"You should sleep, though," Mariel told her, worried about her exhaustion. "They won't be here for a long time."

"I can't sleep now," Amber said, stifling a yawn. "When I finally do get into bed, I'm going to be out for a lot longer than a few hours."

Amber sat between Noah and Mariel on the couch, and they drank their coffee, and they talked about their lives. Mostly, Amber talked. Now that she had spoken to her parents, she seemed to have come alive.

When she had emerged from the bathroom after a five-minute conversation, and after relaying directions, courtesy of Noah, she had excitedly told Noah and Mariel what they already knew: that her father had answered the phone.

He had told Amber that he was staying at home with her mother and had been ever since she disappeared.

Amber asked him if it meant he was home to stay, but he wouldn't confirm or deny that.

It didn't seem to bother her. It was apparently enough, for now, to know that there was still hope for her parents' marriage. The two of them were coming together to New York City. They had refused to wait until morning, but had told Amber that they would be on the road as soon as they got dressed.

Amber had taken a shower and washed her hair, and though she still looked haggard, it was a vast improvement. Her hair fell in soft, sweet-scented waves past her shouders. She wore a pair of Mariel's shorts and one of her polo shirts, and the clothes fit perfectly. Mariel had told her to keep them.

She couldn't help wistfully imagining what it would be like if she had a daughter who borrowed her clothes—a daughter she could shop with, a daughter whose hair she could brush and braid, a daughter she could teach to shave her legs and put on make-up and whatever else it was that mothers shared with their daughters. . . .

Whatever else Mariel had missed, all these years apart from Amber.

As Amber chattered, telling Noah and Mariel what her life had been like, Mariel clung to every detail. Her daughter spoke of things they had already learned: that her best friends were Sherry and Nicole, that she liked to surf the Net, that she had played the lead in the school musical *Hello, Dolly*.

She told them things Mariel had suspected, based on clues she had gleaned from that fleeting visit to the Steadmans' home: that she played the piano, and that she loved to read, especially the Harry Potter series.

There was so much more.

Amber had broken her right arm when she was seven and fell off the monkey bars at school, and her parents had spoon fed her while she was in the hospital so she wouldn't have to move it.

For Amber's tenth birthday, her parents had given her a surprise pool party, inviting ten of her girlfriends. The food was all red, white, and blue in honor of the patriotic date—pizza and Hawaiian punch and blueberry pie with vanilla ice cream.

When Amber was in seventh grade, the school bully had inexplicably threatened to beat her up, and her father had walked her to school every morning, making himself late for his own job, for the entire year.

There were countless stories of a childhood that was largely unremarkable, and for the very small-town normalcy of her daughter's life, Mariel was grateful.

There was a tremendous amount of evidence that Amber had been cherished.

Mariel knew, beyond a shadow of a doubt, that she had been wise to choose the Steadmans. Now, at last, she was able to banish any last shred of concern. Whatever their marital difficulties, the Steadmans had been the kind of parents she and Noah could never have been. Not back then, at least.

As for now . . .

But now didn't matter. Now wasn't really *now;* now was over. It had, in these last hours together, become *then,* a part of the past, along with everything else they had ever shared.

She would be catching the first flight back home as soon as Amber left with her parents.

There was no reason to prolong her leaving. The

longer she dragged out this good-bye, the more it would
hurt.

"Can I visit you both again?" Amber asked suddenly.

Mariel faltered. "If your parents think it would be a
good idea, then I would like that, Amber."

"I don't think they'd mind." Amber looked at her
watch, then at the door. "Don't you think they should
be here by now?"

"It's a long drive," Mariel said, reaching out to brush
back a strand of hair that had fallen across Amber's
cheek.

"You don't think something could have happened to
them?" Amber asked worriedly.

"No, I'm sure they'll be buzzing the door any minute
now," Noah reassured her.

Mariel realized that it was the first time he had spoken
in a while. She looked past Amber, and her gaze collided
with Noah's, but only momentarily. He stood abruptly
and picked up his coffee mug.

"I need a refill," he announced. "Does anybody else
want more?"

"I'll have some," Amber said.

"I hope you're not developing a bad habit," Noah
teased. "Caffeine is addictive, you know."

"Hey, cut me a break," she said lightheartedly. "I
never drink coffee at home. Normally I can't stand the
stuff."

"Well, you'd better go easy on it," Noah said, "or
you'll stunt your growth, and the next thing you know,
you'll be—"

His words were cut off by a loud buzz.

Amber bolted off the couch. "That's them!"

Mariel's heart sank.

She had known this was coming. She had to accept it . . . along with everything that would follow.

Numb, she watched Noah press the button that allowed Amber's parents to enter the building. Then she rose to stand beside him at the door, behind Amber, who peered out into the hallway anxiously.

When hurried footsteps sounded on the last flight of stairs, Amber flew out the door and rushed down the hall.

Mariel watched through tear-filled eyes as her daughter hurtled herself into the arms of her parents.

She felt a hand on her shoulder and turned to see Noah looking down at her, his own eyes brimming with emotion. "It'll be okay," he said softly.

She nodded.

How many times had they said just that?

These past few days . . .

And fifteen years ago, when she was pregnant and terrified, needing to believe that she was making the right choice. Even in labor, when she had writhed in agony and Noah held her hand for hours upon hours, reassuring her whenever she cried out in anguish. He had known that her torture was as much emotional as it was physical, and she had known that he shared that part of the burden. That his words were meant to comfort her as much as himself.

It'll be okay.

But it hadn't been okay.

It had never been okay, until now.

Now, at last, as she watched the three Steadmans tearfully embrace in the dimly lit stairwell, she knew that this much, at least, really was okay.

She and Noah had created a family.

It just hadn't been theirs.

Carl Steadman turned toward them first, his arms wrapped around Amber. "Thank you," he said hoarsely. "I don't know how to thank you. Both of you. You've given us our daughter for the second time in our lives."

Mariel tried, and failed, to find the right words. All she could do was smile through her tears and know that beside her, Noah was doing the same.

When the Steadmans left Noah's apartment, the sun was rising over Manhattan.

He closed the door behind them and went to the window. If he craned his neck, he could see past the towering buildings that lined the opposite side of the block. He could see the sky streaked with pink and gold, and he could tell that it was going to be a beautiful day.

Behind him, there was a clinking sound as Mariel gathered the five coffee cups from the table and carried them to the kitchen. He heard her running water in the sink.

He didn't turn around, and he didn't go to help her.

When the Steadmans were here, he could allow himself to be distracted.

He could make awkward conversation, and he could watch them fuss over their daughter.

Of course, Amber had sat between them on the couch, in the exact spot where she had earlier sat between Noah and Mariel.

He had been conscious of the older couple glancing around his sorry excuse for a home, had felt them weighing it against their own house back in Valley Falls.

Or maybe it was just his imagination.

Maybe he was the only one making a comparison.

They had stayed only a half an hour or so, long enough to assure themselves that Amber was all right, and to drink a cup of coffee to refuel themselves for the road, and to apologize for suspecting that Noah and Mariel had had anything to do with their daughter's disappearance.

"It's all right," Mariel had told them. "We would probably have done the same thing, in your shoes."

And Noah found himself desperately wishing that he *was* in their shoes as they ushered their daughter out the door, with a promise to keep in touch.

Amber's hug still lingered on his shoulders, along with the echo of her parting, whispered words, "Please let me be in your life. Please stay in touch. I want to see you again."

He had nodded.

And he would see her again.

It was Mariel he wouldn't see.

Now that they were alone together, the inevitable loomed.

He heard her footsteps behind him, returning to the living room.

"I guess I should go straight to the airport," she said.

There.

It was finished.

He refused to allow himself to flinch at her words. He simply nodded, still staring out the window at the sky, where a lone bird soared above the buildings.

"I'll take a shower and change my clothes," she said.

He nodded again.

She seemed to be hesitating in the doorway behind him.

He was irritated.

What did she want him to say?

What did she want him to do?

Try to stop her?

Well, he wouldn't. He had tried that already. Twice, in fact.

Twice, he had begged her to spend her life with him.

Twice, she had refused.

He had had enough.

This time, he would let her go.

He heard her footsteps retreat, and then the bathroom door closed quietly behind her.

Mariel felt as though she was living a recurring nightmare as she stood on the street beside Noah, her luggage at her feet.

His arm was raised as he faced the traffic whizzing down Broadway. He was hailing a cab for her.

He was going to let her leave.

Back in the apartment, she had been sure that he was going to try to stop her again.

And she had known that if he did, if he said the slightest thing to convince her, she would stay.

Watching Amber walk out of their lives had been painful. But this . . .

This was torture.

Amber didn't belong with them. She was a beautiful kid, and now that Mariel had found her, she would be as much a part of her life as the Steadmans—and Amber—desired.

But she wasn't really Mariel's daughter. Not anymore. She never had been.

A part of her ached for the loss, yet another part of her was strangely content.

For, in those brief hours with the child she had borne and given up, she had discovered something about herself.

She had discovered a well of maternal longing that she hadn't known was there. At least, not in the sense that she now comprehended it.

For years, missing her daughter, she had thought that the longing stemmed from guilt, and that it was connected only to the child she had lost.

Now, she had realized that there was more to it. That she might actually have what it took to be a mother. That she wanted to have another baby, a baby she would keep and nurture and raise, just as her own mother had.

Yes, she longed for another baby.

For a family to call her own.

She longed for Noah, and for his child. A child they would bring into the world together, consciously, lovingly.

But it was too late for such dreams.

She was leaving, and he was going to let her go.

Unless . . .

Unless she told him how she was feeling.

But even then, he might not believe her.

He might reject her.

If only she knew that he wouldn't.

If only she knew that he loved her.

But he had never said anything about love. All he had said was—

"Taxi!" he shouted, waving his hand wildly as a cab careened in their direction.

For a rash, hopeful moment she believed that it was going to go on by.

She saw that the middle light on the dome that protruded from the cab's roof was lit. She had learned enough about Manhattan cabs these past few days to understand what it meant: the cab was available, and the driver would stop for her.

And even if by chance he didn't, another cab would be along behind it. There was always another cab, in Manhattan. Always somebody willing to take you wherever you wanted to go. . . .

And wherever you didn't.

She was going to the airport, she reminded herself fiercely. She was going to fly back to Missouri. It was the right thing to do, because Noah hadn't asked her to stay.

And he hadn't offered to go with her.

Not for the right reasons.

Sure enough, the cab driver stopped.

Mariel watched, almost in a daze, as he popped the trunk.

Noah picked up her luggage and put it inside.

He opened the back door for her.

The sequence was unfolding just as it had on Wednesday morning.

She could let it happen. . . .

Or she could stop it.

She looked up into Noah's tired, shadowed eyes, hoping to see something there that would tell her what to do.

She swallowed hard.

"I don't want to drag this out," she said, her voice strained.

He nodded. "There's no need. Just go, Mariel. Go. You have to."

She did.

She had to go.

She turned and blindly got into the backseat.

Noah slammed the door closed after her.

"Where to?" the driver asked.

She couldn't speak.

"Where to?"

She wanted to tell him to forget it. That she wasn't going anywhere.

She opened her mouth. Found her voice.

"La Guardia," was all she said.

Back in his apartment, Noah walked from room to room, his shoes sounding hollow on the bare floors, echoing through the emptiness.

This was his home.

This was his life.

Incredulous, he stood again in the living room window, looking out at the street below, shocked that it had come to this.

He was alone now, in this apartment, in this city, in this world.

Even at this early hour on a summer Sunday, people and traffic rushed by. Everybody had someplace to go. Everybody had someplace they belonged.

Somewhere uptown, Kelly was lying in her king-sized bed, maybe alone, maybe not.

In Queens, Noah's mother was probably getting ready for morning mass, and afterward, she would go for coffee with some of the neighborhood women.

His friends were with their wives, some of them with their children, too—perhaps planning a lazy day in the park or at the beach.

Somewhere on a highway leading out of the city, Amber rode with her parents, heading home.

Just as Mariel was heading home.

For a moment, as he had looked at her beside the open door of the cab, Noah had almost thought she was going to waver. If she had—if she had shown the slightest hesitation—he would have asked her to stay.

Or he would have offered to go with her.

Anything, just so that they could be together.

But she hadn't hesitated.

She had gotten into the cab, and she had ridden out of his life, and she hadn't looked back.

He knew she hadn't, because he had watched her, standing on the street until the cab whirled around a distant corner and was gone.

Now he was alone.

He could pick up the pieces and get on with his life . . . .

Or he could go after her, dammit.

He froze at the thought, willing it away. . . .

And then allowing himself to embrace it.

He could go after her.

Yes.

He knew enough about baseball—and about life— to know that two strikes didn't mean that you were out.

There was one last chance waiting for him, and he would be a fool not to take it.

* * *

Clutching a bouquet of red roses he had hurriedly bought on the street outside of his apartment, Noah strode through the terminal at La Guardia. He stopped walking only long enough to check what gate her flight was scheduled to depart from before heading to the security checkpoint.

"Do you have a ticket, sir?" a female uniformed officer asked, stopping him before he could walk through the metal detector.

"No, I'm just seeing someone off. . . ." *Or, with any luck, convincing her not to go.*

"I'm sorry, sir, only passengers holding tickets can proceed past this point."

He opened his mouth to argue. Then he realized it was useless. That was the rule. They weren't going to let him break it no matter what he said. He would only be wasting time.

He glanced at his watch.

Her flight didn't depart for another twenty minutes.

If he hurried, he could make it.

He turned around and rushed back to the ticket counter, where a long line snaked through the velvet-rope concourse.

Distressed, he took his place at the end of it.

It moved faster than he had hoped.

He repeatedly checked his watch for the next fifteen minutes. At last, it was his turn to speak to the ticket agent.

"I need a seat on the seven thirty-five flight to St. Louis, please," he said, plunking his Visa card on the counter. Never mind that it was almost maxed out. With any luck, there was enough remaining credit to charge a plane ticket.

"That flight is leaving on time. It's already boarded. You have only a few minutes to catch it."

"I know."

"Round-trip or one-way?" the agent asked, smiling slightly as she noticed the bouquet of roses.

"One-way," he said decisively.

He was going to convince her that they belonged together. He wasn't going to give up until she believed it. Until she agreed to spend the rest of her life in his arms.

The ticket agent efficiently pressed some keys on her computer terminal, and looked from the screen to him.

"The round-trip fare is two hundred and thirty dollars cheaper."

"One-way," he repeated, his jaw clenched.

He wasn't coming back here. He wasn't going to take no for an answer. Who cared if he had to abandon his rent-controlled apartment and his half-written screenplays and his shabby furniture and a wardrobe that was meant for a job he no longer had?

"I'd recommend that you buy the round-trip ticket," the agent offered in a conspiratorial tone. "It's much less expensive to do it that way. It doesn't mean that you have to—"

"I'm not coming back," he said firmly. "One-way, please."

She shrugged and picked up his Visa.

Moments later, he clutched a boarding pass in one hand and the roses in the other, dashing toward the gate.

He arrived just as the final boarding call was announced.

"I'm on this flight," he said breathlessly, dashing to the attendant beside the open jetway.

"You just made it," the man said, and ripped the stub from his boarding pass. "Go ahead."

Noah raced down the jetway and onto the plane, barely acknowledging the three flight attendants who greeted him as they prepared the galley.

His seat was in the last row. He stood in the front of the plane, his eyes scanning the rows of seats, searching for Mariel. He would beg whoever was seated beside her to switch with him, and if they resisted, he would pay them, for crying out loud. He couldn't wait an entire three hours to tell Mariel all that was in his heart.

"Sir, you'll have to be seated," a flight attendant said, coming up behind him. "We're about to push back."

In numb horror, he realized that Mariel wasn't on the flight.

What the hell . . . ?

Had he gotten on the wrong plane?

"Does this flight go to St. Louis?" he asked the attendant, his mind whirling in confusion.

"Yes," she said with a pleasant nod. "Sir, if you'll just—"

"I'm sorry," he said abruptly. "I'm on the wrong plane. I have to get off."

She gaped at him. "But, sir—"

"I'm not going to St. Louis," he called over his shoulder, fleeing the plane just as two airline workers below flicked a switch on the jetway.

He dashed through it as it folded back toward the terminal, racing by the shocked-looking attendants at the gate.

"Wrong flight," he called over his shoulder.

He hurried to a departures screen and scanned the list of outgoing flights.

The one he had been on was the only one headed for St. Louis this morning. There was another to Kansas City—

Where would she be going?

His thoughts were muddled as he tried to sort things out, struggling to remember whether Rockton was closer to St. Louis or Kansas City. There was a flight to Kansas City leaving in two hours.

He would wait by the gate, he decided.

And when she showed up, he would stop her.

Of course she would show up.

Where else would she be?

Then it hit him.

She could have gone to Kennedy airport. Or to Newark.

He hadn't bothered to ask her what her travel plans were.

For all he knew, she was sitting on a runway at JFK, waiting to take off.

This had been an insane idea, he realized, deflating. He couldn't go after her.

He couldn't.

Because it wasn't meant to be.

He had been an impulsive fool to come here looking for her.

You were wrong. Two strikes, and you're out, he thought glumly, tossing the roses and boarding pass into a trash container as he walked toward ground transportation.

Mariel sat on the stoop of Noah's building, watching the traffic go by, her arms wrapped around her knees.

She had been here more than an hour, and he had refused to buzz her up.

Or maybe he wasn't home.

That was a possibility, she admitted to herself. Yet she couldn't rid herself of the image of him standing in his apartment, listening to her ring the buzzer, sensing that it was her and refusing to reply.

Why should he let her in?

She had left him.

But she had come back, dammit. She had gotten to the airport, and she had realized that she couldn't do it.

She was going to tell him that she wanted another chance. That she wanted to try to work things out. That even if there were no guarantees that they could make it together, she was willing to take the risk.

Because she couldn't live without him.

She shifted her weight on the step, gazing out at the morning traffic stopped at a light on the next corner. Somewhere in the distance, far below the street, she could hear the screech of a subway rumbling by. Pedestrians passed, some solitary, others in couples and in groups—people living their lives against the backdrop of the exhilarating city that Mariel had once thought would be her home.

Until she had realized that Rockton was her home . . . .

Or so she had believed, until she realized, in the airport, on the verge of boarding a flight to St. Louis, that home could be anywhere, as long as Noah was there with her.

She didn't care whether he moved with her to Rockton or she stayed with him in New York or they both picked up and lived in ... in Strasburg, or Paris, or wherever he wanted to go.

She was going to tell him that, just as soon as she was face-to-face with him again.

Sooner or later, she told herself, watching the traffic begin to move down Broadway again as the light changed, he would have to come out. Or come home, if he really was out.

Either way, she was going to wait here until he materialized. No matter how long it took. She had spent fifteen endless years without him. A few more hours wouldn't make a difference in the long run. . . .

Not if he says yes.

Idly staring at the street, she saw a yellow cab pull up on the opposite curb.

She watched as a man got out.

Then her heart began to pound as she realized who it was.

So he hadn't been upstairs, ignoring her.

Noah walked briskly to the corner, glanced at the light, and waited for it to change. His head was down, his hands shoved into the pockets of his khaki pants.

Mariel leaped off the steps and walked hurriedly along the sidewalk to the corner opposite the one where he stood.

"Noah!" she bellowed, as an unyielding current of traffic rushed between them. She waved her arms frantically like someone who needed to be rescued. "Noah!"

He didn't hear her.

She looked impatiently at the light, then at the DON'T WALK sign that still glowed on the opposite corner. She would be a fool to take a chance by stepping off the curb. She had to wait, even though every ounce of her being longed to rush to him, dodging cars and buses and cabs.

"Noah!" she shouted again, just as the traffic slowed and the light changed.

He looked up at it, and stepped off the curb.

"Noah!"

Then he saw her.

His jaw dropped.

She rushed toward him.

He met her halfway across Broadway, swooping her into his arms.

"Mariel!" he breathed, crushing her against him. "I thought you left."

"I couldn't do it. Not without telling you something. Not without telling you that I love you, Noah." The words spilled giddily from her tongue and seemed to dance in the dazzling June sunlight. She couldn't stop saying them. "I love you. I love you and I want to be with you, wherever you are."

"I love you, too," he said, and he bent his head to capture her lips in a sweet, clinging kiss that would have told her everything she needed to know even if he hadn't just uttered the words.

"My God," she said when they broke apart, "I've been such a fool. I had convinced myself that you hated me. That you could never forgive me for choosing to give up Amber. For refusing to marry you."

"I never hated you," he said raggedly. "And I've forgiven you. You made the right decision, Mariel. The most unselfish decision you could make. I was the one who wasn't thinking clearly. I wasn't thinking about what was best for anybody but me. I wanted you so much. I wanted us to be a family."

"We can be a family now," she told him on a sigh. "We can try. And it wasn't just you, Noah. I needed to forgive myself. I didn't realize that I hadn't. You were right. I've been letting life pass me by. My life in Rockton is an escape. But I'm ready to stop hiding. I'm ready to leave it behind. It's time to start living again."

"With me," he murmured against her lips, kissing her again.

A car honked.

And then another.

And then there was a chorus of honking, and a disgruntled cabbie yelled through his car window, "Hey, get a room. I haven't got all day!"

They burst apart and, looking up, saw that the light had changed.

Laughing breathlessly, they dashed to the sidewalk.

"We're on the wrong side of the street," Mariel realized, seeing Noah's building across Broadway.

"Oh, well," he said, pulling her into his arms. "The light will change again. And I know just what we can do while we wait."

With that, he kissed her again.

And she knew, without a shadow of a doubt, that at long last, she was exactly where she belonged.

EPILOGUE

As Leslie and Jed stepped from the white clapboard church into the brilliant July sunshine and a flurry of rose petals, Mariel, standing on the steps beside the door, breathed a sigh of relief.

Her sister was married.

The wedding had come off without a hitch, aside from the moment when Leslie, coming down the aisle on Daddy's arm, had tripped over her train. She had steadied herself by grabbing one of the ribbon-bedecked pews, and Mariel, watching from beside the altar, had given her momentarily flustered sister a reassuring smile.

Leslie hadn't seen her. Her gaze had gone right to Jed, waiting at the head of the aisle, and when he smiled and nodded encouragingly at her, the bride's face had become serene.

That was when Mariel had realized that her sister was going to be just fine without her.

Not that either of them was going anywhere for good—at least, not for the time being.

Leslie and Jed had moved into their new home a few blocks from the old one.

Mariel was leaving, but only temporarily, in a few days, while they were on their Hawaiian honeymoon.

At last, she was going to Europe. She was going to see London, and Paris, and Rome, and she would be traveling with Noah at her side. That was the incredible part, the miracle.

They were using some of Mariel's savings and some of Noah's severance pay from the agency, along with the security deposit he had gotten back on his apartment. Tammy Harper down at All Aboard Travel had nearly fallen off her seat the day Mariel walked in to book the trip.

"Sure is a far cry from Syracuse, Mariel," she had commented.

"Sure is," Mariel had said sweetly.

They would return to Rockton by Labor Day, just in time for Mariel to begin teaching the new term at school. And Noah would have all the time and space and peace he needed to work on his screenplays. Maybe one of these days, he would sell one.

But if he never did, he told Mariel, it wouldn't matter.

Not as long as they had each other.

And she believed him.

She watched her sister and Jed kiss each other passionately as rose petals drifted down around them.

Then she turned her head and searched the crowd of well-wishers gathered on the green lawn below the church steps.

She spotted Noah there, beside her father, his hand on the older man's arm to steady him as he stepped backward to take a picture of his daughter and his new son-in-law.

Mariel caught Noah's eye, and she flashed him a grateful smile, nodding her head toward her father, silently thanking him for looking out for Daddy.

Noah smiled back.

Daddy was beaming, Mariel thought, watching him snap another picture of the newlyweds. This was probably one of the happiest days ever—though he would be even happier when he had a grandchild on the way, as he had reminded Leslie and Jed during his toast at last night's rehearsal dinner.

Mariel and Noah had exchanged a glance when he said that.

Daddy still didn't know about Amber. Someday, perhaps, they would tell him, and Leslie and Jed. When the time was right.

And someday, perhaps, they would have other news to share, Mariel thought blissfully.

The bride and groom descended the steps, and she followed, careful to hold the hem of her pink maid-of-honor gown high above her shoes.

"You look gorgeous, sweetie," Katie Beth said, stopping Mariel. Her youngest child was asleep on her shoulder, and Olivia clung shyly to her hand. Patrick was beside his wife, one toddler in his arms and another clinging to the leg of his dark suit pants.

"You look gorgeous, too," Mariel told Katie Beth, admiring her green dress.

"I do not," Katie Beth said, leaning toward her to whisper in her ear, "This dress is so damned tight around my stomach, I can't breathe. But believe me, there's a good reason."

When her words registered, Mariel gasped, then hugged her friend, and Patrick, too.

"Congratulations," she said whole-heartedly. *'Five* children?"

"Believe me, we were even more surprised than you are," Katie Beth said dryly. "I guess we had a little too good a time when we went away for that long weekend without the kids in April."

Mariel laughed. "Where are you going to put them all?"

"We'll fit them in," Patrick said, and Katie Beth nodded, contentment sliding over her pretty face.

Watching them, Mariel felt strong arms slipping around her waist from behind, and she looked up to see Noah. Her heart beat a little faster. It always did when he was near. She wondered how long this romantic giddiness would last.

Then she looked at Katie Beth and Patrick, who were gazing at each other past their children's heads, and she knew that it could last forever.

"Can I have the first dance at the reception, or do you have to share it with the best man?" Noah asked, his voice low in her ear.

"You are the best man," she said teasingly. "The best man for me, anyway."

He kissed her. "That's right, and don't ever forget

it. Not even when we're old and gray and we have hordes
of children and grandchildren to distract us."

"I won't," she promised with all her heart.

And she didn't.

AUTHOR'S NOTE

If you would like to receive a current Janelle Taylor newsletter, bookmark, and descriptive flyer of other books available with pictures of their covers, send a self-addressed stamped envelope (business size best) to:

Janelle Taylor Newsletter #37
P. O. Box 211646
Martinez, Georgia 30917-1646

Reading is fun and educational, so do it often!

Best Wishes from

Janelle Taylor

Complete Your Collection of
Fern Michaels

Thrilling Romance from
Meryl Sawyer

The Queen of Romance
Cassie Edwards

__Desire's Blossom	0-8217-6405-5	$5.99US/$7.50CAN
__Passion's Web	0-8217-5726-1	$5.99US/$7.50CAN
__Portrait of Desire	0-8217-5862-4	$5.99US/$7.50CAN
__Beloved Embrace	0-8217-6256-7	$5.99US/$7.50CAN
__Savage Obsession	0-8217-5554-4	$5.99US/$7.50CAN
__Savage Innocence	0-8217-5578-1	$5.99US/$7.50CAN
__Savage Torment	0-8217-5581-1	$5.99US/$7.50CAN
__Savage Heart	0-8217-5635-4	$5.99US/$7.50CAN
__Savage Paradise	0-8217-5637-0	$5.99US/$7.50CAN
__Silken Rapture	0-8217-5999-X	$5.99US/$7.50CAN
__Rapture's Rendezvous	0-8217-6115-3	$5.99US/$7.50CAN

Call toll free **1-888-345-BOOK** to order by phone, use this coupon to order by mail, or order online at **www.kensingtonbooks.com**.

Name _____

Address _____

City _____ State _____ Zip _____

Please send me the books I have checked above.

I am enclosing $_____
Plus postage and handling* $_____
Sales tax (in New York and Tennessee only) $_____
Total amount enclosed $_____

*Add $2.50 for the first book and $.50 for each additional book.

Send check or money order (no cash or CODs) to:

Kensington Publishing Corp., Dept. C.O., 850 Third Avenue, New York, NY 10022

Prices and numbers subject to change without notice.

All orders subject to availability.

Visit our website at **www.kensingtonbooks.com**.